INTO THE GRAY

A BOSTON CRIME THRILLER

BRIAN SHEA

SEVERN RIVER PUBLISHING

ALSO BY BRIAN SHEA

Boston Crime Thrillers

Murder Board

Bleeding Blue

The Penitent One

Sign of the Maker

Cold Hard Truth

Into the Gray

The Nick Lawrence Series

Kill List

Pursuit of Justice

Burning Truth

Targeted Violence

Murder 8

Sterling Gray FBI Profiler Series

Lexi Mills Thrillers

Memory Bank Thrillers

Shepherd and Fox Thrillers

Booker Johnson Thrillers

To find out more, visit

severnriverbooks.com

To the real Jaime Doyle and his family. After serving nearly two decades in corrections, he was forced into early retirement after attempting to intervene during an inmate altercation that left him with a broken back. Thank you for sharing your story with me on that hot summer afternoon. Your experience became the genesis for this story and I hope my fictional telling honors that.

A special shout-out to the brave men and women of the Department of Corrections around the country who hold the line within the gray walls.

1

Roland Watt sat in the diner on Savin Hill, the same one his father had taken him to on special occasions, the rare times in their lives when he had a little extra cash in his pocket. It was out of his neighborhood. Over the years, as sections of Dorchester were revitalized, the diner and the people who frequented it weren't the sort he associated himself with. He hadn't been here in a long time, but under the circumstances, today seemed to demand it.

He pushed the empty plate to the edge of the table and dabbed his finger into the leftover crumbs from the crust, tasting the last bit of his favorite dessert since childhood. It was early for cheesecake, and the girl who had served it to him gave him a funny look when he ordered that and nothing else. He wanted to have its taste in his mouth one last time before today's meeting.

He flagged the waitress, who took the plate and refreshed his coffee. When she walked away, he tore open and poured in a few sugar packets, then reached inside his pocket and pulled out a flask, adding a dash of whiskey to the hot coffee. He stirred it gently as he looked outside the window toward the street and waited. A few minutes later, the diner's door chimed. He didn't have to turn and look because he'd just seen the man pass by the window.

D-Roc, head of the Rock Steady Boyz, stood beside the booth. Watt looked up at him. D-Roc was an enormous man, at least twice the size of Roland Watt, who was average in both height and build. What he lacked in size he made up for in intelligence, and everybody knew that. He was as deadly as he was smart.

As big as D-Roc was, he could see the same edginess, the same nervousness that he'd seen a thousand times when meeting face-to-face with those who feared him. "We a little out of our turf, ain't we?"

"Conversations like the one we're about to have call for neutral territory." Watt gestured to the worn bench across from him. "Have a seat."

"Diners really ain't my thing, man. I'm more of a club guy."

"Sit."

"You know, you don't get to boss me around. I run my crew, you run yours. You don't get to tell me what to do."

Watt pulled the spoon out of his coffee and set it neatly on the napkin beside the small saucer where the cup was resting. He then brought it to his lips and took a slow sip, allowing the hot liquid to sting the back of his throat while the whiskey warmed him from the inside. D-Roc postured for a moment longer before grunting and taking a seat. The worn leather cushion let out a slow wheeze of air from under its frayed edges.

"I'm here and it's early, so forgive me if I'm not at my best, but you said this was important, you and I having this little parley."

Watt set the cup down and locked eyes with the man across from him. "You and I have been at this game a long time, have we not? We're young, but in this life, we're reaching the status of OGs."

"Is this where you tell me some shit where we're too old for this game, because your message to me said that you needed my help or something. You looking for an out? You looking for me to take your piece?"

Watt was quiet for a moment. "That's why I chose this place, you know?" He looked around the diner and out toward the street. "Your crew owns the territory west of here, and mine everything east. This diner sits smack-dab on the border between our two turfs."

"Yeah, so what?"

"This is the diner I've come to since I was a child. It's a safe place for me.

It's a good place. My brother and I used to sit in this very same booth. He used to sit where you are now."

"Well, your brother's gone. He's been locked up. Word is they're shipping him off to Susan. Soon, right?"

Watt nodded.

"That's a long haul, man. That's the end game there. Once you go to supermax, you ain't coming home. Not that he had a chance of coming home from Walpole either. You can't kill three men in the middle of the street and beat the rap."

"You're right."

"You know something I never figured out, Watt? All the time you've been at it, you ain't never been caught once. Not once, not even some petty shit, man. Hell, I've done three years up in Walpole, and everybody in my crew has been snatched at some point or another, but you? You beat them all. You're clean."

"You got something to say, say it."

"Just saying. How's someone like you get all the way where you're at without catching no case?"

"Simple. I'm smarter. I'm smarter than the cops, I'm smarter than you."

"Shit! You think you are."

"The proof is right here before you. I've been at this longer than you, and yes, I've never been touched. I'm sitting here with you by myself without protection because I know I am protected, because this is my neighborhood. This is my diner. This is my Dorchester. The Dot belongs to me."

"So, you want my territory?"

"No."

"Then what is it you need?"

"I need your help with something. I need help getting into Walpole."

D-Roc let out a loud, boisterous laugh that caught the attention of the neighboring diners, who turned to look in the men's direction. Watt didn't like the attention. He never had. He didn't like the light to be turned toward him, but today was a different day and he allowed it.

"Why the hell would you need to get your ass into Walpole anyway?"

"I need to see my brother."

"Go to visitation, man."

"No, not like that. I need to see him before they ship him off to supermax."

"Oh shit, man. You thinking some crazy stuff, aren't you? So all this time you avoid getting locked up, and now you want to get yourself put in? I don't get you, man, and I don't know how you think I can help." D-Roc folded his arms across his chest and cocked an eye at Watt. "So what is all this, man? This walk down memory lane? Oh shit. What are you aiming at?"

"You and I have battled long and hard to earn our place on the street. And what? To fight for scraps." Watt pressed into the table. His eyes leveled at his longtime rival.

"So this is an alliance." D-Roc shifted back slightly. A bead of sweat bubbled up on his forehead near his hairline.

"Not necessarily. You mind taking a walk with me?"

"Man, I don't get you. First you tell me to take a seat. Now you tell me to get up and take a walk."

"I'm not going to ask you to walk far, just to the corner. Right there." Watt pointed out to the street.

"Shoot, man. Whatever." D-Roc got up in a huff. The bench seat creaked in annoyance as the big man scooted out and made his way toward the door.

Watt slipped a twenty under his saucer and stood, looking back at the empty bench where his brother had once sat. He took a second to remember the time when he was eight and his brother ten. His father had bought them a vanilla cheesecake to share with the little extra cash he had from working overtime as a bus driver for the Boston Transit System.

It was the last time they saw their father. On his double shift that night, he was stabbed by a deranged crackhead when he refused to give him a free ride. It was the last meal they had together as a family before they had to forge a new one on the mean and unforgiving streets of Dorchester, a family Watt hoped to once again reunite.

The two men stepped out onto the sidewalk and walked slowly toward the corner. Winter had broken early, but a cool morning wind still whipped down the street.

"So, what now? We're outside. What can I do to help you get into Walpole, to help you with your brother's situation, whatever it is?"

"That's the thing. Your gang, they're going to stop selling. Your men, the ones who are willing to, are going to be given an opportunity to work for me, and those who don't? Well, you know how that's going to work out." Watt knew the threat carried weight.

"So now you're telling me you're taking my turf?"

"It was never your turf to begin with," Watt snapped back.

"You've got some nerve coming at me like this out here in the open."

"What better place?"

"Man, you're all twisted up. First, you ask me to sit with you in a diner. Then, you start reminiscing about your brother. Now, you're talking about prison, and then you take me outside and talk about taking my turf, all while asking me to help you get into Walpole. None of this makes sense."

"I just felt you should know your part in all this. You should know how it's going to go from this point forward. Take a look at the two blocks you've owned for the last five years. Take a good, hard look at it, because it's the last time you're going to see it."

D-Roc turned toward the street and then back toward Watt to find that he was staring down the barrel of a nickel-plated handgun.

"Yo, man. What the hell?" D-Roc stepped back and threw up his hands.

An MBTA bus drove by, the exhaust fumes wafting into Watt's nostrils, reminding him of the smell his father used to carry on his clothes after coming home from a long day's work. He fired once, sending a bullet through D-Roc's forehead, dropping the large man to the ground.

Somebody screamed. Cars screeched to a halt, and within seconds, he heard sirens in the distance. Watt ignored it all. He let the gun hang down by his thigh as he stood beside the dead man and waited for the cops to arrive.

2

Sunlight pierced through the slit. No wider than two inches and no taller than ten, that slit had been Kelly's only view for the last eighty-eight days. The eight-by-ten cell, his home away from home, was tucked into the isolation wing of MCI-Cedar Junction, better known as Walpole Prison.

Kelly pushed the breakfast tray toward the cell door, then washed his hands before cupping them under the spout and splashing his face. It had become his morning routine during the past three months of his incarceration in Walpole's isolation wing. He patted himself dry and looked at the solitary picture taped to the polished metal of the mirror. His daughter Embry wore a bright, carefree smile, her teeth coated in a smattering of rainbow-colored Dippin' Dots. A younger version of Kelly sat next to her, his arm pulling his daughter close as they celebrated his birthday at Fenway Park. His world had changed dramatically since that photo was taken. His wife Sam had left him not long after. The marriage hadn't survived the demands of the job, or at least that's what he told himself. But as he looked at the muted reflection staring back at him, he barely recognized the man in the picture.

He'd allowed the job to consume him, to sever his connection to those he loved most in the world. The red jumpsuit denoting his status as an ISO inmate was his new uniform, one he'd donned to further his transformation from cop to criminal, all in the hopes of the long shot of being able to insert himself into the Savin Hill Gang. In the nearly three months since his confinement, Kelly had played out the scenario, continually weighing the cost against its end. Each second without his daughter had called into question that decision.

Connor Walsh, head of the Irish mob, had held the city in his grip. The criminal mastermind had managed to elude capture. His reign over Boston and, in particular, Kelly's neighborhood of Dorchester, had resulted in countless deaths, both in the drugs he dealt and the murders he and his associates committed to maintain their stranglehold on the city. He weighed the scales of justice: his family's needs versus bringing Walsh to justice. The same question permeated his mind as it did every time he looked at his daughter's face. Was it worth the possibility of losing everything he held dear?

His future was on hold while he faced the demons of his past. A chance at a new beginning with Kristen Barnes, his partner who had become so much more. Kelly pushed away the image of her face when he'd cleared his desk and prepared for the road ahead. He had been unable to tell her of the department's plan to use him to infiltrate the mob, a secret known only to three men who now held his fate in their hands.

Kelly pushed back from the sink. He shook his shoulders loose as he stared at the colorful drawings taped to the wall. He didn't want his daughter to see him like this. He didn't want her impressionable mind to ever have the image of her father in prison garb. Sam had tried to convince him otherwise, but ultimately she'd honored his request. It didn't stop his eleven-year-old from sending him drawings and letters, though. He always responded in kind, although his drawings didn't come close to hers. Three months was an eternity, and he tried not to let the thought of the missed time plague his mind.

The only thing capable of muting his raging inner conflict was the one thing he'd always turned to in times of need: boxing. The cell had become his new ring. The gray concrete walls were the ropes. He closed his eyes, inhaling deeply as he pictured the gym he'd called home. He could see the hardwood floors stained with sweat. Leather heavy bags swung under relentless pounding delivered by the next up-and-comer. As he walked himself through Pops's gym, he stopped at the ring. The tattered ropes and worn turnbuckles carried memories of his growth, not only as a boxer but as a man. The smell of sweat permeated his nostrils. He was no longer inside a prison cell.

Kelly opened his eyes. He heard Pops delivering one of his sermons. *Speed is the weapon against size. To take the bigger man, you must outmaneuver and outsmart.*

He bent his knees slightly and shifted to the balls of his feet. Leaning forward and distributing most of his weight to the front foot, Kelly brought his hands up. His head dipped low. His fists, wrecking balls of flesh and bone that had served him well over the years, rose up to protect his head. Looking over the knuckles of his left hand, he shot out a jab at the imaginary opponent who danced in front of him. In his mind's eye, the opponent's face was his. He'd been fighting this mirrored version of himself since he set foot inside these four walls. A bout without rounds. A timeless battle waged in the stale air he'd become accustomed to.

He unleashed a flurry of punches into the air. Kelly could see his target move and counter. He did the same. With each torque of his hips, he felt the release accompanied by the jabs, crosses, and hooks. His head bobbed as he slipped his invisible opponent's attack, an unchoreographed dance scripted by the memories of the thousands of times he'd done this.

Sweat took shape on his brow, gathering momentum and trickling down his cheeks as his relentless pacing increased. Right now, he was no longer a prisoner. He was as free as any man could be.

His imaginary opponent threw a heavy overhand right. Kelly dipped his body low, bending at the knees and stepping off to the side. He struck a body blow before rising up and firing off a left hook with enough force to level a building.

Three sharp knocks on the door were followed by the rattle of keys. His round was over.

Kelly turned from the door and walked slowly to the far wall, placing his palms flat against the concrete. He rested his forehead against the wall, the cold penetrating from the March wind outside wicking the sweat from his forehead.

He heard the latch release and the heavy door slide open.

"Kelly, you're good."

Kelly turned to see the smiling face of Jamie Doyle, fifteen-year veteran of the Department of Corrections and one of the officers assigned to the ISO wing. He wiped the excess sweat onto the sleeve of his jumpsuit. "What's new?"

"Same old." Doyle looked Kelly over. "I see you've got a jump-start on your morning routine."

"You know me." He gave a half-cocked smile. "Speaking of routines, you're a little early today."

"It's supposed to snow later. Thought you might want to get in some yard time. The bag's available."

Several cages separated from the general population were set aside for ISO prisoners. Most were empty spaces, not much bigger than the cell where he stood. One of them had an old heavy bag that had become Kelly's sanctuary on the days he was able to use it. Doyle knew this and had been good about getting him time.

"Sounds like a plan." Kelly grabbed his jacket, a canvas overcoat with DOC stamped across the back. It wasn't insulated, but the heavy material worked well enough to stave off the cold.

Doyle dangled a pair of cuffs. "You know the deal."

Kelly stepped forward and extended his arms. Doyle attached the cuffs to his wrists, keeping them loose. With his shackles clicked into place, Kelly lowered his hands like a churchgoer approaching for Communion. The chain dangled underneath.

Doyle put a hand on Kelly's elbow and escorted him out of the cell. Kelly stepped onto the red line painted along the floor—or the racetrack, as it was called by inmates and guards alike. The line, centered along the hallway extending through the ISO wing, provided enough room for a guard to walk along either side, or in the case of a volatile inmate, two guards. As Doyle had explained to Kelly when he first arrived, the line was designed to ensure minimal exposure of ISO inmates to the other cells' inhabitants. This cut down on the trash-talking and threats that often led to bloodshed.

Kelly kept his head and eyes forward, all part of the rule structure for those wearing red jumpsuits. Doyle closed the cell and locked it before resuming his position alongside Kelly and guiding him down the hall.

"How's the wife and kids?" Kelly kept his voice at a whisper, knowing that small talk between inmates and guards, especially the kind that was personal in nature, was often frowned upon.

"Sal's good. She's been picking up the slack on our plow business since they got me pulling doubles."

"Looks like she'll be bringing home a little extra scratch with the coming storm."

"I hope. My oldest is looking at trade school in a year."

"That'll be good."

"Yeah, unless his dumb ass keeps smokin' pot." Doyle shook his head. "I know we all dabbled when we were young, but my wife caught him smoking in the house. What happened to the day when kids would sneak off and just lie to their parents, like we did?"

"Different world."

"Ain't that the truth. At least my youngest has got her head screwed on straight. She's got her sights set on becoming an architect."

"Maybe she'll build you a house someday." This got a chuckle out of the guard.

"Speaking of. I think I saw another letter from your daughter down in the mailroom. I'll bring it to you after they've cleared it."

"Thanks." And like that, Embry rocketed to the forefront of his mind. He needed the heavy bag more than ever, snow or not.

Kelly and Doyle continued their journey down the long hallway leading to the passage tunnel connected to the yard used exclusively for the ISO inmates. They passed several empty cells along the corridor. The unit was rarely at full capacity, which Doyle said was a good thing, as it limited the amount of guard presence and bolstered his opportunity for catching the much-needed overtime shifts.

A low grumble, like an eighteen-wheeler roaring to life, arose from a cell off to Kelly's right. The small window was cast in the shadow of the man behind the thick door. The prisoner's hulking figure lowered, giving way to the menacing face behind the glass.

Kelly slowed his walk and locked eyes with the giant. Doyle gave a light tug of his sleeve, ushering him forward.

"No need to go poking that bear. Goliath there has proven himself enough trouble as is," Doyle said in a hushed tone.

"He's right where he belongs." Kelly quickened his pace to match that of his escort.

"Rumor mill has it you single-handedly brought him down."

"The rumor mill, eh. Not sure I'd trust everything you hear."

"What I heard is that you stood toe to toe with him and came out victorious."

That was the same story that circulated around the department as well, no matter how many times Kelly tried to minimize the sensationalism. "The truth is often never as interesting as fiction."

"Let me hear it from the horse's mouth and I'll be the judge."

"Goliath was the muscle for the Rollin' 9s, a local gang around my old neighborhood known for knocking off other dealers and stealing their stash. The big man had a reputation for violence. Did some minor stints for your garden-variety crimes."

Kelly shot a glance back at the cell. Goliath's eyes continued to track him, a predator salivating after his lost prey.

"He stepped up to the big leagues when he caught his girlfriend cheating. Went ballistic. Killed them both with his bare hands."

It was Doyle who now slowed their pace. "No shit?"

"No shit. Brutal scene. He caved their heads in. Tough one, even for the saltiest badges."

"He didn't run?"

"He did. Just not very far." Kelly cleared his throat. The vent system, running constantly, sucked the moisture from the air. "I was on patrol at the time. My partner and I got a tip on his whereabouts. We hunted him down, but he didn't go peacefully."

"I can't imagine a guy like that would."

"He tried to escape. My partner and I separated in an effort to cut him off. I had the luck, or misfortune, of running smack-dab into him." Remembering that night, Kelly felt the fear rising inside him again. Most cops wouldn't talk about it, and if they did, it was dismissed as the kind of macho jocularity that was commonplace among those in uniform. But Kelly never dismissed or minimized those fight-or-flight moments. Instead, he embraced them. Accepting fear as part of the job and recognizing its power, Kelly time and time again channeled it to give him the fighter's edge when facing off in a life-or-death situation.

"But you bested him?"

"I arrested him. But bested—not sure that's ever been decided. For me, at least." Kelly saw that Doyle was hanging on his every word. Not one for showboating or ego floating, the conversation left him feeling uneasy. But inside the prison, with nothing but the slow ticking of time, conversation was the closest thing to freedom one could find. Especially when stuck in isolation.

"I tried to bring him in easy. But he wasn't having it." The cool night air swept across his face. He could see the intent in Goliath's eyes that day, same as it was now. There was only one thing on his mind. Murder. "I had him at gunpoint. He wasn't armed. Regardless of the violence he'd just shown, the attorneys would've ripped me limb from limb if I'd fired that shot."

"Sounds like it would've been justified." Doyle cocked a smile. "Would've saved the taxpayer a chunk of change housing that beast for the rest of his godforsaken life."

"Even so, I saw how it would've played out. Plus, I was a bit headstrong at that time in my career."

"Looks like not much has changed."

This evoked a rare chuckle from Kelly. "Maybe so. I called for my partner but he didn't hear or was out of range. Can't really remember. Doesn't matter now. At the time, what did matter was the fact that I had a decision to make. Stand and fight or make my retreat."

"I don't see you as the type of guy who backs down from a fight."

"Probably why I've been stuck in here for the last ninety days."

"Eighty-eight. Two days until you're breathing that fresh air on the other side of the fence."

"Who's counting?" Kelly got a laugh from Doyle and then continued. "I holstered and decided to go hands-on. The story told countless times by others who weren't there is that I fought and won."

"Well, he's wearing a jumpsuit for the rest of his life, so I guess when it's all said and done, you did."

"Guess so." Kelly could feel the exchange of punches like it was yesterday. "I've been fighting my whole life, inside and outside of the ring. But to this day, I've never had a tougher bout. We banged it out, each getting our pound of flesh. I'd hit him with a punch that wobbled him. I made the mistake of thinking I had him where I wanted. And that mistake still haunts me."

They reached the access door to the stairwell, but Doyle stopped and waited for Kelly to finish.

"I went for the knockout but overplayed my advantage. And he took his. The punch he hit me with felt more like a sledgehammer than a fist. Dropped me to my knees. At this point, with darkness closing in from the corners of my eyes, I went for my gun. Problem was, I was looped. Couldn't get my brain to access the holster's retention lever."

"What'd you do?"

"Prepared for the coming onslaught. To be honest, I prepared to die." Kelly's heart rate had increased. He felt the blood rush to his face as his mind replayed the near-death experience. "Goliath reared back and was preparing to deliver a blow that I'm certain would've been my last. Just as he was about to drop the hammer, my partner appeared."

"You've got the angel touch. Something my mother used to say. When you're swooped from death's door by an unforeseen act of grace."

"Whatever it was, I'll take it. If my partner hadn't rounded the corner when he did, I'm pretty sure I wouldn't be standing here today. And the story told about that night would've had a much different ending."

"Hell of a story. I think this time, truth trumps fiction." Doyle pressed his key card against the reader on the wall. An electric buzzer sounded, and the door released. "He won't be our problem anymore. Your friend Goliath is being shipped off to supermax."

"No kidding. 'Bout time."

"Transfer orders came through last week. He'll be gone by next week."

Kelly followed Doyle into the stairwell and was hit with cold air from the tunnel leading to the yard.

As he made his way through the prison's dank underbelly, Kelly's mind remained locked in the thralls of that night. He now had a new face to put to his invisible sparring partner. Kelly planned to unleash his demons from his encounter with Goliath on the duct-taped canvas of the cage's heavy bag.

3

Kristen Barnes sipped her coffee, now lukewarm, before setting it back down on her desk amid a sea of papers. She typed the last few lines into her supplemental report and sat back. Her eyes skimmed the document, and she made a final pass before tapping the icon and uploading it to the digital filing system.

She pushed her legs out, rolling the chair back past her cubicle dividing wall and arching her back to complete the stretch. Her attention turned to the empty desk on the other side, heart sinking, as it always did since Kelly had made his exit. She wondered how much time had to pass before she no longer felt his presence in every inch of this space. Barnes doubted any amount would ever truly mask the hole his absence left.

The door to Boston's Homicide Unit opened and Mark Cahill walked in. Kelly's young protégé had been handed off to her upon his departure. The newest addition to the unit showed real promise in the months since coming over from his time in Narcotics.

"Trying to catch that worm?"

"Just trying to follow your lead. I guess you're still the early bird." Cahill strode through the office and tossed his coat at the hook on the wall before making his way over to their station.

Barnes stood and twisted her shoulders, loosening her lower back. Her early morning run followed by an hour of deskwork left her body tight.

"Brought you some Dunkin'. Medium regular."

Barnes accepted the offering, never one to turn down a cup. The warmth felt good against her palm as she popped the lid and took a long pull of her morning addiction. "Kissing ass won't change the fact you still owe me those notes from the victim interview you did the other day."

"Never thought it would." Cahill flashed a coy smile. "You still writing up the summation?"

"Just finished."

"You'd have been great in the military. You live that old slogan about getting more done before nine a.m. than most people do all day." Cahill plopped into his seat and threw his hands behind his head. "Another slam dunk for us."

"Not that hard when the doer was caught on three different cameras with one showing him still holding the knife."

"True. But you nailed him to the wall with that interview."

"He was a junkie hurting for a fix. His addiction did more to elicit the confession than anything I did."

"Just take the damn compliment. It's not gonna kill ya." Cahill flipped through a file on his desk. "And junkie or not, he killed a man. Over what? Sixty bucks and a stupid watch? And in front of his girlfriend too. Whatever they hit him with, it won't be enough."

Barnes shrugged. The truth was, nothing really worked to satisfy the void. Since Kelly had ended things with her and embarked on his ninety-day sentence, everything she did fell flat. The cases she poured herself into lacked the luster of before. Even the morning runs became long stretches of tedium. What used to fill her with energy just left her missing Kelly's huffing and complaining as he fought to keep up.

"Why don't you come out for a drink after work tonight? Thirsty Thursday."

"Leads to Friday funk."

"C'mon." Cahill put his hands together as if he were Oliver begging for a spot of porridge.

"We'll see."

"You said that the last ten times I asked you." Cahill sat forward in his chair and then wheeled himself around the corner to face her. "Plus, Mainelli said he's buying."

"That'll be a first."

"Exactly! Alligator arms is finally going to put some cash on the table. Or at least he says he will."

"Tell you what—you finish that report and I'll think about it."

"Gotta do better than that if you want these fingers to dance a jig on that keyboard."

Barnes could see Cahill wasn't going to back down. The truth was, it just felt wrong. Going out and enjoying herself while Kelly was locked away didn't sit well with her. Even though he'd ended things, Barnes still hadn't fully accepted the terms, and doubted she ever would.

She took another sip of coffee, ignoring Cahill's expectant look for a few more seconds before answering. "Fine. You finish the report you should've completed a day ago and I'll meet you guys for a drink."

"Hot damn! If I had known that's all it would've taken, I'd have been bustin' my ass to get those reports done all along."

"What are you so excited about?" Mainelli sauntered in with several of the other detectives punching the timeclock by arriving at eight o'clock on the dot.

"Barnes here finally decided to grace us with her presence tonight."

Mainelli staggered back as if he'd been shot. His dramatic improv skit nearly knocked the mug out of Sergeant Halstead's hand. "Sorry, Sarge."

"Don't stop dying on my account." Halstead, the Iceman, delivered his line with the flat affect that had become his hallmark, thus earning him the nickname carried forward from his days as an Internal Affairs supervisor.

Mainelli feigned shock before righting himself and moving toward the coat rack. "You should join us too, boss. A little celebration to cap off our perfect closure record for the year."

"It's only March."

"It's still perfect." Mainelli looked pleased with himself.

"Who's buying?" Halstead asked.

Cahill nearly shot out of his seat as he pointed a finger at Mainelli.

Halstead paused for a moment and sized up the veteran detective. "If you're buying, then I'll have to stop by."

As Halstead headed into his office, Cahill gave a half spin of his chair and leaned toward Barnes. "See? Even the Iceman himself is coming. Now there's no backing out."

Barnes began the tedious process of setting her desk back in order. Completion of a case meant clearing the slate for the next one. In Homicide, as in any investigative unit, there was never a shortage of casework. Being short-staffed since Kelly's departure had only added weight to the volume of their small group. She looked up at the rotation board. The other teams were already tagged with ongoing investigations, which meant her team was on deck once again.

Halstead reappeared from his office almost as soon as he'd entered. He had the grim look that always permeated his stony exterior prior to giving the news of another body. He pocketed his cellphone and approached the cubicle station where Barnes and Cahill were sitting. Mainelli still hadn't taken up his post and was busying himself at the coffee maker in the back room.

"Might have to put drinks on hold for tonight." Halstead delivered the news in his usual monotone.

"Damn." Cahill spun in his chair to face their boss. "I guess that'll make Mainelli happy. He can go back to hiding his wallet."

The joke did little to change Halstead's demeanor. "What do we got?" Barnes asked.

"Shooting death. Just happened in Dorchester."

"Any leads on the shooter?" Cahill sat up straight and dropped the cocky banter.

"He's in custody as we speak. Patrol's bringing him in now."

"That was quick. Guess we've got another slam dunk in the hopper." Cahill smiled.

"Let's not get sloppy just because we've got one on the hook. There's still a scene to process and a case to build."

"Just sayin'. It's a lot easier when we've got the perp on lock."

"What do we know so far?" Barnes chimed in.

"Not much yet. But it appears our shooter dropped the guy in the open. Then he waited around until patrol arrived."

"Not sure I've ever heard of something going down like that before." Cahill was already up and gathering his notepad.

"I need you both to head down to the scene. Work it like you would any other. We'll piece the puzzle together once we have a better handle on things." Halstead shot a glance back toward the breakroom. "I'll have Mainelli hang back in case our shooter gets chatty before you return."

Barnes opened her top drawer, grabbed her duty weapon and extra magazine, and slipped them into the holster on her hip. Her knees popped as she stood.

"I'll drive. My car's still warm," Cahill said, grabbing his coat from the hook.

Barnes met Cahill by the door. The younger detective turned back to Halstead before exiting. "Maybe there's still a chance for that beer after all."

"Don't count on it." The Iceman spun on his heels and headed for Mainelli.

"He's a real Debbie Downer," Cahill whispered to Barnes as he pushed through the door.

"The body beat has that effect on people." Barnes looked at her desk, the clean space about to be littered with another case. The never-ending wheel continued to spin.

4

Kelly sat on his bunk, his upper body still tingling from the energy he'd unleashed on the heavy bag. The letter Doyle had told him about was under his cell door when he returned. The envelope was thicker than normal.

The intake officers had already opened and examined it in the mail-room. They'd made a half-assed attempt to reseal it, as they always did. He picked at the thin piece of tape on the back of the envelope and dug inside to retrieve its contents. In an instant he realized it was far too bulky to be from his daughter. After he unfolded the thick stack of papers, the letter-head confirmed it.

Stapled on the front was a handwritten note from his ex-wife.

Mike, I'm sorry to do this to you, but I have decided that under the current circumstances, you pose a significant risk to the well-being of our daughter. She's at an age where your influence could negatively affect her future. I know in the past, you've always been able to find a way to balance your job with your respon-sibilities as a father, but in light of recent events, we think you're no longer in a position to do that. We've filed a request for full custody with the court. Attached is the documentation. We'd like to make this as painless as possible for Embry. By signing it, you'll save us the ordeal of having to drag Embry through the legal process. If you choose to fight it, a court date will be set once you're released from prison. Sorry to do this to you while you're incarcerated, but we're just doing what we think is best. —Sam

Kelly dropped the paperwork to the floor. The tingle in his shoulders and arms now burned with the blood coursing through his veins. He fought the urge to scream as the words from Sam's message swirled in his head like flurries before a blizzard.

His detective mind activated, and he began picking apart the language she'd used. Her words were guarded. Instead of *I*, she phrased everything with *we*. If he didn't know better, Kelly would've thought she was coerced. And maybe to some degree she was. Her new husband was an attorney and Kelly knew without a doubt that he had assisted in carefully crafting the damning note.

Nothing like kicking a man when he was down. His eyes wandered the confines of his cell. The gray walls closed in, constricting his ability to breathe. He knew going into this assignment the potential impact on his personal life, and most importantly his daughter. It was weighed against the greater good. But now, after receiving the letter that lay in a heap by his DOC-issued, laceless sneakers, he realized he had greatly underestimated the fallout from his decision.

He thought about reaching out to Halstead or Sharp to tell them the deal was off, that the cost to his family was too great. Then his mind shifted to the other families, past, present, and future, and the losses they faced. The answer that had seemed so clear three months ago now eluded him.

Three quick bangs on the door shook him free of his thoughts as he turned to face the window on his cell door. Behind the glass, Kelly saw Doyle's face.

He assumed the position. Touching the wall was a tangible reminder of his circumstances. The door rolled open and Kelly turned.

"Got a visitor."

Doyle looked pleased, as he always did when delivering such news. Kelly did not return the look and only offered a sigh. Not many people had come through over the last ninety days, except a visit here or there from Pops. His old crew from the neighborhood had come by a couple times in an effort to keep Kelly's spirit up with little effect.

Kelly didn't bother to ask Doyle who it was as he shuffled forward and extended his wrists.

"Let me see the latest Embry masterpiece."

"No pictures today." Kelly cast his head down to the paperwork on the floor. "Probably not for a long time to come. My ex is gunning for full custody."

"I'm sorry to hear that." Doyle gave a long pause before continuing. "Doing a bid, no matter how long or how short, is never easy. You lookin' at the light at the end of the tunnel and you probably feel like it's gotten a little dimmer. Don't let it get to you."

"Easier said than done."

"I get it. But from experience, I can tell you that things change once you're back on the other side of these bars." Doyle gave Kelly a friendly pat on the shoulder. "Have faith."

Faith. Kelly's very understanding of the word had been challenged to its root. But Doyle's words did serve a purpose in giving him something he'd found little of lately. Hope. No matter how infinitesimally small it was, hope had a way of moving things forward.

Kelly stepped onto the line while Doyle closed his cage. The two then set off in the opposite direction, heading for the private visitation rooms allocated for ISO prisoners.

The walk took them through a set of secure doors connecting the isolation wing to D-Block, one of the general population sections. The inmates were grouped by the degree of criminal activity that led to their incarceration while also taking into account past history. A-Block contained the minor offenders. The progression stopped at D-Block, where the most dangerous were housed.

Kelly had a good working knowledge of the prison's layout, having come through for interviews and case follow-ups, but being on this side of things still felt odd. The passage of time played tricks on his mind, and he started feeling less connected to his old life. He'd rationalized it by telling himself that mindset was the single most important thing in taking on an undercover assignment. He couldn't pretend to be someone else. He must become an alternate version of himself. For Kelly, it meant going back to his youth and taking the other path when the road had forked. The problem with undercover work was being able to find your way back. Having an anchor was essential. Embry was his, and now his ex was doing her best to sever it.

Kelly and Doyle came to a T-intersection. The connecting hallway led to the second-floor access door of D-Block. Each of the blocks had a two-tiered housing of cells with a common space on the bottom floor. The second floor of each block contained a guard room overlooking the section that lay just beyond the secure door.

A couple of inmates were mopping the hallway. The white jumpsuits of D-Block inmates were stained and tattered, an indication of their time inside. Kelly didn't recognize either man but they definitely recognized him, either through past contact or by reputation. Didn't matter the how— the look on each man's face left little doubt to their feelings for the former cop. A pure, unadulterated hatred danced in their eyes as they paused their tasks to stare down Kelly. They looked as though they were deeply considering ditching their responsibilities in lieu of delivering an old-school ass-kicking.

Doyle must've caught wind of the same negative energy. His pace slowed and Kelly felt his body stiffen. "Lock it down, boys. Unless you want me to snatch your privileges."

Doyle didn't yell. He didn't have to. His words, delivered with the evenness of truth, were enough to achieve their purpose. Both men offered a mumbled, "Yes, boss," before returning to the work of scrubbing the hallway.

"You're a real celebrity around here," Doyle said as they continued toward the visitation rooms. A few short paces ahead was the door to the prison's central hub, where free men conducted the day-to-day operations of managing the overpopulated and understaffed facility.

"Celebrity? More like target."

"That, I can't argue. Hard for most inmates to accept responsibility. Easier for them to blame those responsible for bringing them in. And whether you personally saw to it or not doesn't factor in. The badge you carried makes you the emissary of their misfortune."

"Glad I have you around to keep them in check."

"Easy enough. I use mutual respect. I find it goes a lot further than a more totalitarian approach."

"I wish every guard saw it your way."

"I can only assume you're referring to Gladstone."

"You said it, not me."

Doyle chuckled. "If I'm speaking honestly, he's an asshole who's created more problems than he's solved. But that's his burden."

"It's a fine line. Not much different from anyone else who wears the badge."

"True. Only difference is that I'm inside with them too. Hell, I spend more time with inmates like you than I do my own family." Doyle tapped the leather belt holding his radio and weapons. "Plus, the big difference is I'm armed with some OC spray and an extendable baton. Not much in terms of intimidation when facing down a convicted murderer. Respect is my best defense. Don't get me wrong: given the right set of circumstances, those guys would gut me in a second."

"Same on the street. Treat everyone like a prince but have a plan to kill them."

"I'm glad you're one of the good guys."

"Doesn't feel that way anymore."

"It should." Doyle brought him to a halt outside a visitation room marked ISO 4. "Doesn't matter what brought you in, I can see the man you are. I can see the love you have for your daughter. And I know you're gonna rise above all this."

"Thanks."

"Plus, you punching out Lincoln White was about the best thing I've ever seen. I've rewatched that knockout a million times." Doyle had a big, shit-eating grin on his face. "Most of us guards in here agree you got the shaft. White's a real piece of work."

"Had dealings with him?"

"Not directly. But I listen. I hear from the inmates the methods he used to get his results. One or two bitching about a cop who set them up doesn't get much traction with me." Doyle shook his head, the smile disappearing. "The volume of complaints against White lends them credibility."

Kelly did nothing to sway Doyle's opinion, because it was all true. He assumed the position, pressing his chest against the wall while Doyle unlocked the door. "What do they say about me?"

"That you were always fair. Treated them with respect. And the ones who required a more hands-on approach said that after the dust settled, you never held a grudge."

"Good to know."

"All you've got to do now is ride out your last couple of days. The rest will sort itself when you get out."

"Not for nothing, your treatment of me over the course of my stay has made these past months more bearable."

"Respect is a double-edged sword. If you need anything on the other side, don't hesitate to reach out. For the select few I deem worthy, my service extends beyond the bars."

"I appreciate it."

Doyle opened the door and escorted Kelly inside. He removed the shackles before Kelly sat in a chair at the polished metal table, both bolted to the floor. Every time he entered these rooms, Kelly took a moment to adjust his mind to the position he was in and how it stood in stark contrast to the life he'd worked so hard to build.

"Who's the visitor?"

"Robert McDonough."

Bobby. His closest friend from the old neighborhood. The two had taken far different paths, and the decisions each had made forced a wedge in their relationship. The road Kelly now traveled shrank that divide.

"Sit tight. I'll bring him in."

Doyle disappeared into the hallway, shutting and locking the door before stepping off to fetch his oldest friend. Kelly hadn't seen Bobby since entering Walpole, and he wondered what had brought him now. He'd have the answer shortly.

The clock braced in a cage against the wall ticked off the passing seconds in metronomic fashion as he waited.

5

Barnes held on, bracing herself as Cahill took a hard turn. The light snow that had begun to fall did little to slow the junior man's race through the morning traffic.

"If this is how you drive to a scene, I'd hate to see what a code run looks like with you behind the wheel."

"Drive it like you stole it. A motto I live by." Cahill approached a city bus, almost kissing the bumper before sliding into the adjacent lane.

"If you only did paperwork with this kind of energy, maybe those reports would be done."

Cahill turned his head, displaying the cocky smile she'd come to accept as his trademark look of satisfaction. "You clear your head by running. For me, it's driving."

Barnes released her white-knuckled grip as Cahill brought his unmarked to a stop inches from the crime scene van. She let out a long, slow exhale after realizing she'd been holding her breath toward the finish.

Cahill put the car in park and opened the door. Barnes got a whiff of the overworked engine as she stepped out into the cold air. "Next time I drive."

"A little adrenaline dump never hurt anyone."

"If you say so." Barnes felt the thrum of her heartbeat resume its normal rhythm as she saw a familiar face in the crowd of blue uniforms lingering about.

"Sergeant Bostik, what brings you out on such a fine morning?" Barnes asked as she approached her former street boss.

"You know me, I love to have my morning cup while standing over a puddle of blood. It adds to the ambiance." Bostik cradled a steaming mug in front of his barrel chest as he looked over the scene. "Nice to see you, Kris. I see you've got a new partner. Don't think I've had the pleasure."

Bostik turned toward Cahill and gave him a quick once-over. Barnes knew through experience that the crusty street sergeant had a softer side. But like a Tootsie pop, it took a lot of work to get to it.

"Sarge, this is Mark Cahill. Came over to us not long ago from Narcotics."

"Name's familiar. You had that big bust a while back, right?"

Cahill only nodded in return.

Barnes had noticed from working with him that Cahill had dialed back on the macho bravado he had when first entering their unit. It was a nice change. He'd proven himself to be a good detective worthy of his position. And if Barnes was honest with herself, he'd grown on her.

"Get us up to speed on what we're looking at here," Barnes said.

"Sure thing. We don't want this stiff getting any stiffer." Bostik gave Barnes a wink.

"From what we were told, the shooter popped our guy and then, what, waited for patrol to arrive?" Barnes looked beyond the yellow tape. Plastic sheeting covered the body near the corner of the intersection where the curb met the street. Traffic was being redirected, adding a bottleneck to the morning commute.

"Sounds about right. Strange as hell, if you ask me. Been doin' this gig a long time. Never have I seen a banger stick around after poppin' a cap in someone's ass. Sure, plenty have been caught after the act by some twist of fate. But it was like this guy wanted to get caught." Bostik gave a shrug of his thick shoulders and took another swig of his coffee.

"Who was first on scene?" Barnes asked.

Bostik pointed to an officer leaning against his cruiser outside of the scene's boundary. "McDougal."

"Don't recognize him. New guy?"

"Green as they come. Finished his field training yesterday."

"First day solo and he catches a shooter. Hell of a start," Cahill said while dusting off the snow accumulating on his jacket.

"Every day's a crapshoot, from your first to your last." Bostik heard his name called by a pale-faced lieutenant stepping out from an SUV. He looked past Cahill, directing his attention to Barnes. "Got to go tend to the man-child who thinks he's in charge. Let me know if you need anything."

"Will do. Thanks, Sarge."

"Cahill, you've landed yourself a hell of a partner. You'd do well to listen to what she has to say. Kris here is one of the good ones. Less of that going around these days." Bostik leveled a gaze at Cahill before walking over to the lieutenant.

"At least he likes you. I'd hate to see what he'd be like if he didn't," Cahill said under his breath.

"Not a pretty picture, I can tell you that." Barnes led the way over to the rookie officer. "We'll get it from the horse's mouth before working the scene. I like to have an idea of what we're dealing with before we get into the processing."

"You lead, I'll follow."

"No leading. You're no dog. Besides, we're partners now."

Something lightened in Cahill's step as he walked alongside Barnes. She wondered if all the bravado was his way of looking for the same thing they all were. Acceptance.

"McDougal?" Barnes asked.

The patrolman pushed himself off the cruiser, his body snapping to a modified position of attention. Barnes could see the academy's militaristic teachings were still fresh.

"At ease, soldier. We're Cahill and Barnes. Homicide," Cahill said.

"We already spoke to Bostik. Got the gist of things but wanted to get your perspective." Barnes noticed the tremble in the rookie's hand. She knew it well. Some compartmentalized it and moved forward. Those who couldn't fell by the wayside, swallowed by the grit of the city they'd set out to protect. Time would tell which fate would befall the young man standing before them.

"Heard it was your first day solo? Nothin' like getting a murder pinch out of the gate." Cahill slapped a hand on the rookie's shoulder, sending a cascade of light snow swirling in the air around them. "Look, kid, we just need you to take us step by step through what you saw from when you first arrived on scene to the point you slapped on the cuffs."

"Sure. No problem." He looked over to the tarp covering the body and then back to the detectives. "I wasn't far away when the call came through. Down the street grabbing a coffee. I got here quickly."

"Define quickly." Barnes held out her notepad, hunching her body slightly to deflect the falling snow from the exposed page. "If you had to guess, how long did it take you to get here?"

"From call to arrival, minute-thirty. Two max."

Barnes made the notation. She knew the specific response time would be verified by the dispatch records, but having it in hand, or at least a rough idea, benefited the investigative thought process. She shot a glance at Cahill. His face told her he was thinking the same thing. Why didn't the perp run?

"Did you run code or silent?" Cahill asked.

"Code. Lights and sirens. Traffic was a real bitch at that time. I knew I'd have a better chance of catching the shooter if I came in low profile but figured it was just as important to get there quickly for the victim's sake."

"A minute-plus is plenty of time to duck out before you arrived." Barnes said this more to herself.

"That's what I thought too. Figured the boss would have my ass for blowing the opportunity to snag the doer."

"Tell us about what you saw when you first hit the corner," Cahill said.

"I parked over there. Backup was a couple blocks away. I moved up, using a parked car as my cover. When I popped up, the shooter was right there." McDougal pointed to where the body lay. "I mean, shit you not, the guy was just standing there, gun in hand."

"Did he see you?" Barnes asked.

"Not sure. Don't think so. At least not until I made my first call out to him."

"Can you describe what he was doing at the time when you first saw

him? In those seconds before you made contact." Barnes tried to put herself
in the rookie's shoes, to see it from his perspective.

"Nothing."

"Describe 'nothing,'" Cahill said.

"I mean nothing. He just stood there. The gun was down by his side. He
just stared out toward the street in front of him."

"Did he look to be in shock? Maybe dusted?" Barnes asked.

The rookie shook his head slowly and then shrugged. "I don't think so. I
guess anything's possible. I don't have much experience with either of those
things."

"Best guess," Cahill prodded.

"No. He seemed the opposite. If I had to describe him in one word, it'd
be calm."

"How did he react when you first addressed him?" Barnes asked. "Did
his demeanor change?"

"I gave him the commands I'd learned for conducting a felony stop.
Told him to drop the gun. Which he did. Told him to take several steps
back from the weapon. He did. Proned him out. By the book." McDougal
shook his head in disbelief. "To be honest, when they taught me that shit in
the academy, I never thought it'd work on the street. Hell, even the instructors gave me a harder time than this guy."

"Sounds like you handled your business like a veteran." Cahill delivered
the compliment and the rookie's face brightened.

"Did my best." McDougal gave a sheepish shrug. "I waited for backup,
which arrived shortly after I got the shooter on the ground. We got him
cuffed and stuffed. That's all she wrote."

"Good work, kid." Cahill followed with a smile. "Make sure you put all
of that in your report."

Cahill started walking to the officer assigned to the logbook, the gatekeeper of the crime scene, in charge of noting any and all officers or investigators who entered.

Barnes lingered for a moment and then spoke in a lower voice. "Do me
a favor and give yourself some time to process what you went through this
morning. And I'm not talking about meeting the shift for beers. I mean
real time, real reflection. Moments like this take their toll. If you don't

address them, they have a tendency to sneak up on you and bite you in the ass."

The rookie exhaled. His shoulders drooped as if a burden had been lifted. "I had him in my front sights. I pulled the slack on the trigger."

"Sometimes the shot not taken plays on the mind just as much."

As Barnes followed after Cahill, the rookie called to her. "Detective Barnes, one more thing."

Barnes turned back as a gust kicked up the glittering white into the air between them. "What's that?"

"I forgot to mention. Not sure it even matters. But when I put him in the back of the cruiser, he did something strange. He smiled."

"Thanks. Every detail matters. It's where the devil lives." She had arrested a lot of people in her time as a Boston cop. Few, if any, ever smiled when the bracelets went on.

After signing into the logbook, Barnes and Cahill dipped under the tape and made their way over to the body. Ray Charles, senior crime scene technician for the department, stood a few feet back with his younger protégé Dawes. Charles had a notepad out and was making a rough sketch of the scene.

"Top o' the mornin' to ya, boys," Cahill said while giving a tip of his imaginary hat.

The two technicians turned. "Well, if it isn't the dynamic duo," Charles said. "You guys are the new go-to team, it seems."

Cahill's bravado made a subtle return in the form of a smile that stretched across his face. Barnes knew the comment was meant as a compliment, but the flipside only served as another reminder that the old one, the Kelly and Barnes team, no longer existed. Both on the job and in her personal life.

"Where are we at?" Barnes asked.

"Just noting the scene. Then we'll begin the overall shots before collection," Charles replied.

"Why the drawing? Why not just use the tablet? Doesn't it create a 3D render and make your job a lot easier?"

The pencil stopped and Charles cocked his head in Cahill's direction. "I see we've still got a bit to learn. No amount of technology trumps the true nature of an investigation. Making this scribbled notation of the scene does something beyond the image itself. Each of the thousands of sketches like this"—Charles turned the pad toward the detectives—"connects my mind to the scene. Something about physically transferring my perception to the page enables me to recall it more clearly. I can go back into my notes, dating back thirty-plus years, and when I run my eyes across drawings like this one, I'm transported back to the scene. Brings my mind to days like this, where I'm standing in the freezing cold looking over another body."

"No shit? Never thought of it that way," Cahill mused.

"Most don't. Most think every new gadget is the magic bullet that'll enable subpar investigators to become rockstars."

"And obviously, you don't feel the same."

Charles shook his head. "Detectives, the good ones, were solving crimes long before any of these so-called advances."

"Maybe so, but it makes things a hell of a lot easier."

"Easy means you didn't dig deep enough." Charles gave Cahill a once-over. "Your predecessor understood that."

Cahill took the blow to his ego in stride. "Point taken."

"Let's take a look." Barnes shifted the focus from the lesson to the task at hand.

Charles and Dawes pulled back the tarps covering the dead man. The shape of the head was distorted. Blood darkened the white canvas coating the ground, a nightmarish Rorschach painting. The body was contorted by the curbing where he'd fallen.

"Shell casing's already been marked," Dawes said as he pointed a few feet from the body.

A thin layer of snow masked the brass. The plastic triangle with the number one identified the evidence. Barnes knelt and examined the damaged skull. "I'm seeing a single gunshot wound to the head."

"Execution-style," Cahill muttered under his breath.

"Appears so. Based on the powder burns and stippling around the entry wound, looks like our shooter was standing beside or slightly in front when he fired." Charles spoke while putting the finishing touches on his sketch.

"Able to locate an ID?" Barnes stood.

"License was in his wallet. Near the gun that was tucked in the small of his back," Charles said matter-of-factly. "Both items have already been photographed and collected."

"Looks like our dead guy was no innocent," Barnes said.

"Not even close," Cahill said. "Dealt with him many times when I was in Narc. Didn't recognize him on account of his balloon head. But he's a bad dude, no doubt about it. Runs a local band of shitheads in the neighborhood."

"I hope this isn't the beginning of a turf war," Barnes said.

"I was hoping this would be an open-and-closed case with the shooter already in custody. Guess we'll have to do some digging." Cahill shot a wink at Charles.

"Looks like we've got a teachable one here." Charles's lips curled upward in a barely perceptible arc. "Each body comes with its own lessons. And its own story."

"Guess we'll get a clearer picture once we have a little chat with our shooter."

Barnes surveyed the scene, gathering a mental snapshot. "We've got some work to do here first. Let's get our ducks in a row before we step into the interview room. And that's assuming the guy hasn't lawyered up already."

"These bodies have a lot to say, just as long as you're willing to listen," Charles said as he slipped the notepad into his satchel and walked to the crime scene van to retrieve his gear.

Barnes focused on the dead man sprawled at her feet, opening her mind to the tale he had to tell.

6

The door opened and Bobby McDonough stood alongside Doyle. Kelly's friend strode inside and took up the seat across the table from him. Doyle waited until the guest was seated before stepping back into the hallway.

"I'll be outside." Doyle looked to McDonough. "You've got thirty minutes."

The door closed, leaving them alone for the first time since Kelly's incarceration. "What brings you in?"

Bobby let out a sigh. "Meant to."

Kelly gave a dismissive shrug.

"Work had me away on business. You know how it is." McDonough shot a glance toward the video camera in the corner of the room.

"Still at it?"

"Not much in the way of choice in that regard."

"Not much of a retirement plan either."

McDonough gave a soft chuckle. "Who needs it? Retirement's for suckers."

"Especially with your employer."

"'Bout that. What's your plan for when you get out?"

Kelly shrugged. "Probably see if Pops has got some work for me."

McDonough was quiet for a moment before leaning forward. "You think coaching some young pups and mopping up after they're done is gonna pay the bills?"

"At least it's honest work."

"From the guy wearing a jumpsuit."

"I can see you're not pullin' any punches today."

"Never do."

"I guess I should've expected nothing less."

"You serious about Pops? I mean, shit, you could do a hell of a lot better."

"I've got Ma's packy as an option. Talked to Brayden a few weeks ago. He's got it running like a well-oiled machine. Even building out some online distribution that's bringing in some new revenue."

"Working in a boxing gym or at a liquor store. Those are the two options you see for yourself?"

"From inside here—yeah. Maybe something'll turn up once I get through the gate. Who knows?" Kelly cast the first line and began the process of slowly reeling his friend in. "Why? You got a line on a job?"

Bobby's eyes cut to the camera again. "I put a word in."

"You did what?" Kelly feigned annoyance and hoped it came across as genuine.

"Why not?" McDonough threw his hands up.

"I can think of a thousand reasons." Kelly shook his head. "I can't imagine mentioning my name to your boss went well. Hell, I'm surprised he didn't put you out just for asking."

"I'd be lying if I said he was elated at the idea. But after the dust settled, he saw my reasoning."

"And what's that?"

"You mean beyond the fact you're blood?"

Kelly's jaw clenched. Connor Walsh, head of the Irish mob, was his biological father, something he didn't learn until late in life. The thought of it still haunted Kelly. "You know I spent the majority of my career trying to bring him down? Or has that little tidbit been forgotten?"

"Bygones." McDonough smirked. "Plus, you're in a much different position now."

"Doesn't change the past."

"Does if you see your past as an opportunity."

"For what?"

"Think of what you know. All the insider information you've got locked away in that thick skull of yours. You'd be invaluable."

"How so?"

"All those connections. It'd be better than having someone on the payroll."

"Fat chance. I'm on the outside now. Blacklisted. Nobody's gonna feed me info if I'm not in the game anymore. Doesn't work that way."

"I'm sure there'd be a few who would—knowingly or not."

"Do you hear yourself when you talk? This idea you've got rattling around in there's one of the dumber things I've heard come out of your mouth." Kelly folded his arms across his chest. "And that's sayin' a lot."

"You're missing the big picture."

"And what's that?"

"It can be a chance at a second life. A new road going forward." McDonough's face softened. "The one I always thought we'd take together."

"I didn't take it then. What makes you think I'll take it now?"

"Because things are different."

"You think me being in here changes who I am?"

"Who you were. And yes, I do. Because I haven't met a guy who's walked into the gray and didn't come out a different person." McDonough looked around the room. "These walls have an effect on everyone. You're no different. You're just still holding onto the belief that you're the saint. To the outside world, you're now a sinner. Like the rest of us."

"Maybe you're right." Kelly looked down at the red jumpsuit. "Doesn't mean I can't climb back out."

"True. If anyone can, it's you. But I'm playin' the odds. And I'm not seeing the upside to you passing on this opportunity. One like this doesn't typically have a second offer."

Kelly let the silence hang in the space between them. He knew turning down an offer to work for Walsh's crew would send Sharp into a frenzy. His incarceration had been staged to create this exact opportunity. What Kelly knew that Sharp didn't was that pushing back would give credibility when he accepted. All that hinged on whether another would come. Everything he stood to gain or lose hung in this moment. He prayed he made the right move. Otherwise, his sacrifice was for naught.

"I've got to think about my daughter. Bad enough I'm in here."

McDonough looked hurt. "You saying your daughter hates her Uncle Bobby?"

"No. You know better than that. But she doesn't know what you do. She doesn't know what I know."

"Exactly. Why would it be any different for you?"

"It's not just her. It's her mom."

"What's Sam got to do with any of this? She start payin' you conjugals?" McDonough's eyebrows bounced and a shit-eating grin overtook him.

"No. Nothing like that." Kelly let out a frustrated breath. This was something he didn't have to fake. "Got a letter today. She's filing for full custody of Embry."

"The hell she is!" The levity gone, McDonough slammed his fist into the table.

The door immediately opened, and Doyle stood at the ready.

"Sorry about that." McDonough put up his hands in mock surrender. "That was all me."

Doyle looked to Kelly, his hand lingering on the door handle.

"We're all good here," Kelly said.

Doyle retreated into the hallway and closed the door again.

"I'll go have a talk with her. Get her head straight," McDonough said.

"The last thing I need is for you to show up at her door to plead my case."

"She's from the neighborhood. Sam knows how this kind of shit's supposed to go down. You don't take a kid away from their father, prison or not. Those are the rules."

"Sam's different now. The neighborhood doesn't have the same pull as it used to."

"Probably 'cause of that prick lawyer she married."

"Maybe. Or she's really just trying to do right by our daughter."

"How's taking you out of the picture helping anyone? Especially Embry. You're her world."

Kelly's head dipped low. "Haven't been for the last few months."

"Time is irrelevant. The bond you two share is unbreakable."

Three months ago, Kelly would've agreed. Since making the choice to take on his new assignment, he felt the first fracture. He wondered how wide the chasm had grown in his absence.

"I won't stick my nose where it doesn't belong. But you have a change of heart, I'll step up for you."

"I know you will. Let's hope, once I'm out of here, that I'll be able to talk some sense into her."

"She already file?" McDonough asked.

"Got the papers today."

"Couldn't wait until you were out? Sorry, Mikey, that's some cold shit."

"I'm just hoping we can avoid the courts."

"If it gets to that point, let me know. I've got an attorney who'll put this to bed. Might even be able to get sole custody over to you."

"I'd never take my daughter away from her mother."

"And that, my friend, is why good guys finish last."

"Don't think that applies to me anymore."

"That's why the offer I made with regard to your new career path still stands."

"I already told you—"

McDonough waved a finger in the air. "Doesn't matter what you say now. It'll be different once you're out. You'll see."

"It's not going to change anything."

"Like I said, wait until you're free and clear of this place before you decide." McDonough cracked his knuckles and straightened in his chair. "Looks like our time is running out. I heard the boys stopped by a few times."

"They did." Like four leaves of a clover, Kelly, McDonough, Donny O'Brien, and Edmund Brown had been inseparable since their youth. Each had taken a different path, but they all found common ground in the neighborhood they'd grown up in and the gym that gave them the skills to carry them through life.

"I'll have a cold one in your honor tonight."

"Didn't even realize it was Thursday. The days blur together in here."

"Our sparring rotation's been thrown into chaos with you being inside.

Be nice to have you back." McDonough gave Kelly a once-over. "I'm gonna have to whip myself into shape to get ready to take you on again. Geez, you look like you're in condition to grab another Golden Gloves belt."

"Not much else to do inside."

"Don't have to worry about that much longer. One day and a wake-up before you're breathin' that free air."

Kelly nodded.

"I'll be here waiting for you on the other side as soon as they open the gates." McDonough stood. "You've almost done your final round in this place. Keep your chin tucked and your guard up."

McDonough walked to the door and knocked while Kelly remained seated.

"Give what I said some thought and we'll talk about it later," McDonough advised as the door opened.

"I'll take him out. Sit tight. I'll be back in a couple minutes," Doyle said.

Kelly absorbed the silence. He'd taken the first steps toward his objective. Each move held consequences. Criminal or not, McDonough was a good friend and the offer he'd made was done out of the kindness of his heart. Kelly would have to use that to his advantage. The damage would be irreparable.

He weighed the scales of justice in his mind. They continued to teeter. And Kelly once again questioned the choice he'd made.

7

Barnes and Cahill made the slog of a commute through the afternoon buildup, aggravated by the steady snowfall that continued as they processed the crime scene. She shook out her coat before hanging it along with the others on the back wall, then dumped her notes onto her desk, the new case already adding its disarray to the established order.

Mainelli, gracing the room with his presence, walked over to their cubicle station and took root by the partition wall next to Barnes. "Our shooter has been booked and processed. He's sitting in interview room four."

"He lawyer up?" Barnes asked.

"Nope. Not yet, at least."

"Is he talking?" Cahill peeked around the partition.

"Just in answering the formalities. As far as the shooting goes—not a peep. You ready to take a crack at him?" Mainelli cracked his knuckles. "If so, I can warm him up a bit before you take the seat. Ya know—give him the speech that you're a human lie detector. That kind of stuff. Put his nerves on edge a bit before you go at him."

"Nah. Let's let him stew a bit while I get my thoughts together." Barnes flipped open her notepad and began reviewing the facts she'd gathered while working the scene. Her mind kept returning to what McDougal had said. The smile he'd seen on the shooter's face.

"From what I heard, it's about as straightforward a case as we could land. Broad daylight. Witnesses to confirm. And the doer in custody with the gun still in hand." Mainelli gave Barnes and Cahill a self-satisfied look.

"Looks that way." Cahill cast a glance at Barnes.

"Agreed," Barnes said while running her eyes over the pages. "I guess we've got the who and how pretty much locked down. It's the why that's nagging at me."

"Probably some turf thing. These guys are always banging it out for control of the market or some corner they claim as their own." Cahill stood up from his chair and rolled his neck. "I'm gonna grab a cup before we go in. Want one?"

"I'm good." Barnes looked at Mainelli. "Has he had anything to eat or drink since arriving?"

Mainelli shook his head. "I try not to feed the animals."

"Good. It'll give me something to work with." Barnes stood and walked over to the vending machine in the breakroom, Cahill joining her.

"So what's the plan of attack?" Cahill depressed the Keurig, and the coffee maker hummed as the brewing began.

"I think we play it straight. He was caught red-handed. Getting a confession would be icing on the cake."

"Agreed. Not that we need it, but it would be nice to hammer in the nail." Cahill stirred in three packets of sugar and one creamer before lifting the steaming beverage to his lips. "But he's a hardcore banger who just committed a cold-blooded murder. My hopes he's going to talk are about as bleak as me getting you out for beers."

This forced a laugh from her. "True."

"Let's put a wager on the table. We get a confession, drinks are on."

Barnes dallied on answering as she forced a crinkled dollar into the vending machine slot. After two attempts, the bill was accepted, she made her selection, and a bag of potato chips fell to the tray below. "Fair enough. Full confession and beers are back on."

Cahill smiled as he took another sip. "Ready whenever you are."

"No time like the present." Barnes stepped back to her desk to grab her notepad and recorder. Stacking the chips on top, she headed to the room where their suspect waited.

Cahill used his key card to unlock the door. He held it open for Barnes and the two entered.

Barnes took a seat across from the shooter, with Cahill beside her. She set her stuff on the table, placing the chips beside her notepad. Before proceeding, she pressed the ON button and activated the recorder.

"This interview is being recorded by both audio and video." She pointed to the camera in the righthand corner of the room. "The recording device in front of you is a secondary system used as a backup."

Roland Watt's face was devoid of any reaction. He sat with his arms folded, his body relaxed.

"I'm Detective Kristen Barnes and my partner is Detective Mark Cahill. We're assigned to Boston Police's Homicide Unit and we're the primary investigators into the shooting death of Larry Rockland. You probably know him better as D-Roc. You've been arrested in connection with that murder."

Watt remained unmoved. He stared into Barnes's eyes as she spoke but offered nothing in return.

Barnes continued. "I understand that you've been read your rights under Miranda. But for the purposes of this interview, I'll advise you of them again, after which I'll request that you sign a document attesting to the fact that you understand them."

Barnes spent the next several minutes carefully reading the rights document verbatim, stopping after each and providing an opportunity for Watt to sign his name. This continued until it was completed in full.

"After being advised of your rights, do you wish to continue speaking with us?"

He set the pen down and folded his arms, then shrugged.

"You'll need to verbalize your answer for us to proceed." Barnes maintained a cool demeanor in her delivery. Cases like this were viewed under the microscope of defense attorneys, and she wanted to leave nothing to chance.

"What my partner means is, open your mouth and speak if you've been asked a question." Cahill's voice had the edge commonly found among those investigators who worked the gang beat.

"I know what verbalize means, Detective Cahill. I'm no idiot. Don't make the mistake of treating me as such." Watt leveled his gaze in Cahill's direction.

Barnes was caught off guard by the articulate manner in which Watt spoke. His tone was calm, and his voice never wavered.

"Again, and for the record, do you understand the rights you've been read and are you willing to speak with us regarding the incident that occurred earlier this morning outside of Kenny's Diner on Savin Hill?" Barnes matched Watt's delivery.

"Yes. And yes." Watt unfolded his arms, his palms coming to rest on the table between them. "Go ahead and ask your questions so we can get on with it."

"You're agreeing to speak with us under your own free will."

"I am."

"And at this time, you've not requested a lawyer to represent you during this interview?"

"There isn't a lawyer in the world who could undo what I've put in motion." Watt sneered. "Hell, Johnny Cochran wouldn't be able to get this charge dropped no matter how many gloves he couldn't get to fit."

Neither Barnes nor Cahill caved to the attempt at levity. "Now that's out of the way, let's talk about what happened this morning."

Watt's stomach rumbled and he looked over at the bag of chips. "Those for me? Or did you plan on having a snack while we talked about my future in prison?"

Barnes slid the chips across the table. "We can get you a drink too, if you'd like." She did this by design. The chips would make a suspect thirsty and thus provide another opportunity to offer help. The exchange of food and drink was a timeless technique used in the building of rapport.

"What do you want to know?" Watt tore open the bag and stuffed several chips in his mouth.

"Not gonna lie, the evidence is pretty damning. We've got plenty of witnesses who saw the shooting take place. Two surveillance cameras in the area caught the act on tape."

"Not to mention you were arrested with the weapon in hand," Cahill interrupted.

"Guess you got it all figured out then," Watt said between crunches. "So what do you need from me?"

"We're hoping you can explain why you did it," Barnes said.

"It's the street. Law of the jungle."

"Don't give me that bullshit. You popped him in the head, at close range." Cahill leaned forward, pressing his elbows against the table. "That wasn't survival or self-defense. It was an execution."

"You from the streets, Detective?"

"Mattapan."

"I didn't ask where you grew up. I asked if you're from the streets." Watt finished the last of the chips and tipped the bag up, shaking the remaining crumbs into his mouth. He then crumpled the bag and tossed it on the floor. "You think you know, but you don't. You're just another punk-ass bitch with a badge and gun."

Barnes could see the effect Watt's words were having on Cahill. "Detective Cahill, would you mind grabbing Roland a Coke?"

Cahill sat back, weighing the question in his mind. He then pushed himself back in his seat, stood, and walked to the door.

Just before the door closed, Watt called out to him, "Make it a Sprite."

Barnes heard Cahill curse under his breath. She was now alone with the killer. He posed no threat to her, at least not directly. She aimed never to take things said during these verbal sparring matches to heart. Nothing was personal, something she needed to convey to her partner.

Watt sat with a smug look on his face.

"Is this a game to you?"

"Everything's a game. Problem is, not everybody knows the rules."

"Then explain it to me. 'Cause from where I'm sitting, it looks as though you've lost."

"It's all a matter of perspective."

"Then help me understand. Help me see it from your side of things."

"D-Roc was a problem. I did the city a favor today."

"How so?"

"I removed a dangerous criminal from the streets. Permanently."

"Did he threaten you? Or your family?"

"Is that what you're looking for? You gonna dig into my past and find some reason for what I did that justifies it? Are you some kind of bleeding heart who needs to know that everything has a reason?" Watt's expression became serious.

"The why gives answers to the family whose lives you've destroyed." Barnes matched him look for look, mirroring the criminal's attitude.

"There isn't a reason I could give that you'd understand."

"Try me."

"He was just a pawn." He had a matter-of-fact manner of speaking. "Nothing more. Nothing less."

"Not sure I understand."

"Didn't think you would. Because you're not playing the same game."

"I need you to give me something." Barnes played with the pen in her hand.

She knew the delay in Cahill's return was because he and Mainelli were watching from the live feed in Halstead's office. She'd just received a text from Cahill and looked down to her thigh to read it. *You've got him on the ropes. Go for the knockout.*

"You want me to tell you I killed him. I did. Ain't no refuting that. And I plan on telling the judge the same thing tomorrow morning at my arraignment."

Another text. *Looks like beers are on for tonight!*

Barnes closed her notepad. Before turning off the recorder, she asked, "Is there anything else you'd like to say?"

"Yeah. Where's my Sprite?"

"I'll check on that. As for your future, prison will afford you plenty of time to work on your chess game. Because it looks like you've checkmated yourself."

"That's 'cause this game's got a different set of rules. Maybe someday I'll teach you."

"Doubtful." Barnes walked to the door and opened it.

"I'll be sure to say hi to Detective Kelly when I get there." Watt's lips drew up into a broad smile. "He and I have a lot to catch up on."

Barnes felt a tingle run down her spine. She ignored the comment, not giving in to the baiting. But she'd be lying to herself if she said it didn't have an effect. Barnes just hoped her expression hadn't betrayed her feelings.

As she walked out into the hum of investigators, Barnes tried to dismiss the shot at Kelly as nothing more than tough talk from a man about to face some tough time. The clock was winding down on Kelly's stay at Walpole and she doubted the two would cross paths. Until he was a free man again, she'd continue to worry. Even though he'd distanced himself from her, their relationship wasn't over—not in her mind, at least.

She closed the door and was greeted by Cahill and Mainelli as they stepped out of Halstead's office. Barnes turned to the patrolman standing by. "He's all set."

The officer nodded and entered the interview room. A moment later, Roland "Killa" Watt was escorted in cuffs from the office and down the hall, where he'd be placed in a holding cell until his arraignment hearing in the morning.

"Looks like beers will be flowing tonight." Cahill chuckled and then gave Mainelli a playful shove. "Get that wallet ready 'cause I've worked up quite a thirst."

Mainelli groaned while giving an exaggerated roll of his eyes.

"A deal is a deal," Barnes acquiesced.

"Not my fault if you're too good at your job." Cahill gave a mock salute.

Halstead exited his office. "Nice work, Kris. Way to lock him in."

"Didn't do much. He pretty much served himself up on a silver platter. Almost like he wanted to get locked up."

"Maybe he did. Who really ever knows what makes these guys tick?" Mainelli shrugged. "Don't overthink it. Take the win and move on."

"We don't catch the smart ones," Cahill said as he started for his desk.

"That's the thing. From what I gathered, he's no dummy." Barnes followed.

"Well, today he proved otherwise."

"Get me the report before you leave. They'll need it for tomorrow." Halstead turned and disappeared back into his office.

Barnes had just begun typing up her report when her attention was called to the two men entering the unit. Lieutenant James Sharp and Chief Ryan strode through the maze of cubicles and headed toward Halstead's office. The chief made a detour and stopped at Barnes's desk while Sharp continued on.

"Heard you guys made quick work of that shooting from earlier. Any luck getting something out of the shooter?"

"Just wrapped the confession."

Chief Ryan leaned in close and lowered his voice. "That's why your unit's my go-to team for the big ones." He stood erect and raised his voice as he continued, "Good policework in bringing that one to resolution."

"Thanks." Barnes's fingers hovered above the keyboard.

"I'll leave you to it." The chief moved along to Halstead's office. Before entering, he turned back slightly. "I keep hearing good things about you, Barnes. If this continues, I may be forced to promote you."

Barnes felt her face redden as the other detectives scattered around the office took notice and looked her way. She ducked lower in her seat, disappearing further into her cubicle space.

The chief entered Halstead's office and closed the door behind him. This was the second time this week she'd seen the three men meet like this. Halstead never spoke about it with their unit, and she'd dismissed it as some administrative wranglings. Seeing them meet again made her think it was something else. What that something was, she couldn't put a finger on.

She set her overactive mind to rest and focused on the task at hand, resuming her documentation of the case. Tomorrow Watt would be sent off to Walpole. A day later, Kelly would be out.

Two days didn't seem like much when compared to the last few months, but with time winding down, her confliction over the unresolved feelings she had was beginning to weigh heavily. Maybe a night out was exactly what she needed.

8

Halstead stood immediately, waiting until Chief Ryan had taken his seat. He glanced out his office window toward the cubicle station where his unit was putting the gift wrap on the murder case before turning his attention to the senior men in the room.

"You've really proven yourself worthy of the position." Ryan gave a nod.

"A coach is only as good as his players. And in that regard, I've been blessed with some of the best this PD has to offer."

"Can't argue there." Ryan shifted in his seat toward Sharp. "The ball is in motion on our other project. I'll let you take the helm."

Sharp nodded. "Kelly's a couple days away from being back out on the street. And his timing couldn't be better."

"How so?" Halstead asked.

"Word on the street is that Walsh's crew is about to make some big moves. A shipment of drones went missing from Hanscom Air Force Base about a week ago."

"And Walsh is responsible?"

"Don't think so. My guys are still running down leads, but it looks like another crew may have been behind it." Sharp rolled a quarter between his fingers as he spoke. "But Walsh wants it. We received a tip that he's trying to broker a deal. The problem is we don't know with who."

"Why drones?" Halstead asked.

Sharp shrugged. "Don't know. Maybe the mob's looking to up their countersurveillance operation."

"Or maybe they're planning on weaponizing them?" Halstead thought of the implications. There were enough guns on the street as it was; the prospect of adding unmanned aerial attack capabilities to the mix was unsettling to say the least. "I can see if my guys have anyone in their snitch Rolodex who might be able to get you that answer."

Sharp shook his head. "Might do more damage than good. The wrong nose goes sniffing around and it's likely to throw up a red flag. Could push the deal off."

"We can't afford to have those drones find their way into Walsh's hands." Ryan lowered his normally booming voice to a whisper. "There's another problem. We think there's a mole."

"In this office?" Halstead felt himself rear back at the thought of it. He'd spent years working as an investigator in Internal Affairs before getting tapped for his supervisory role in Homicide. He'd uncovered enough corruption to know, better than most, the influence money could have in getting officers to cross the line. Regardless, each time one came to light, it rocked the foundation of the job he'd devoted the better part of his life to serving.

"We don't think so." Sharp tossed a look at the chief.

"Don't think or don't want to say?" Halstead fired back with a bit more edge to his voice than he intended.

"We really don't have a finger on the who. We're working on it."

"Then how do you know there's a leak?"

"Too many coincidences with missed opportunities." Sharp stopped the quarter between his thumb and forefinger. "Walsh has deep pockets and it's not much of a leap that he's putting some of that money in blue hands. We've been monitoring it for a while but still haven't been able to dial in on the who."

"But you're sure it's a cop?" Halstead asked.

"As sad as it is for me to say this, yes." Ryan's anger simmered just beneath the surface.

"That's a problem." Halstead pushed back in his chair.

"With Kelly getting out in a few days, I'd say it's a really big one," Sharp offered.

"That's why we want to ensure that we remain the only three who know about Kelly's status and our plan to capitalize on it." Ryan shot a glance toward the Homicide floor. "You haven't mentioned anything to Barnes, have you?"

Halstead tried not to reveal his disappointment in the question. "No. That was part of this arrangement. She's been kept out of the loop, as has everyone else."

"I just had to ask."

"No. You didn't." Halstead let his words hang in the air between them.

"I think what the chief is saying is that armed with the new information we've received, we can't afford the risk of exposure."

"You want to talk about risk? Kelly volunteered for this operation. In doing so, he's sacrificed his relationship with his daughter, with Barnes, and for the moment, with this department." Halstead's normally icy demeanor melted away under the rush of warmth filling his cheeks.

"You think we don't know that? Trust me when I say that it weighs on my conscience every single day since we first asked him to do this." Ryan's face darkened. "I made a promise to him that once the dust settled, we'd make it right."

"Kelly hasn't been in contact with us since arriving at Walpole. We can't trust the recorded line at the prison. And we haven't wanted to risk making in-person contact. Prison's got eyes all over and we couldn't chance it, regardless of how remote." Sharp began rolling the quarter again. "I know the original plan was to have me be his point of contact, but the chief and I have discussed this and decided you'd be a better relay."

"Why's that?"

"I've crossed paths with Walsh and his crew on too many occasions. Somebody happens to catch sight of Kelly and me meeting up—he's a dead man."

"So I've become the de facto handler?"

"Pretty much." Sharp shrugged. "If you two were seen together, he'd at least have enough of a back story to lend to his credibility. Plus, you worked in IA. It would be easy enough to say you had opened an investigation into one of his past cases in light of his recent conviction. All we need to offer is plausible deniability."

"Sharp will closely coordinate with you prior to any meetups and will be your source for intelligence," Ryan said. "Although with the potential mole, we'll need to proceed carefully to ensure it's not being used to flush out Kelly."

"How does this play into the plan going forward?" Halstead asked.

"With the recent intel about the weapons, we're going to have to push the pace on Kelly's insertion into Walsh's crew," Sharp said.

"I thought we had discussed letting him take his time. Establish himself in the old neighborhood. Put some time between the job, prison, and the like. The plan was to give him a wide berth and let him slowly work his way forward."

"Not anymore. The clock is ticking on those drones."

"Explain how you think Kelly will be able to do this. Besides your needs, what changes things?"

Sharp stuffed the coin in his pocket and scooted forward. He pulled a file from his leather binder and slid it across the table to Halstead. "We've been tracking Kelly's visitors during his time inside."

Halstead scanned the sparse list of names. "Not much in the way of company."

"And prior to today, none of those visitors registered on our radar." Sharp tapped his finger against the most recent entry. "Two days before his release, Bobby McDonough shows up."

"This means what? Kelly grew up with him. Doesn't seem like such a red flag to me."

"McDonough is Walsh's top enforcer now. Basically his number two."

"This isn't new information."

"No, it isn't. But coupled with the fact that McDonough just got back in town from Maine makes the timing of his visit more interesting." Sharp cocked an eyebrow.

"Not sure I understand the significance. What's in Maine?"

"We believe it's where the stolen drones are being kept. My guys were running surveillance on McDonough. Followed him as far as Bangor but lost him a few days back. Never nailed down the stash location."

"Maybe you're onto something or maybe not."

"I—" Sharp cut a look at the chief. "We feel the timing of his visit could be the opening we've been hoping for."

"Hope is always a big leap to reality."

"True. But if my guy is right on this, McDonough might be trying to reel in Kelly before the big score."

"Why would he do that?" Halstead worked double-time trying to sync his brain to the thought process behind the Organized Crime lieutenant's logic.

"Because it's what I would do. A cop's insider knowledge would keep Walsh and his guys one step ahead. This would be a situation that would not only call for it—it would demand it."

"If what you say is true, and McDonough did stop by today in an effort to recruit Kelly, I wouldn't be so sure it's progressing the way you hope."

"How so?" Sharp wore his frustration.

"If his friend had tried to rope him in, Kelly would never accept a first offer."

"And why not?"

"Because Kelly's smart enough to know what that would look like." Halstead leaned into his desk. His forearm rested on the visitation list. "You don't think McDonough hasn't been knocking on that door for the better part of their friendship? Each and every time, Kelly's pushed back. Held the line. If he was to flip the script too soon, McDonough would smell it a mile away."

"Then you think McDonough was testing him?" Ryan weighed in.

"If he did ask Kelly to join his merry band of thieves and cutthroats, then yes. McDonough may love Kelly like a brother, but he fears Walsh. In the world McDonough's spent the entirety of his life, fear trumps friendship every time."

Both men sat quietly. The excitement in their voices and expressions at first mentioning McDonough had subsided.

"There's a silver lining to all of this." Halstead watched the jolt of interest return. "If McDonough did ask, and Kelly answered the way I assume he would, then McDonough will ask again."

"You may be right." Sharp had a pensive look. "But what makes you so sure?"

"Because it's what I would've done." Halstead looked out toward his team. "Gentlemen, I have my marching orders and will make contact with Kelly shortly after his release. Keep me posted if anything changes with the stolen drones. But for now, I must wrap up things from earlier because I've got a crew of my own that's in desperate need of a night out."

"I couldn't agree more," Ryan said as he stood and made his way to the door.

Sharp rose from his chair and extended a hand to Halstead. "Thanks for reining me in. I get a bit overzealous at times."

Halstead shook hands with the lieutenant. "We're all on the same team. And we're seeking the same end. Just gotta make sure we do it in a way that ensures we bring our man back in one piece."

Chief Ryan and Lieutenant Sharp moved toward the exit, slowing enough to make small talk with the detectives they passed. As Halstead stood in his office doorway, he noticed Barnes peek up from her desk. She offered a smile that he returned with a nod.

As he stepped back inside, he couldn't help feeling the guilt of the secret he'd been keeping from her over the last three months. Barnes had poured her frustration and anger into the cases she worked, often staying late and coming in early. As her supervisor, he was thrilled that her newfound work ethic had resulted in an unprecedented case closure rate, making both their unit and him look like rock stars. As a human being, and knowing the source of her drive, he hated himself for contributing to it.

9

Calvin Johnson—or Cut, as he was better known on the street—sat on the worn couch in D-Roc's apartment. He and his crew had been drinking and smoking weed since receiving the news about D-Roc's murder. Cut had slowed his alcohol intake, and his painful climb to sobriety left him with a splitting headache that wrapped around his skull like a vise. The numbing effect receded. His nerves were raw and the tremble in his hand became more noticeable with each passing minute.

"Get the bitches out of here," T-Roy boomed. The de-facto leader pounded the last drops of a forty-ounce before tossing it to the floor.

The girls who'd been keeping the vigil with them wasted no time in grabbing their stuff and making their way to the door of the third-floor apartment. When T-Roy spoke, people listened. Those who didn't felt the swift wrath of his hand. Today, his eyes, bloodshot and glossy, burned with rage.

The door slammed. Scrub, the smallest member of their clan, immediately set the two-by-four wood board into the brackets attached to the frame.

With D-Roc gone, it left them five strong. Bounce, a skinny kid with a hyperactive fidget that normally gave way to T-Roy's annoyance, sat uncharacteristically still. It could have something to do with the oversized joint hanging out of his mouth.

Flex stepped into the living room from a back hallway. His thick muscles contracted as he posted up against the wall and waited, as they all did, for instructions.

"The Rollin' 9s did us dirty today." T-Roy leaned toward Bounce and snatched the joint from his mouth. He took a long hit and then tossed the weed onto the table. "D-Roc popped by Killa. Broad daylight. After calling for a parley."

"What's the play?" Bounce asked.

T-Roy released the hit. Smoke encircled his head in a gray cloud. Cut could see the storm brewing in the man's face.

"They broke the truce. Hell, they didn't just break it, they started a war!" T-Roy's voice rumbled. "And that's just what we're going to give them."

His words evoked a ripple of "hell yeahs" and "let's do this" from the others in the room. Cut added his supportive battle cry to the mix, though his voice was weaker than the rest. His heartbeat increased, and panic over what was coming permeated his every thought.

"This is our neighborhood. Our streets. Ain't nobody gonna stop us from keepin' what's rightfully ours." T-Roy walked over to the window and looked down on the street below. "They don't know the trouble comin' their way."

"What're we waitin' for?" Scrub asked. He stood near Flex and looked like a chihuahua standing beside a pit bull.

"Whatcha gonna do, little man?" Flex asked, looming over him.

"I gonna bring the pain."

"Hell yeah you are!" Flex pulled Scrub under his massive arm, wrapping his bicep around his neck and noogie-rubbing the top of his head.

Scrub wriggled himself loose and straightened his T-shirt. Laughter broke out among the group but was quickly silenced by the pounding of T-Roy's fist against the wall.

"Stop jackin' around. We got business to tend." T-Roy pulled a pistol from his waistband, his nickel-plated .45 he loved to brandish. He pulled the slide back, chambering a round.

The others began gathering their weapons. Scrub went into the bathroom and came out a few seconds later with a long-barreled revolver. The gun seemed larger than it was in the small hands of its carrier.

Bounce rose from the couch and then flipped the cushion he'd been sitting on. He retrieved a sawed-off shotgun and brought it up to rest on his shoulder. Cut rocked forward in his seat and pulled the small .25-caliber semi-automatic from the back of his pants. Unlike T-Roy, he didn't need to chamber a round. He always kept his loaded.

Cut looked down at the pistol resting on his thigh. The serial number had been filed off. He worked to control the nervous energy pulsing through his veins and causing his leg to bounce. He liked the cash and girls that came with being a part of his crew, but the gun stuff never sat well with him, though he never dared mention it to any of the others.

"They may have taken our king, but we're going to take their castle," T-Roy said, letting the gun hang loose by his thigh.

"We gonna have the 9s' streets runnin' red," Bounce said in jittery fashion.

"Killa was dumb enough to get picked up. That leaves his crew to receive the punishment." T-Roy stared down each man gathered before him until his eyes came to rest on Cut.

T-Roy's gaze seemed to linger longer on him, or maybe that was just in his head. But to Cut, it felt as though T-Roy was peering deep into his soul.

"How we doin' this?" The question came from Flex, who was no longer leaning against the wall. His body was rigid and the intensity with which he stood was evident in the ripples of muscle pulsating along his wide jawline.

"Hard and fast." T-Roy stood like a battlefield general addressing his troops. "We takin' the van. Roll-up smash-and-grab style."

"We doin' a pop and roll?" Scrub asked.

"Ain't no drive-by tonight." T-Roy was deadly calm. "No way I'm takin' a chance on this comin' back on us. Tonight, we bangin' that nail."

"Hammer time!" Bounce exclaimed.

"Have your ratchet on ready, 'cause this is poppin' off." And with that, T-Roy started for the door.

Cut stood and shot a glance at his watch as their new leader approached. This earned a snarl from T-Roy, who leaned close. His breath stank of malt liquor and marijuana as he spoke in a harsh whisper. "You got somewhere to be, Cut? Because I can't figure anything's more important than the business we got right now."

"Nah. My bad. Baby momma shit, ya know." Cut could feel T-Roy's intensity like steam from a radiator as he took a moment to process. "T-Roy, you know me. I'm down. Time to blaze, right?"

"Time to prove up." T-Roy stepped back and continued on.

The others followed. Just as Scrub reached for the wood brace, a loud knock came from the other side. The group froze in place.

"Boston Police with a search warrant! Open the door!" a deep voice boomed.

T-Roy spun on his heels. In a low whisper, he barked, "Shit! Po-Po! Scrub, take the guns. Stuff 'em in the spot. Bounce, make that powder disappear."

Cut looked on as members of the crew, including him, handed their firearms to the little man. Scrub scurried off down the hall to dump the weapons behind the wall they used for hiding their gear. Bounce grabbed the bags of cocaine from the cupboard and ran to the bathroom to flush it. Five thousand dollars' worth of product was about to enter Boston's sewer system.

Cut stood by the door, frozen in place. Another blast of pounding came from the other side. T-Roy frantically moved toward the window. He threw it open and looked down the fire escape to the street below.

"No blue on this side. Time to bail," he called out.

Flex moved in behind their leader as they prepared to make their escape. The big man growled at Cut, "Get yer ass movin' unless you want to take the pinch."

Cut shifted uneasily. His heart pumping added to the throbbing in his head. Yet, he didn't join the fleeing felons; instead, he turned to the door and reached for the wood brace keeping the police at bay.

"What the hell you up to?" T-Roy's attention was now redirected to the door.

"Sorry," Cut mumbled, unsure whether it was received, not that it would matter afterward anyway.

He then pulled up on the plank, releasing it from the steel brackets holding it in place. Cut tossed the board aside and stepped back from the door, edging over to the kitchen area.

T-Roy and Flex paused at the windowsill, staring in total disbelief. There was a crack as the frame splintered and the door swung wide. A swarm of uniforms filled the void, entering the apartment with guns drawn. Black masks covered their faces as they barked commands, telling everyone in the room to get on the floor.

A sudden stillness fell over the room as both sides faced off. It was short-lived, as one of the men in the tactical unit brought a shotgun up and aimed it at T-Roy. No further commands were issued. A deafening blast erupted from the gunman.

The shot struck T-Roy in the thigh, spinning him. He collided with the muscle-bound Flex and the two fell against the nearby wall. T-Roy slumped to the ground, holding his leg as he let out a scream.

Another member of the tactical team fired a burst from his automatic rifle, punching several holes into Flex's massive chest. His white sweatshirt darkened as blood seeped from the wounds.

Flex let out a roar and charged toward the enemy, staggering when another round of bullets found their mark. By some unseeable force, Flex continued to press on. He rounded the couch, clutching the back for support as his strength waned. Six holes and he was still coming. He launched himself at the nearest member of the tactical team, arms outstretched like a linebacker going for an open-field tackle. His target stepped back just out of reach. Flex landed flat on the floor, his head just inches from the man who'd fired the last volley of shots, the last exhale releasing from his body.

Gunshots rang out from the hallway. One found its mark, striking Flex's killer in the shoulder. The man fell back as Scrub found cover in an adjacent room while he continued to pepper the tactical team.

The men dove out of the way and the rounds riddled the wall behind them. As Scrub stepped out from his cover and began approaching, the team readied themselves for the next wave of attack. One of the team members crawled through the kitchen and positioned himself at the edge of the hallway.

Scrub entered and took aim at a man hiding behind the couch. His weapon clicked. Cut watched the horror fill the little man's face. It was short-lived. The gunman closest stepped forward and placed a single shot into the side of Scrub's head.

"One missing. Where's Bounce?" one of the tactical team members shouted.

In the quiet that followed, the sound of a toilet's tank refilling gave away the last of the crew's position. Two of the tactical men silently approached. They brought their weapons up and fired into the door. A whimper leaked out from the other side.

One of the men kicked hard and caved the door inward. The other stepped inside and fired four more shots at a downward angle. Cut heard no further sounds.

"What the hell? I'll kill you. I'll kill your families." T-Roy's threats were met with laughter.

One of the tactical guys walked over and stepped on his wounded leg. T-Roy let out a howl. He spat blood and swung wildly at the man standing over him.

"No. I don't think so." He leaned down and pressed a revolver against T-Roy's head. "Say hi to D-Roc when you see him."

The gunshot caused Cut to jump. T-Roy's dead eyes stared up at him. One of the tactical group members moved in beside Cut.

Cut tried to steady himself. He knew what he'd signed on for when he'd agreed to the Rollin' 9s' request. Even so, his life seemed less valuable in the wake of this bloodshed. "Survive at all costs" were his father's last words. It didn't seem worth it now. But the street carried different rules, and you either lived by them or suffered the consequences.

"We owe you one." The man's voice unnerved him. It was eerily calm in light of everything that had just transpired. "I guess we'll have to pay you back in another life."

Cut never felt the bullet enter his brain. The nerves leading up to this moment funneled out of the hole in his head as he gave way to nothingness.

10

Barnes had finished and submitted the case report before leaving the station. She made a quick detour on her way to the bar to check on her cat, Bruschi. After adding some dry food to his bowl and filling his water dish, she made fast work of changing into something more casual.

The drive to the bar was stop-and-go traffic, but she used the time to clear her head, telling herself she deserved the night out. Part of her felt guilty, thinking about Kelly locked away. He'd have been in the seat next to her right now. She could almost hear his voice. His presence was everywhere, and though she would never admit it, she felt lost without him.

No street parking was available, and she pulled her car to the back lot, wedging between a work truck and a Prius. The morning snow had died off. The March wind followed, nearly blowing her door shut on her as she exited.

She stopped at the pub's back entrance, the smell of food seeping into the night air. Music and laughter reverberated through the walls as she stood and gave one last thought to turning and heading back home, but the incessant ribbing she'd endure tomorrow wasn't worth the effort. Pushing away her reservations, Barnes opened the door and stepped inside.

She paused as she scanned the well-dressed after-work crowd who sat and stood shoulder-to-shoulder with the more hardcore locals. The bartenders were busy retrieving drinks for the thirsty bunch when Barnes caught sight of Cahill.

He must have sensed her looking at him, because he swiveled on his stool and smiled brightly at her. He held a half-full mug in the air and waved her over.

"The stars have aligned." Cahill downed the last of his beer and stuck his hand out in Mainelli's direction. "Pay up."

Mainelli begrudgingly fumbled with his wallet and, after a moment of hesitation, retrieved a twenty-dollar bill, slapping it in Cahill's open palm.

"What was the bet?" Barnes asked as she stood at the table between her two colleagues.

"Whether you were going to be a no-show." Cahill pocketed the money.

"Ye of little faith, Mainelli." Barnes gave him a playful shove. "What's your wife going to say when you come home broke?"

"Probably be sleepin' on the couch." Mainelli shrugged. "Nothing new there."

"Where's the sarge?" Barnes asked, seeing an extra mug at the table.

"Draining the lizard."

"Geez, Cahill. There's a woman present."

"Nah, Barnes is no woman. She's a cop."

Her nerves faded as the banter continued and she was reminded of the importance of cutting loose, especially given their recent caseload. "Where's mine?"

Cahill put his fingers to his lips and let out a loud whistle. It got the attention of a nearby waitress, and she approached the group.

"What can I get you?" she asked.

"Same." Barnes thumbed toward the beer in Mainelli's hand.

"Sure thing."

As the waitress turned, Cahill caught her by the elbow. "Might as well bring a pitcher." He shot Mainelli a devious smile. "Better make that two. Maybe throw in a round of shots."

The waitress gave a nod. Barnes also noted the look she gave Cahill. She did little in the way of hiding her interest. Offering a wink and a smile, the waitress disappeared into the crowd as she snaked her way to the bar.

"Looks like you've got an admirer," Barnes said.

"Her? Nah. She's not my type."

"Not your type? I thought your only requirement was a pulse." Mainelli nearly spat his beer as he laughed at his own joke.

Cahill's face reddened. Barnes couldn't remember a time when she'd seen the newest member of their squad embarrassed.

"I see the team is all here." Halstead appeared behind her. "I'll grab another round and get you a glass."

"No need. Already done. Mainelli's been extremely generous tonight." Cahill smiled and patted the pocket containing the twenty.

"I've only got one more in me," Halstead said while checking his watch.

"Early bedtime, Sarge?" Mainelli asked.

Halstead shook his head. "Sergeants' rules. Or at least mine. Never stay too long. I don't want to be around when the real stupid comes out. Plausible deniability."

"Don't have to worry about that with us, boss," Cahill said.

"Plus, it gives you guys time to vent about me."

"Never happens. You're one of the good ones," Mainelli offered.

"Now that's the beer talking." Halstead gave an uncharacteristic smile.

Libations had melted the Iceman's unreadable façade. Barnes was happy to see he had another side to him. And she knew he was right. Good boss or not, staying too long and drinking too much with subordinates never panned out well for either side.

The waitress returned, carrying the tray on her shoulder. Barnes was impressed with the petite girl's ability to handle the weight of it while navigating the gauntlet of drunkards lining her path. She set the drinks on the table. Barnes noted a small, folded piece of paper under the shot glass she placed in front of Cahill. She mouthed the words "call me" before moving on to another table of thirsty patrons.

"Damn you and all your boyish charms," Mainelli said as he refilled his mug.

"Luck o' the Irish, my Italian friend."

"Who said we're friends?"

Cahill's bravado was immediately dashed. Mainelli kept a deadpan expression for only a moment longer before letting the junior detective off the hook and slapping him on the shoulder. "Just kidding. You're starting to grow on me."

"Good. 'Cause I may be crashing on your couch with you tonight."

"The hell you will. Last thing I need is for my wife to learn there's a young stud in my unit. I'm barely able to keep her satisfied as is," Mainelli said into his mug.

Halstead picked up his shot glass and held it at eye level. "I'd like to propose a toast. To the best damn squad in BPD. Hell of a job today!"

Barnes and the others scooped up their shot glasses and said in unison, "Hear, hear!"

"Sláinte!" Cahill said, and slammed his empty glass on the tabletop.

The whiskey burned the back of Barnes's throat, causing her eyes to water. Warmth spread across her cheeks as she filled her mug and took a sip to neutralize the sting. The liquids hit her empty stomach and reminded her she'd forgotten to eat. Cases had a way of staving off hunger, and she was victim to it once again.

Halstead did what he'd promised, hanging out long enough to finish another beer before readying himself to leave. "I'm heading out. Enjoy yourselves tonight. You've definitely earned it."

"Thanks for coming out, Sarge. We'll have to do this more often," Cahill said.

"I'd like that." Halstead threw on his coat. "Remember, tomorrow's business as usual. Prepare yourselves for some fallout from today's shooting. The other crew's going to be looking to make things right. And that's never a good thing for us."

And like that, the Iceman was back. Calm, cool, and collected, he made his exit.

"He's right, ya know. Gonna be a real shit show when D-Roc's boys decide to get their pound of flesh," Mainelli said.

"Well, it ain't tonight. We've got plenty of beers between now and then." Cahill topped off his beer and took a swallow.

The three spent the next couple of hours trading war stories. Cahill and Mainelli had some witty repartee during their back-and-forths, the latter working tirelessly to one-up every story Cahill threw out. The junior detective, not one to take the abuse lying down, fired back with comments about

Mainelli's ancient tall tales. Neither crossed the line and all of the verbal sparring was friendly in nature.

Barnes was a bit more reserved, but as the hours dragged on, she began to loosen up. The beer had found its mark and she was able to set aside her angst over Kelly and enjoy the company of the two men bookending her at the bar table.

Mainelli's phone vibrated on the lacquered tabletop next to his nearly empty mug. He picked it up and thumbed the screen open. He squinted at the message, which resulted in another insult from Cahill about the senior detective's age.

"That's it for me, kids." Mainelli pounded the last of the beer and grabbed his coat. "Wife's pissed. Told her I was going to be home an hour ago."

"Looks like it's the couch for you," Cahill said as he raised his glass in a final salute.

"Don't do anything I wouldn't do," Mainelli advised as he departed.

"Maybe you'll actually beat us to work in the morning for once," Barnes called out to Mainelli as he made his way through the bargoers, much less gracefully than the waitress.

"And then there were two." Cahill eyed his mug and then Barnes.

She swirled the beer in her mug. "Probably a good idea we head out too."

"Why? Don't like the company?"

"Not that. It's just getting late is all."

"They haven't made last call yet." Cahill emptied his glass.

"If I'm setting my clock to bar time, we're already screwed." Barnes offered a conciliatory smile.

"All work and no play."

"You saying I'm dull?"

"Furthest thing from it."

Barnes heard a slight slur to Cahill's words. But what caught her off guard was the look in his eyes. He stared at her with an intensity she hadn't seen or maybe hadn't wanted to notice before. She lifted her glass, using it as a shield as she finished up the last swig.

"You hide behind the work. You know that, right?" Cahill let out an exasperated sigh. "Not that we don't all do it to some extent. But you've been going at it harder than most. Especially lately."

"The cases demand it." Her words lacked conviction, and she knew it. Cahill did too.

"Not saying they don't. Just don't lose yourself to it."

"Thanks, Dad."

"Not my place, I guess." Cahill traced a watermark on the table with his finger, breaking eye contact. "I'd hate to see you look up from those case files and find yourself ten years older and nothing but the job to show for it."

"Not gonna happen."

"I've seen it before. And I've heard the same. Sometimes it just does."

"Well, I'm not going to be one of those cops."

"Just worried about you."

"Didn't know you cared."

"I do. I guess I always have." Cahill lifted himself from the stool he'd been rooted to for the better part of the night and picked up his coat. "Not that it matters anyway."

"I appreciate it. I really do." Barnes felt herself fighting for the words. She blamed it on the alcohol but knew it was something else.

"But?"

"It's complicated."

"Not from where I sit." Cahill was serious now. "It shouldn't have happened. Kelly's a hell of a cop. One of the best I've ever worked with. But things broke bad. He's on a different path now."

"I know." That deep sadness she'd pressed down for the past several hours was resurfacing.

"He let you go. Problem is, you haven't let go of him."

She knew he was right but offered nothing in return. Instead, she distracted herself by grabbing her coat.

"Sorry. I overstepped my place."

"I'll figure it out. I always do."

"At least let me walk you to your car."

Barnes offered a shrug. "Suit yourself."

Barnes noticed Cahill left the waitress's number on the table. They made their way through the thinning crowd and down the hallway to the back door. The blast of cold air felt good against her face as she stepped out into the lot.

She walked over to her car. The work truck was gone, making it a lot easier to open the door. She turned back to Cahill, who was standing close.

"If you ever need an ear, I'm here to listen." Cahill rested a hand on top of the car door, steadying it against the gusting wind.

"I'll keep that in mind."

Cahill's hand lingered. "You know I used to give him crap about shitting where he ate. Never date a cop, ya know?"

"He told me."

"But I get it now." Cahill had a nervous edge to his voice. "I mean, you're not just any cop."

"I'll take that as a compliment."

"You should. I mean, you're worth it. Worth breaking the rules for." Cahill leaned in closer, his body nearly touching Barnes. "If you ever want to grab a bite or a drink, or whatever, let me know and I'll be there."

"Not sure you could fit me into your busy after-hours schedule." Barnes gave a weak laugh. With Cahill only inches away from her, she felt a nervous tingle run through her body. Her mind raced and she couldn't discern whether it was good or bad.

"I'm looking for something more than all of that. I see a better option." Cahill moved even closer. "I see that in you."

Cahill leaned in, his lips pursed. Barnes's heart nearly jumped out of her chest. She stood frozen, turning her head at the last second and redirecting Cahill's kiss to her cheek.

He stepped back and stumbled with his words. "I'm sorry. I misread things. I didn't mean—"

"No. I'm sorry if I gave you the wrong impression." She could see the pained look in his eyes. "It has nothing to do with you personally. You're a good-looking guy. A great cop. And a good friend."

"Oh man. The F-word. Kiss of death." Cahill stepped back a bit.

"I've got to get my head around things first."

"But you're saying there's a chance."

"I'm saying let's give it some time."

"Fair enough." Cahill straightened.

The cellphone in Barnes's pocket vibrated. Grateful for the distraction, she pulled it out and then looked at Cahill. "It's Halstead."

"Great."

"Hey, Sarge, looking to find us for last call?"

"There's been another shooting. Sounds like a real shit show."

"Watt's crew take a hit?"

"No. It was D-Roc's."

The phone was on speaker and Barnes held it up so Cahill could hear.

"Doesn't make sense. Unless the 9s are trying to do a preemptive strike," Cahill said.

"Not sure who the shooters are at the moment. May be unrelated." Halstead paused for a moment. "But doubtful, knowing the players."

"Where do you need us?" Cahill asked.

"Not tonight. Sergeant Belkin's crew is taking lead on this one."

"Shithead Acevedo. He and his partner couldn't find a clue if it was shoved up their ass," Cahill muttered.

"No matter. They're up on rotation. We'll pick up the pieces in the morning. Get some rest because there's going to be plenty to do tomorrow." Halstead hung up.

An awkward silence followed. Barnes slipped her phone back into her pocket. "You heard the sarge."

"About that kiss—"

"Don't have to explain. Beer gets the best of us sometimes." Barnes slid around the door and put one foot inside.

"I'll see you tomorrow." Cahill stuffed his hands deep into his pockets.

"Tomorrow it is. Partner."

Barnes entered her car and closed the door. She let out a long, slow exhale. As she drove out of the lot, she tried to clear her mind. Winding through the city streets, she thought of only one person. And the two days until he was home.

11

His stomach rumbled. The breakfast tray had never arrived. It was unlike Doyle—or any of the other guards, for that matter—to skip a meal delivery. There'd been times over the course of his stay where the food had arrived late. This was different. Aside from the yard time, meals were one of the things he looked forward to. The food was terrible, although his palate had adjusted over time. He liked it for a different reason. Each serving marked the passage of time. Today was his last full day inside these walls. The fact that his meal hadn't been delivered threw off the internal clock marking his final countdown, and he found the irregularity disconcerting.

Setting aside his annoyance, Kelly forced himself to focus on his most reliable distraction. Boxing. For the second time since winter's gray light filtered in through the slit of a window, Kelly dropped to the floor. His palms slapped the concrete as he locked into a rigid plank position, then lowered himself into a push-up and launched himself back up. He finished his twenty-fifth burpee and then shook out his arms, taking up a fighter's stance and bringing his right fist close to the right side of his temple. His left jutted out in front of him, just below his eye.

He imagined the sixteen-ounce gloves he used to wear and positioned his hand accordingly, as if they were still there. He tucked his elbows tight to his ribs and rolled his shoulders forward. He began rocking with his hips and brought his weight up to his toes to begin the dance, moving around the small square space that was his gym now.

He thrust forward a double jab followed by an overhand right, and then shifted his weight quickly, twisting, bobbing, weaving, fighting the imaginary opponent as he danced with his shadow cast by the sunlight. He wasn't in the cell when he was throwing punches. He was back in Pops's gym. His home. He could smell his sweat, reminding him of the sweat he'd poured into those thousands of hours of punches being thrown and absorbed.

The lessons learned there helped him now to temporarily ease his mind of the burden he was carrying. In the nearly three months that Kelly had spent inside Walpole, he'd trained as if he was going for the Golden Gloves, minus sparring partners and heavy bags. Kelly was in the best shape of his life, or at least his life since becoming a cop.

The three meager meals a day had left him wiry, and the training had left his muscles taut. He swung at the imaginary opponent, ducking the blows that no one but Kelly could see, slipping, dipping, bobbing, and weaving, and then sending a hail of uppercuts and hooks. Downing one opponent as another would rise, turning to face each foe, moving through the gauntlet in his small space, transporting himself to the bigger ring, transporting himself beyond the bars.

There was a bang at the door that took him away from the ring, brought him back to the cold concrete surroundings. The metal frame of his twin cot bed, the steel of his toilet and sink, the one picture of Embry taped above the faucet.

"Prisoner 14362, Kelly, step back to the wall."

Kelly stopped his momentum. Sweat seeping from his body, he complied, waiting for the door to open. A buzzer sounded and then a manual key was inserted in the lock, turning the heavy bolt and releasing the seal on the door.

"Enter cell 31."

The voice belonged to Derek Gladstone, an oversized gorilla of a guard who had made no bones about his dislike for Kelly. Apparently, Kelly had arrested his brother years ago on a minor drug violation back when he worked Narcotics. Gladstone was overjoyed to see Kelly among the prison's jumpsuit-wearing population.

"Step forward, Kelly."

Kelly took three steps forward as Gladstone entered the cell, dipping his head slightly below the doorframe.

"Turn around. You know the drill. Hands on the wall."

Kelly did as he was instructed and Gladstone ran a full search of Kelly's body, starting at the wrists and working his way down the back and then up the front of his legs. He checked between his crotch and buttocks, moving up the jumpsuit before slapping him once on the back with his meaty hand.

"Good to go. Ready to walk?"

"No room service today?"

"Not today."

Kelly followed Gladstone's enormous frame out onto the landing.

"Pin your hands."

Kelly, like a military soldier preparing to march, pinned his fists alongside his seam lines and stood at a modified position of attention.

"And move," Gladstone said, taking up step behind Kelly.

He drummed his thumb loosely on an extendable baton at his waist, the way he always did. Kelly knew men like Gladstone. He'd seen them in the ranks of his own PD. The ten-pound badge, the draw of the power, he despised it all, and in turn despised Gladstone.

"One more day," he said to himself as they made their way to the sealed doors that provided access to the D-Block wing and general population. Kelly stood by the door as Gladstone waved to the camera. A buzzer sounded, and Kelly entered.

The prison was structured like a pentagon, each wing branching off a central hub and network like a roundabout. At its center was a guard control tower, and passageways led into the five blocks of the prison system.

As the door sealed behind them, Gladstone said, "Open D-Block." Another buzz and hiss, and the door released. Gladstone pulled the door open, and Kelly entered.

Gladstone followed, sealing the door just like before, and the two walked down the corridor. Kelly could smell food cooking but couldn't discern what today's meal would be. It usually tasted as it looked: gray.

Several of the inmates catcalled as Kelly entered the room, lobbing threats and taunts his way. He'd heard them all before. Since he'd been processed in, there had been many opportunities for some of the general population to lay eyes on him, although no one had ever touched him. The guards were vigilant about keeping the prisoners back.

Kelly headed for the chow line. Up ahead, a young, thin man with a light brown complexion and neatly groomed fade was grabbing a tray. Kelly eyed him, seeing something familiar but unable to pinpoint what. It had been like that since he entered the prison on day one. Many of the hardened faces he'd passed were men he'd encountered in his life before the jumpsuit—he was personally responsible for arranging many of their current sentences. Few, if any, held anything but contempt and hatred in their eyes when catching sight of him. Even now, he felt their cold, ruthless stares from all sides.

An inmate bumped into him from behind, knocking Kelly into a nearby table. Heavy body odor trailed the thickly muscled man responsible as he proceeded past, chuckling to himself and cutting his way up the line until he came to the smaller inmate Kelly remembered but couldn't place.

He grabbed the tray from the smaller man and smacked him on the side of the head, dropping him to the ground. The man fell into a fetal position, and the aggressor continued his unsolicited rampage and began kicking the downed prisoner.

"Do something," Kelly said to Gladstone.

"It'll sort itself out. Sometimes these boys just need to blow off some steam. Keeps things from bubbling up."

Kelly shot him a glance. "Looks like this has reached its boiling point."

"Mind your place, Kelly. You're not a cop anymore."

Kelly disregarded the warning and left the red line he'd been conditioned to stand on. Out of the corner of his eye, Kelly saw Gladstone reach for him, but he managed to slip the guard's grasp. He bypassed the other prisoners in line, making a beeline for his target.

He lowered his shoulder as he closed the gap. The bigger inmate was winding up for a big finale, his right foot drawing back. Kelly slammed his shoulder into the center of the bully's back.

The big man lurched forward, his body off-kilter from the one-legged stance, sending him into the cafeteria line's tray rack. Momentum did the rest of the work, hurtling him over the rack and onto the hard floor of the kitchen beyond.

He wasn't down for the count. A roar erupted as the enraged inmate shot up from the linoleum. Seeing that Kelly had been the cause only furthered his rage. He kicked the rack out of his way, sending trays skidding across the chow line, and charged forward, his massive hands telegraphing the destruction they sought.

Kelly lowered his center of gravity at the last second, ducking the bigger opponent's wild swings and catching him by the waist. Using the charge to energize his movements, Kelly lifted the big man, then spun him and slammed him down, letting gravity do the rest.

His attacker was flat on his back now, his bald head smacking the hard flooring. Kelly seized the opportunity and swooped down on the dazed man. He gripped him by the collar, cinching it tight around the inmate's thick neck as he lifted his head and prepared to deliver a knockout blow.

His fist was cocked and ready to strike when Kelly was suddenly jerked back from behind. Caught off balance, Kelly dropped the inmate and spun, ready to take on the next attacker only to find it was Gladstone who had intervened.

"You want to do another ninety days?" Gladstone shouted, yoking Kelly up close. Frothy spit fell from his mouth onto Kelly's uniform. "When I say leave it be, you leave it be."

"Let go of me." Kelly's hands were still, his fists relaxing. He thought hard about laying out the guard but knew that he was too close to the end. Gladstone saw that his opportunity had passed too, but he held on for a moment longer before releasing his tight grip.

"Get back in line. You too!" Gladstone ordered the inmate who had started the fight.

Before Kelly took up his tray and got back in line, he bent down and reached out a hand to the man on the ground. He took it and Kelly pulled him to his feet.

"You all right?"

He nodded. "Thanks."

He picked up another tray and set it on the railing, then began moving down the chow line. Kelly worked his way down the line with Gladstone now close at his heels. He could still feel the heat of anger emanating from the man's mere presence.

Gladstone wasn't angry that the other inmate had attacked the younger, smaller man. No, he was angry that Kelly had defied his authority and done something he should've done, something he was paid to do, which was to protect the inmate. Kelly wanted nothing more than to gift the poor excuse for a corrections officer the devastating overhand right he'd intended for the bully. If nothing else, he hoped Gladstone's actions, his true character, would be noticed by his superiors and his badge ripped from his uniform.

Even in the darkest of situations, truth had a way of finding the light. He hoped the same held true here.

12

Barnes thrust out her hand from beneath the thick comforter and blindly felt her way across the nightstand. The incessant beeping of her alarm clock was amplifying the pounding in her head. Her finger pressed the raised button and brought blissful silence. It was short-lived, as the vibrations of her cellphone rumbled along the wood surface.

She pulled the phone under her covers, illuminating her dark cave of blankets. It took a moment for her eyes to adjust to the brightness before she could make out the caller ID. It was Halstead.

Panic blitzed her mind as she saw the time. Nine a.m. Barnes shot up into a seated position against the headboard. The room spun and she fought against the queasiness in her stomach.

"Sarge." Barnes did her best to hide the fact that moments ago she'd been in a beer-induced coma. "My apologies. Running late this morning."

"That makes two of you. Cahill's MIA as well."

She heard the terseness in his voice. Or maybe she was hypersensitive to it under the circumstances and in her current state.

"I guess I made the right choice in cutting out early," Halstead said.

"This is why I don't go out after work."

"Happens to the best of us."

"Not me." Barnes fished around the floor until she found the Gatorade bottle and was happy to see it still had a swig left. She gulped it down. The lukewarm sugary liquid worked its way down and cleared the dryness of her throat.

"Don't beat yourself up."

Barnes cradled the phone between her shoulder and neck as she scooted off the bed and over to her dresser. "What's the word on the shooting from last night?"

"It's a cluster. We've got five dead."

"Five?" Barnes stopped moving. "That's a bad hit."

"Bad as they get. They're just breaking down the scene now. We'll get a better picture once Belkin's crew gets back."

"I'm on my way. Out the door in thirty seconds." Barnes stepped out of her pajamas and pulled up a pair of khakis.

"Get here as quick as you can. Briefing's going down in thirty minutes."

"Got it. I'll be there." Barnes switched sides with the phone as she threw on a button-up shirt.

"See if you can get hold of Cahill." Halstead's voice faded out for a second. "Disregard, he just walked in. I'll see you when you get in." Halstead ended the call.

Barnes finished dressing. In her haste, she nearly forgot to grab her gun. The only thing worse than showing up late was showing up late without your duty weapon.

She holstered her Glock, made quick work of brushing the chalky taste from her teeth, then grabbed her coat and bolted out the door.

The drive to headquarters took less time than usual, but every second ticking by felt like another slap across her wrist. Barnes had never received a mark in her personnel file. Not once. This morning, she felt the demerit punching a hole in her perfect record.

The cold air bit at her face as she exited her vehicle and raced toward the back entrance of Boston PD Headquarters. The wind acted as a wet washcloth, temporarily cleansing the remnants of last night's overindulgence now seeping from her pores.

She opted for the stairs, taking two at a time as she rushed to the second floor. Barnes slowed her mad dash to a brisk walk when she entered the hallway. Up ahead she saw Acevedo exit the elevator and walk into the unit's office. Closing the gap, she caught the door before it shut.

She took a moment to catch her breath as she scanned the busy room. It was an all-hands-on-deck situation, and her late arrival made her the odd man out. The hum of chatter was louder than the norm as she moved toward her desk.

Mainelli leaned against the wall outside of The Depot, the unit's conference room typically used as a workspace for major crimes. It was already being organized as such by members of Belkin's team.

"Well lookie here. 'Bout time you rolled in." Mainelli beamed.

"First time you've beat me in. It'll be the last," Barnes muttered.

"I guess you and Cahill took the same bus."

Barnes tossed her coat over the back of her chair. She heard the squeak of wheels as Cahill slowly stood from his desk. He looked as bad as she felt. Seeing him again after the way things ended last night filled Barnes with shame. She kicked herself for not bailing when grumpypants had departed.

"Grabbed you a coffee." Cahill nursed a sip from the cup in his hand.

Barnes saw the medium Dunkin' on her desk. She picked it up and popped the lid. Steam wafted into her face as she raised a toast. Her stomach rumbled as she brought it to her lips.

"Sorry if it's a bit cold. Been sittin' for a couple," Cahill said.

"It's perfect. Thanks. Just what the doctor ordered."

Cahill slid around his cubicle and moved in close to Barnes. She felt the return of the uneasiness of where they'd left things.

"Hey, Kris. I just wanted to apologize again for last night," Cahill whispered.

Barnes shook her head. Unable to meet his eyes, she buried her face in the coffee. "Nothing to apologize for."

"We're good, then?"

"Right as rain."

Halstead exited his office. Lincoln White, head of BPD's Narcotics Unit, stood beside him. White had his hands on his hips and was puffing out his chest like a battlefield general surveying his troops. The sight of him stirred the liquid contents of Barnes's stomach.

"Head into The Depot. Belkin is going to give us a rundown on last night's incident," Halstead said.

Barnes grabbed her notepad and made her way to the room. Mainelli gave a bow and stretched out his arm in grand fashion. Barnes ignored the gesture and slipped inside, finding a seat at the far end of the room. Cahill snuck into the seat beside her. Normally she would've welcomed his presence, but now it only compounded her annoyance by serving as an unnecessary distraction to the business at hand.

"Five dead. That's a lot of bodies to work," Cahill said under his breath.

"That's a lot of grieving families calling for justice."

"These boys weren't no angels, I can tell you that. Spent the better part of my time in Narc putting cases on them. Or at least trying."

"Here we go. Telling stories about the good old days when you were thumping heads with the goon squad?" Mainelli plopped noisily into the seat on the other side of Barnes.

Cahill rolled his eyes.

The seats filled quickly, leaving several detectives to stand. White entered, followed by Halstead. The door closed and the room fell quiet. For a group of Boston detectives, moments of silence like this were a rarity.

"As you know, yesterday morning we had the shooting death of Larry Rockland, age twenty-eight, better known on the street as D-Roc. His killer, Roland Watt, is already in custody, but the fallout from that incident appears to have bled over into the shooting that occurred last night," Halstead said.

"We got any leads on perps?" one of the younger detectives asked.

"Not exactly, but we're working toward that end." Halstead looked over at White. "My team was primary on the first murder. Sergeant Belkin's team is handling the second. From the looks of it, they're related, and we'll be working together to bring those responsible to justice. Sergeant Belkin will give the details gathered from last night's investigation so we're all on the same page."

Halstead stepped aside and Belkin moved toward the center of the room. Belkin's eyes were bloodshot and his slacks were wrinkled, the telltale signs of an all-nighter.

"Ladies and gents, we had a real bloodbath last night. Five men were gunned down in a third-floor apartment near the intersection of Talbot and Helen. The first call came in just after one o'clock this morning. Units were on scene a couple minutes later. None of the suspects were on scene at that time." Belkin rubbed his pointer and middle fingers together; they were stained a light yellow. His smoker's fidget was on full tilt as he spoke. "Multiple gunshot wounds of varying types leads us to believe we're dealing with more than one shooter."

"Any possibility we're looking at a contained shooting?" Mainelli asked. "Is it possible these guys got into a beef and banged it out?"

"We looked at that as a possibility but ruled it out."

"No way these guys shot each other. The body positions don't jive with that. Plus, we found a blood trail in the hallway." Detective Acevedo twisted in his seat toward Mainelli.

"All of the men killed last night were Rock Steady Boyz, members of D-Roc's gang."

"We know the 9s and RSB have been beefing for control of that section of Talbot's drug trade for a long time now," White interrupted.

Belkin gave a weary nod. "That said, all fingers point to the likelihood this was carried out by members of the Rollin' 9s. As far as who the actual shooters were—that we don't have at this time. It's one of the reasons we've brought in the lieutenant here. His unit is very familiar with all the players, so his insight into our list of possible suspects will be invaluable as we build our case."

"Cut the head off a snake and the body still moves," White boomed. "With Watt pulling the trigger on D-Roc, the 9s must've figured it's better to strike first rather than wait for the retaliation, which was sure to come."

"Lieutenant White has compiled a list of the Rollin' 9s' known members." Belkin signaled to Acevedo, who immediately began disseminating the intel packets.

Barnes took one and examined it. Each page had a mugshot accompanied by their government name and street identifier. The last page contained Roland Watt's information. She stared at the killer's eyes, remembering how coolly he'd taken the fall for the murder.

"Is it possible last night's hit was planned?" Barnes asked.

"Of course it was planned. You don't go guns blazin' into a banger nest without one." White's tone mocked the question.

"Not what I meant." Barnes held back the flash of anger washing over her. "I'm saying, is it possible last night's hit was planned prior to Watt's killing of D-Roc?"

This time White didn't have a quick-witted response lined up. His face screwed up in confusion and annoyance.

"We're entertaining all possible scenarios at this time," Belkin said. "I guess it's one possibility that both acts of violence yesterday could have been part of a bigger plan. Not sure how much effort I'd expend in that direction, though. Is there a reason you think this is the case?"

"Nothing of substance. Just thinking about something Watt said during his interview. He was talking about it like it was a chess match."

Acevedo and his partner chuckled like schoolboys, making comments under their breath.

"Something funny you'd like to share with the class, gentlemen?" Halstead leveled his Iceman gaze over the two detectives sitting in front of him.

"Just that Watt is going to have plenty of time for chess at Walpole," Acevedo said. "Just got word they shipped his ass off a couple minutes ago."

Barnes gave Halstead a questioning look. He responded with a slight shrug.

"You didn't hear?" Acevedo seemed pleased with himself. "He was first on the docket. Took the murder hit without missing a beat. No lawyer. Represented himself. Judge sent him packing. Sentencing will be in a few months, but that little turd just got flushed. So whatever his plan was, doesn't seem like it was a good one."

And the hits kept coming. Barnes would've known that had she been in on time. The fact that Acevedo knew about the status of her case before she did added insult to injury.

"The motive behind these latest killings can be determined once we've rounded up those responsible. Right now, our goal is to hunt them down as quickly as possible," Belkin said.

"My team will be running down our snitches. We'll flip this city upside down. By the end of the day, I expect we'll have them pegged." White's confidence gave way to cockiness in the smile that followed.

"We'll be working it from our end, going through the evidence and searching for potential witnesses," Belkin added.

"Any so far?" Mainelli asked.

"Evidence, yes. There's a shit ton. Figuring out how it all plays into it is another story. As far as witnesses go, nobody heard or saw anything."

"Figures as much. How the hell can we get these shitheads off the street if everyone turns a blind eye?" Mainelli huffed.

Halstead gave a subtle wave of his hand, quieting what was sure to be another one of Mainelli's longwinded rants about the failed state of things.

"That's where we're at right now. This is going to require a lot of hands and I expect everyone in this room to do their part." Belkin turned to White. "Keep us in the loop should you come across any leads on your end."

"I'll give you a call when my team's got 'em scooped up." White smiled at Cahill. "Bet you wish you were still runnin' and gunnin' with me."

"Same team, as far as I see." Cahill stiffened.

White gave a dismissive laugh and turned toward the door. Belkin gave an odd-looking salute as he dismissed the room.

"Miss working with him?" Barnes asked Cahill as they stood.

"Not for a minute. I do miss the hunt, though. Kicking doors and rattling the cages is always a good time."

"There's room for that here."

"You might be right." Cahill slowed as they walked by the dry erase board with the list of dead. He tapped his finger on the third name from the top. "I think this is a good place to start."

Barnes read the name. Calvin Johnson. "Don't know him."

"Goes by the street name Cut. Not a bad kid, just grew up in the wrong place. He used to be one of my more reliable snitches when I worked for White."

"I wouldn't think guys in a crew like that would work with the cops," Barnes said.

"Everybody snitches when they're in a jam. Everybody." Cahill stared at the name. "But not Cut. Sure, I came across him on some lightweight drug stuff. Nothing I would've bothered putting a case on. Yet, he still worked for me."

"Why's that?"

"Not sure. But what I am sure of is who his girl is. And she might be able to give us something to go on." Cahill cocked an eyebrow. "Feel like shaking the trees?"

"Won't that step on White's toes?"

"Probably."

"Then hell yes."

Barnes and Cahill updated Halstead, telling him that they were going to be running down a couple potential leads. Neither offered much more, and Halstead didn't dig any deeper.

They made their way out of the building toward the lot. Cahill spun his keys on his finger. Barnes pulled her set out and detoured to her car.

"No way I'm letting you drive again. Not with my hangover." Barnes slid into the driver's seat.

Cahill climbed in and gave her the address for Cut's girlfriend. They slid out into the flow of downtown traffic and headed toward Dorchester.

13

Watt tensed his bicep against the grip of the guard walking him from in-processing to his cell block. He held the folded blankets and sheets against his chest as the guard guided him along. He'd exchanged his Jordans for a pair of laceless white tennis shoes. The lack of cushioning brought him back to his childhood when his grandmother used to get him sneakers from the donation center. Back then he'd been grateful. Now it only served as a reminder of the achievement he'd made, from surviving the streets to running them.

The guard halted him with a tug of his arm as they neared a secure door. Stenciled white lettering on the steel door read D-Block.

"Press the wall, inmate," the guard said.

Watt heard the tough-guy tone, but underneath it he could smell fear in the gruff guard's voice. He didn't offer a challenge to this new authority. He simply complied, leaning forward against the wall adjacent to the door.

The guard swiped a key card, and a buzzer sounded from the door. He tugged on the handle but the door didn't open. His failed effort was followed with a curse.

"This is Sheffield. I'm at the second-floor access to D-Block. Door's on the fritz again."

"Stand by," the voice on the other end of the radio responded.

"I guess if you can't open it, you'll just have to set me free." Watt gave a wink in the flustered guard's direction, which only seemed to add to his frustration.

"Shut your stupid mouth." The guard turned to Watt and leaned in close, his nose nearly touching Watt's forehead. "You ain't been in here but a minute and you're already runnin' your mouth like the words comin' out of it are worth a damn."

Watt had numerous responses queued up but held back. No need to push. Not yet, at least. He offered a simple shrug and looked away, staring at the wall in front of him.

"All you hard-asses come in here thinking that what you did on the street makes you somebody in here. I'm here to tell you it don't."

"Doesn't."

"What the hell'd you say?"

"It's not 'don't.' The word you were looking for was 'doesn't.'"

The corrections officer balled his fist, and for a moment Watt thought he was going to hit him. Sheffield's breath smelled of stale coffee and cigarettes as he glared in disgust. Watt had been on the receiving end of men like this for the better part of his life. Intimidation only worked if you were willing to follow through. It was one of the last things his father said before being stabbed to death. Watt was six at the time, but he never forgot the words. And now that he was a man, he lived by them.

"When this door opens, you're about to find out who the real kings of the jungle are. And it ain't you!" Sheffield pressed the back of Watt's head, forcing his face against the cold concrete. "You see, in there, you're just fresh meat."

"Thanks for the welcome speech. I'll keep it in mind." Watt's voice remained calm.

"It's acting up on my end too. I can't activate the remote release." The voice on the radio crackled. "You're going to have to do it manually."

"Shit," Sheffield said under his breath before keying the mic. "Umm— can you have someone meet me at the door. I don't have my keys with me."

"Will do."

A minute of awkward silence followed as Sheffield waited for someone to arrive to unlock the door. Another corrections officer appeared on the other side of the door and waved at Sheffield through the cloudy glass. Keys clanged noisily and a moment later the door slid open.

"Who do we have here?" the new officer asked.

"Just another shithead who thinks he's gonna run this place." Sheffield spat the words, punctuating them by shoving Watt forward.

Watt stumbled, nearly colliding with the other guard. His name tag read *Doyle*.

"I've got him from here," Doyle said.

"You sure? This guy's got trouble written all over him."

Doyle jutted his chin back toward the large crowd of inmates milling noisily about the unit's main space. "Got a room full of 'em. I'm sure our newbie here—what's your name?"

"Watt."

"Got a first name?"

"Roland."

"I'm sure Roland here will figure it all out soon enough," Doyle said with a smile. "Right?"

Watt gave a slow nod.

"We'll see." Sheffield turned and stepped back into the hallway. He pulled the door closed and lingered for a moment, staring at Watt from the other side of the glass.

Watt shot a parting glance at Sheffield, giving him one last wink before turning his back on the overzealous guard. Doyle put his hand on Watt's elbow. Unlike his counterpart, Doyle didn't try to muscle him around.

They paused on the second-floor landing. Doyle fanned out an arm as if he were Vanna White revealing the final letter. "Welcome to D-Block. This will be your home for the duration of your time inside. What you make of it depends on how well you can adapt."

"No different than the street."

"One big difference. Everybody in here's doing time. And that means everybody here comes to this place with some pretty heavy baggage. Whether they set that baggage at the door or brought it in with them makes a big difference in how things go here."

"How so?"

"Whatever crew you rolled with or whatever beef you got outside needs to drop." Doyle's face went from pleasant to serious in the blink of an eye. "And I mean, right here, right now. Think you can do that?"

"I'll be all right."

"That's not what I asked."

Watt scanned the rows of cells lining both the lower and upper floors of the block. Most were open, either all the way or partly. Some inmates remained inside their cages. Others roamed about. A metal staircase connected the second floor to the common area below.

The inmates who weren't lingering in their cells were in the common area. Some were hunched over a game of chess. Others were huddled close in what looked to be an impromptu rap session. What became instantly clear to Watt was that most of the general population segregated themselves by color. A group of white inmates hung outside a first-floor cell tucked in the far corner. One of the men looked up at Watt. He folded his arms, his face twisting into a sneer. The inmate turned, exposing a green tattoo covering the left side of his neck, and whispered something to the larger man standing next to him. The big man chuckled.

"Don't let them scare you."

"Takes more than a couple of potato-eatin' has-beens to shake me."

"It's not a pissing contest. A lot of what you see out there is more bark than bite." Doyle shot a glance toward the cluster of Irish inmates. He locked eyes with the leader and gave a slow shake of his head. The group dissolved. "See what I mean."

"Guess they're not so tough."

"Far from it. That guy who was mean muggin' you, that's Danny McCormick. Goes by Nickel. Used to be one of the Irish mob's most ruthless enforcers." Doyle's tone conveyed the seriousness of his words. "He's definitely got some bite left in him."

"Nickel won't be a problem."

"You got history?"

"No. But I've got enough experience to know when I can handle a problem."

"There doesn't need to be a problem. Take Bull down there." Doyle pointed to a thick, bald black man whose massive frame stretched the seams of his white jumpsuit. "He runs a Bible study for a small group and is part of the prison choir."

"Sounds like a good time. Where do I sign up?"

"I hear the sarcasm in your voice. Laugh all you want but Bull's serving three consecutive life sentences. No chance he'll ever get out. But that didn't stop him from finding his way inside."

"Why do you care so much?" Watt assessed the middle-aged guard beside him. "I mean, shit, we're just a bunch of caged animals when you get down to it."

"I don't see it that way. I see it as one large family. Dysfunctional? Yes. But what family isn't these days?" Doyle chuckled.

"You've got a strange way of seeing things."

"Not really. It's a matter of survival, for inmate and guard alike. To do that comes down to one simple rule: mutual respect. You've got to give it to get it. And once that happens, getting along falls into place."

"Where I come from, respect is earned."

Doyle let out a slow sigh. "I didn't expect you to get it on your first day. Nobody ever does."

"Then why bother?"

"Planting seeds. Growth takes time."

"I'm more of a weed."

"We'll see about that." Doyle took a step back. "Let me give you the guided tour before we make the walk."

"The walk?"

"You'll see. Anyway, this landing we're standing on is home to the guard station."

Watt looked past Doyle at the enclosed room, which featured a secure door on each side and a large window stretching across the front that over-looked the cell block. Inside, two guards were seated around a console of monitors.

"The station is manned twenty-four hours a day. There's also guards who move about the floor at all times."

Watt looked at a guard who was jaw-jacking with a couple of inmates seated around a table playing a card game. "Doesn't seem like a lot of manpower."

Doyle shrugged. "It's the way it's always been. That's why the rule is so important."

"Mutual respect."

"Exactly. There's hope for you yet, Watt." Doyle smiled. "As far as the guard station is concerned, any inmate wishing to approach must first wait for authorization at one of the lower stairwells located on either side."

"Why would an inmate want to go to the guard station?"

"Personal requests regarding visitation, phone calls, or issues of clothing and bedding are handled through the tower guards."

"Got it."

"First-floor inmates are prohibited from going to the second-floor cell area."

"But second-floor inmates are allowed on the first floor?"

"You're a bright one. Not many catch that." Doyle gave an impressed bob of his head. "First-floor inmates are affiliated."

"So you house gang members with gang members? Seems a bit backwards to me."

"At first, yes. But we do it for a reason. Clustering inmates with known gang affiliation enables us to better control movement."

"I'd think there'd be constant wars."

"First rule, again, mutual respect. These guys can't bang it out like they would on the street. We've got cameras. Things pop off, people get time in ISO. Don't care who you are, ISO breaks the toughest of men."

"My brother's in ISO. Has been for a long time. There isn't anything that can break him."

"Who's your brother?"

"Damian Watt."

"Goliath's your brother?"

Watt nodded.

"I hate to see a family reunion under this roof." Doyle paused, looking pensive. "Not sure you heard, but your brother's on his way out. Shipping off to Souza-Baranowski Correctional next week. Supermax is a big change from the ISO wing here."

"I know."

"Not sure I can make it happen, but I'll try to see if I can get you some time with him before he goes."

"You'd do that?"

"Family is important. More so in here. Like I said, not sure the powers that be will approve it, but it's worth a shot."

"Thanks."

"I guess it's that time. I'll show you to your quarters."

"Quarters. You make it sound like I'm at a resort."

"Five stars on Yelp." Doyle laughed at his own joke. "The food, on the other hand, isn't going to win any awards. But you'll get used to it."

Doyle tapped on the guard station glass. "Making the walk." The closest guard to him gave a nod. Doyle placed his hand on Watt's elbow and guided him to the stairs.

"Mind if I say something?" Doyle asked, lowering his voice.

"Your world, boss."

"You seem like a smart kid."

"Do smart people end up in here?"

"Mistakes can topple the best of us." Doyle offered a consolatory smile. "What I meant by the question is that you're more articulate than most of our other guests."

"What you're really asking is, why don't I sound street."

"Yeah, I guess."

"My grandmother pushed me to read. Got hooked. Never stopped learning."

"Sounds like a good woman."

"She was," Watt muttered.

"Sorry. Well, you'll be happy to know we've got a library. Pretty decent selection of books. Anything in particular?"

"I'm partial to Sun Tzu."

"*The Art of War*, right? Never read it, but it's often referenced by our instructors during some of our combative courses."

"Everything's a mental game. Just like chess."

"We've got that too." Doyle looked down on the inmates intently focused on the gameboard in front of them. "You any good?"

"No. I'm great."

"Have to see about that. Chavez down there is undisputed champ around here."

"Not for long." Watt gave a half-smile.

The two made their way down to the first floor. Watt's entrance caught the attention of the other inmates. The murmuring grew louder as inmates stepped out from their cells and lined the rails of the second deck. Those below slowly congregated, forming an ad hoc receiving line.

"You're about to receive some abuse. It'll be verbal only. Try not to let it faze you," Doyle said apologetically. "Just part of the indoctrination."

Watt said nothing. He stopped for a brief moment when his feet touched the linoleum floor and scanned the onlookers. The catcalls and jeers grew in volume.

Watt stepped forward. The crowd's intensity grew. Their words and taunts blurred into one incoherent roar. Through it all, he kept his head held high and never broke stride.

"Easy does it. One step at a time," Doyle whispered.

A voice rose above the rest. "Killa in the house!"

The chanting took on a different tone. The taunts turned to cheers. Several of the prisoners began clapping as Watt passed through the gauntlet.

Doyle guided him to his cell and pointed to the open bunk. The inmates dispersed and the noise subsided. Doyle leaned close. "That doesn't happen often."

"Like you said, mutual respect." Watt set his sheets and blanket on the thin mattress of the lower bunk.

"Guess so."

"There's a new king in the castle." Watt looked out at some of the gang members he recognized. Some friends. Some enemies. All under the same roof. He eyed one in particular, Dominguez "Domino" Rodriguez, head of the East Street Locos. "They just don't know it yet."

Doyle opened his mouth to speak but held his tongue.

"What, no parting words of wisdom?"

"Wisdom? No, advice. Slow roll picks up the most traction around here."

Watt nodded. Doyle turned to the last couple of inmates still lingering close to the cell door. He spoke in the same calm, easy-going manner he'd used when talking to Watt. The group hesitated for only a fraction of a second before separating.

Watt sat on the bunk. The springs creaked under his weight. A tall, thin man appeared at the cell door and posted up against the steel bars.

"Killa makin' his debut. Never thought the day would come, my brotha."

"Been a minute. How you holding up, Slim?"

"Tick-tock on that slow-movin' clock. You know how we do." Slim gave a toothy grin.

"That clock's about to move a little faster." Watt's expression was deadly serious. At the sight of it, Slim dropped the happy-go-lucky look from his face. "Everything all set?"

"Good to go. Just waitin' on you to give the order."

Watt gave a nod followed by a long, slow exhale. "I'll let you know. Pass the word, I need to parley with Domino."

"That crazy ass? We don't need his chalupa-eatin' loco."

"Does it sound like I'm asking for your opinion?"

Slim dipped his head and muttered a barely audible "no."

"Good. Then set the meet. Tell the others the time is almost at hand."

With that, Slim shuffled toward the main space and slunk over to the table where Domino was intently focused on the game board. Watt watched as Slim spoke to one of the bigger men standing in a protective circle around their leader. Like a game of telephone, he dipped low and whispered in Domino's ear.

The East Street Locos' leader knocked over his opponent's king. His queen dangled from his fingertips as he turned his head in Watt's direction. In a world where every move was watched, either by guard or by camera, Domino's eyes answered the question.

Watt sat back against the cold concrete. His mind drifted from his new surroundings to other, more important things. His mental chessboard put pawns in play.

Watt looked at the clock on the far wall. The second hand took its laps around the numbers. *Strategy without tactics is the slowest route to victory.* Sun Tzu's words echoed in his mind. Watt had no intention of taking a slow path. Checkmate was on the horizon and fast approaching.

14

Kelly's escort had remained silent since they departed the cafeteria. Gladstone made no effort to hide his annoyance at Kelly. The oversized guard squeezed his arm with more force than necessary as he tugged him through the hallway, leading him toward the visitation room rather than his cell block.

"Not heading back to the cage?" Kelly asked.

"Gotta get you all squared away for your big return to the world."

"Come again?" Kelly was growing tired of Gladstone's constant jabs and snarky innuendos. The tone of his response conveyed it and caused the corrections officer to halt, the sudden stop nearly causing Kelly to stumble.

"It's out-processing time, you thick-headed mick."

"Easy, big fella. Just asking. No need to get your panties in a bunch."

Gladstone swelled. His body pushed against Kelly's. As he stood sandwiched between the musclebound guard and the concrete wall, Kelly offered no resistance.

"You think you're somethin' special. You got a raw deal, is that it?" Frothy spittle bubbled in the corners of his mouth. "Some of the guards 'round here treat you like you are royalty. One of the good guys."

"But not you." Kelly met the anger in the man's eyes with an intensity in his own. "You got a problem with me? 'Cause I don't remember doing anything to earn it. You've been riding my ass any chance you got since the moment I walked in here."

"I've got my reasons."

"Not good enough. Not for this kind of bullshit. On the street, I'd—"

"You'd what?" Gladstone turned fire-engine red. He leaned in closer, his sweaty forehead pressing against Kelly's. "You wouldn't do shit, in here or out there."

Kelly played out the sequence of events running in a loop in his mind. Bend his knees. Drop his weight, forcing Gladstone forward while launching upward. The image of the guard's nose breaking brought a smile to his face.

"Somethin' funny about what I just said?"

"Just running the numbers and I don't think you're going to like the math."

"You threatening me?"

"I don't make threats. I usually let my actions do the talking." Kelly could see the coolness of his delivery only further added salt to wounds inflicted by his words.

Gladstone raised a balled fist, keeping it tight to his body. He then shot a glance at the camera covering this portion of the hallway. Kelly watched as the bigger man weighed the consequences. The fist dissolved and the large hand lowered.

"Guys like you don't get it," Gladstone muttered under his breath as he took a step back.

Kelly inhaled deeply once the pressure from the guard's chest released. "Guys like me?"

"You think your shit don't stink. You're out there with your badge and gun. High-fivin' your buddies after you make a pinch. Never givin' a thought to what happens after."

"Never took you for a bleeding heart."

"I'm not," Gladstone grunted.

"Then this is something personal? What'd I do to earn your wonderful treatment over the last couple of months?"

Silence filled the gap between them.

"Seriously, Gladstone, whatever I did, or you think I did, should end here and now."

"You remember a Freddy Marcum?"

Kelly ran through the thousands of names and faces in the space his mind kept for such things. He'd always had good recall, better than most, but the sheer volume accrued over time muddied the waters. "Not sure I do. He go by a street name? Sometimes those stick better."

"No. Just Freddy."

"Sorry. Name doesn't ring a bell."

Gladstone deflated. He cast his eyes downward. "Figures as much."

"What's the deal with Freddy? And how am I involved?"

"He's my brother. Well, half-brothers: same mother, different father. But we were closer than most."

Kelly picked up on the tense change. He pulled open his mental filing cabinet and once again searched for a connection. Nothing.

"For the life of me, I can't recall him. Maybe if you told me more about what happened."

"You popped him for some dope. Couple bags of heroin."

"How many years back?"

Gladstone counted on his fingers. "Seven."

"I was a Narc at the time. We made a ton of small-time arrests. Looking for bigger fish, ya know?"

"Except my brother was just a messed-up kid. He didn't have any bigger fish to connect you with. He also knew enough not to snitch." Gladstone looked to be in some state of limbo between anger and despondency. "When someone works for you as a snitch, what typically happens?"

"We dump the charges and throw them back in the water."

"And what happens when they don't?"

"They stay in the net. Take the pinch." Kelly read between the lines. "So Freddy didn't want, or wasn't capable of, working off his charge? And I'm guessing he took the ride?"

"He did."

"How long?" Kelly rarely ever followed up on minor case sentencing. There were too many other things to focus on. Bag 'em and tag 'em, move on to the next.

"Eighteen months."

"A year and a half for a couple bags of dope? Seems a bit excessive."

"I guess the judge wasn't in a charitable mood. Plus, the arresting officer wrote a report that painted a skewed picture of my brother. Made him out to be a piece of trash. And that officer was you."

Kelly swallowed hard. "I try to give everyone a fair shake. I don't know what I put in the report that you deem so damning, but I never inflate or embellish. City's plenty busy without me adding fiction to reality."

"Doesn't matter. He never served the full term of his sentence."

"That's good." Kelly felt Gladstone's weight shift. "So he got out early and then what?"

"I didn't say he got out. I said he never completed his sentence." Gladstone's baritone voice cracked. "Took twelve jabs with a shiv during a scrap. Died before they got him to medical."

"Damn." He now understood. Gladstone, however misguided his thought process, blamed Kelly for his brother's death. In processing death, anger is often displaced, easier to point the finger outward, and in this case, it had been pointed in Kelly's direction.

"You couldn't let him slide? Couldn't give him a pass? No, you just tossed him aside and let the system devour him." Gladstone choked on his words.

"If I had ever imagined that outcome, I would've never put those cuffs on." Kelly rested his back against the wall. "If there was a crystal ball capable of showing me the future of my actions, I'm sure there'd be a million choices I'd make differently." One, in particular, came to the forefront of Kelly's mind. The decision he'd made to walk into the gray and the ripple effect it was now having on everything he held dear.

"Guess that's one way to clear your conscience. But it doesn't change the fact that Freddy's dead." Gladstone's anger bubbled just beneath the surface, his muscle-bound shoulders tightening against his uniform. "My brother's death is on your hands. Just thought you should know before you walk out those gates tomorrow and start your life again."

Kelly saw the burden lift from Gladstone and settle on him. The weight of it stacked neatly atop the other lives for which he paid a daily penance, like Baxter Green, the young boy caught in the crossfire during a hostage standoff. His lifeless body still haunted Kelly's nightmares.

"For what it's worth, I'm sorry."

"Your words aren't worth shit to me or my family. But I believe in karma. And she can be a real bitch."

They heard a loud clang down the hallway. The door connecting the isolation wing to the visitation rooms where Kelly stood slammed closed. Standing beside a lanky guard was the hulking figure of Goliath.

"Maybe karma's on her way now," Gladstone said. "I heard the stories about you and our beast over there. I've wondered how true they were. Maybe I can set a rematch. Interested?"

"My title fighting days are over."

"We'll see about that." Gladstone stepped to Kelly's side, unlocked the room, and opened the door.

Kelly turned and saw a portly older guard hunched over a stack of paperwork stretched out across the metal table. He looked at Kelly over the top of reading glasses clinging to the end of his bulbous nose.

"I'm Officer Hopper and I'll be handling the paperwork end of things." Hopper held a paper cup to his lower lip. Brown spit from the wad of dip bulging from his left cheek dribbled into it.

Kelly caught the mass of red approaching from his left and cut his eyes in that direction. Goliath now stood along the same wall. Less than ten feet separated Kelly from the monster when he heard the deep, rumbling growl.

"Don't go making things worse for yourself. You're about to face a whole different world. And it's a lot better if you start off on the right foot at Souza. It'll be a while before you get yourself cleared for visitors." The lanky guard's voice quaked. "Your sister's here to see you. Keep this up and you'll be back in your cage. You want that?"

Kelly could hear the fear in the guard's delivery and smell the green wafting off him. To a monster like Goliath, the scent of it must've been like blood in the water. His muscles tensed and then released beneath his jumpsuit, his rage barely contained.

"He's just hungry, Larry," Gladstone belted out. He rested his big mitt on Kelly's shoulder, giving him a tug. "Ain't that right, big fella?"

"Shit, Gladstone, you're gonna rile him up!"

Kelly watched from the corner of his eye as the lanky guard worked unsuccessfully to control Goliath.

"Just havin' a bit of fun, is all." Gladstone leaned close to Kelly's ear. "Ain't that right, Kelly?"

Kelly ignored Gladstone and stepped into the room, freeing the guard's grip. He moved to the opposite side of the table, his cuff chain rattling.

"Go ahead and have a seat," Hopper said, then looked over at Gladstone. "We taking his cuffs off for this, right?"

"All he's got to do is sign some things."

"Yeah, but we normally—"

"He's a big boy, aren't you, Kelly?"

Kelly could feel the big corrections officer's eyes on him. "Makes no difference to me."

"Thought so." Gladstone took a step back into the hallway. "And, inmate, just know the clock on your sentence doesn't stop until you walk through those gates. A lot can happen in that time."

The door slammed closed. Kelly listened as it locked from the other side.

"He's a real pain in my ass too." Hopper rolled his eyes. "These big guys come in here and think muscling inmates keeps things in line."

"You don't see it that way, I guess," Kelly said.

"Take a good look at me." Hopper slapped his gut and gave a mock flex of his biceps before breaking into a laugh. "But I got that jughead by twenty-four years of experience."

"Playing the long game."

"Only way to play. Retirement's just around the corner." Hopper picked up a pen from the desk. "But you're not here to listen to me prattle on about my coming golden years. You are steps away from breathing that fresh air."

Kelly nodded.

"Then let's get to it." Hopper slid a small stack of papers across the table to Kelly. "This is your release packet. First item of business is your personal belongings. This sheet here lists what you came in with. The other is a list of the items you'll be taking with you from your cell. Typically, these are things sent from loved ones during your incarceration."

The only things he'd received were the pictures Embry had drawn and their accompanying letters. He made quick work about filling it out, the cuffs interfering as he wrote.

"Anybody going to be here when you get out?"

"I've got a friend who said he'll pick me up."

"Good to hear. No sadder thing for me than seeing somebody who's done their time having to sit outside and wait for the bus 'cause nobody cares enough to get them."

Kelly nodded absently, half-listening as he thought about the people in his life. He knew they each carried the torch for him in their own way, regardless of how much his current assignment had worked to douse the flame. Or at least that's what he told himself every single day since stepping foot inside his cell.

15

Barnes followed Cahill's directions to the street where Cut's girlfriend lived. Aside from the instructions, Cahill offered little else in the way of conversation. The banter she'd grown accustomed to was lost after last night's folly. She hoped the interruption to the norm was only temporary. Time would be the test.

"Pull in here." Cahill pointed to a spot along the curb between two cars. "This neighborhood has a lot of eyes. Better if we avoid pulling up in front."

Barnes did as instructed and parallel-parked the Caprice. The space was tight but she managed to squeeze in, leaving about six inches between her front bumper and the station wagon ahead of her. Easy-peasy for a native Bostonian. Six inches was like a mile when it came to city parking.

"She lives on the third floor. We'll use the back entrance."

"Sounds good." Barnes twisted and grabbed her notepad from the backseat.

"No need for that." Cahill stripped off his department-issued windbreaker and swapped it for a hoodie he pulled from the bag by his feet. "The less we look and act like cops, the more likely we'll get some traction."

"Got it." Barnes tossed the folder back where she'd found it and rifled around the floorboard behind her seat. Digging under an old blanket, she found the winter coat she kept on hand. A second later, she was changed too.

"Priscilla isn't going to be happy to see us. Not sure she'll be willing to talk. Worth a shot, though," Cahill said.

"Those who hate us have a tendency to need us more often than not." Barnes cut the ignition and stepped from the vehicle. "Funny how that works."

"Only one way to find out." Cahill's breath danced in the cold air. "Follow me."

Barnes walked beside Cahill. He'd thrown his hood over his head and stuck his hands in the sweatshirt pockets. Barnes didn't have anything to add to her subterfuge and opted to keep her head and eyes down. Both detectives kept their badge and gun concealed from view as they made the trek down the alley.

Cahill climbed the broken steps to the back of the apartment building. Barnes slipped on a layer of ice coating the top step and caught herself against Cahill's back, grabbing him by the arms to avoid falling.

"Easy now. I can't have you falling for me." Cahill righted Barnes, offering his trademark half-cocked smile.

And with that, things suddenly felt right again between them. She returned his smile. "Thanks."

Cahill pulled on the knob. The door didn't budge.

"Guess we use the front?" Barnes shrugged.

"There's no door in this city I can't access." He made an overly exaggerated show of cracking his knuckles. Then he reached into his back pocket and withdrew a tattered credit card from his wallet. "Here she is. Good old Gerty."

"You name your credit cards?" Barnes observed the nicks and bend marks tattooed into the plastic.

"She's not just any credit card, are you, baby?" Cahill spoke gently and gave it a kiss. "This ol' girl is my key to the city."

Cahill took up a half squat in front of the tarnished knob. He gripped it and pressed the door inward, sliding the card into the sliver of space between the frame and door. He twisted the knob with one hand while manipulating the card with the other. Less than fifteen seconds later, Cahill stood. The door swung outward.

"Impressive, MacGyver."

"You should see what I can do with a couple paperclips and a rubber band." Cahill slipped the card back into his wallet and stepped inside.

Barnes slid in behind him and closed the door. The air in the building was just as cold as the temperature outside. The only difference was the lack of wind.

"Guess they missed trash day," Cahill muttered.

Bags of trash were stacked in messy piles outside a lower-floor apartment. The cold worked magic against the wide assortment of odors that came with the job. Barnes was suddenly grateful for the lack of heat.

They ascended the stairs. As they crossed the second-floor landing, music passed through thin walls into the apartment building's common space. The pulsing bass thrummed inside Barnes's head, serving as a painful reminder of last night's overindulgence.

"Here we go." Cahill pointed to a door marked 302. "Fair warning, she's probably not going to be overly excited to see us."

"Shocker. Not a big fan of the badge?" Barnes snarked.

"Not a big fan of me."

"I thought you said Cut was one of your snitches?"

"He was. Helped me build some good cases."

"Why do I feel like there's a 'but' coming?"

"One of the last cases I worked, the big bust, was largely due in part to intel Cut had fed me." Cahill kept his voice low as they lingered along the hall a few feet from the door. "I was supposed to return the favor by getting the prosecutor to look the other way on some minor drug charges."

"Forgot? Or failed to follow through?"

"I wish it were that simple. With Lincoln White, nothing ever is."

"I hate that guy," Barnes grumbled.

"You and me both."

"I thought you were one of his bright shining stars. Is it because of what happened with Kelly?"

"That bullshit with him pressing charges on Mike was just the icing on the cake. But I'd formed my opinion of my former boss long before." Cahill kicked an orange needle cap away from his shoe. "After the massive seizure went down and everyone was arrested, I went to pay my dues and honor my promise to Cut. But when it comes to getting favors at court, a supervisor needs to make the call. Otherwise, with over two thousand cops working the streets, the court would be inundated with requests."

"White dropped the ball?"

"Not only dropped it, he punted it down the street and into the sewer drain." Cahill cursed under his breath.

"He ever give a reason why he wouldn't make the call?"

"Nothing that stood to reason. Said something about *not everybody gets a free pass.* I've seen that guy cut loose much bigger fish on much bigger charges."

"How long was Cut's bid?"

"Three months."

"That's not bad." Barnes caught herself. Three months, when compared to five years or a life sentence, was a drop in the bucket. But the last three months of Kelly's incarceration felt like an eternity. "Could've been worse."

"It wasn't the time. It's what Cut missed during that time." Cahill stared at the door. A baby's cry filtered into the hallway. "He missed the birth of his daughter."

"Hard to make that one right."

"I tried. Really did. When I learned White was going to let Cut's case ride, I went to the prosecutor myself. Made the push, but no joy. Nobody crosses White. Apparently, his reach extends beyond the department."

"You ever get a chance to let Cut know your hands were tied?"

"Tried. Went over like a fart in church. Apologies are just words. On the street, action is the only acceptable currency."

"Any fallout from going to the prosecutor behind White's back?"

"I'm here now, aren't I?"

Barnes felt her brow furrow. "I thought you pushed for it after making the big bust. Homicide was your dream gig, or am I not remembering things correctly?"

"Homicide is great. And now, after working the body beat for a minute, I'm glad to have made the jump."

"But it wasn't a jump you'd planned on making?"

"Nah. It was definitely more of a push." Anger flashed across Cahill's eyes. "White set my transfer out of the unit. Created the *rising star* bullshit. Even wrote me a glowing letter of recommendation. The rest is history."

"Did you ever figure out why he was so quick to launch you from the catapult?"

"No." Cahill stiffened a bit as a woman's voice drew closer to the door. "One thing's gnawed at me ever since. Cut not only gave the intel that led to the big bust, he also told me he had an even bigger fish."

"And White knew about this?"

Cahill nodded. "Never found out who or what Cut was talking about. The transfer hit me hard and fast. But one thing I know for sure is that whoever Cut had in his sights, it had to be legit."

"How do you know without verifying?"

"Because he didn't need the leverage. Guys like Cut know the credit big scores earn them with our unit."

"Then why wouldn't White want the intel? Why would he punish you and your informant?"

"That's the million-dollar question. And one I've been rattling my brain to answer ever since."

"Only two possibilities I see. Either White had an informant of equal or greater value already capable of delivering and was just bent about you going behind his back." Barnes hesitated on offering up the other consideration. "Or White had a vested interest in whoever this target is."

"It's been rumored for a long time that White's dirty. Whispered in the locker rooms but never spoken aloud. He's Teflon. Nothing's ever stuck. Pressing it would've likely landed me elsewhere."

"What you're really saying is that you'd end up on the wrong end of a *whitewash*."

"I guess his reputation carries beyond the streets he enforces."

"I think that's something we're both well aware of," Barnes said as she stuffed her hands into her pockets, feeling the warmth of her thighs. "We doing this? Or just trying to cool our hangover in this icebox of a hallway?"

Cahill was uncharacteristically hesitant and now Barnes knew why. She could see that his nerves, or maybe the weight of guilt, had slowed his resolve. Being the partner she'd promised to be, Barnes stepped in front of him and raised her hand to knock when the door opened.

A dark-skinned girl who looked no older than twenty stood holding a baby. Her head was turned back as she called out, "Back in a split. Seein' if the bodega got some formula."

The floorboard underneath Barnes's foot creaked and the young mother spun. Fear immediately transitioned to curiosity as she eyed Barnes cautiously while gently bouncing the baby nestled against her chest.

"Can I help you?" Attitude in her posture and delivery.

"I'm Detective Barnes with BPD Homicide." Barnes opened her jacket just enough to expose the badge before immediately zipping it back up.

"Hey, Priss. Long time." Cahill slid in beside Barnes and leaned against the door frame.

"The hell you doin' here, you slick-talkin' prick?" Priscilla attempted to shut the door but Cahill's foot, already inserted into the threshold, served as a jam.

"Who dat, girl?" A male's voice, gruff and loud, boomed from the unseen recesses of the apartment.

"Just some Jehovahs," Priscilla answered.

"Tell 'em God been skippin' this neighborhood for years. Ain't no point now!"

Priscilla looked down at Cahill's foot. It remained in place. He folded his arms across his chest to indicate he wasn't going anywhere, but his eyes were downcast and the smile was gone.

"Sorry about Cut."

"You should be." Priscilla's baby began to cry, and she patted her back while making a cooing sound. "Gotta go. Baby needs to eat."

Barnes observed the bloodshot eyes and dark lines snaking down the young mother's face. No tears fell now. The well was dry. Barnes had seen it too many times to count in the span of her career.

"I want to make it right. The way things went down, before all this—I still owe him one," Cahill said.

"Maybe if you'd done right by him then, we wouldn't be in this mess now."

"Priss, you still talkin' to them Bible slingers?" the unseen voice called out. "They don't get to steppin', tell 'em I'll put a boot in they ass!"

Priscilla rolled her eyes. With the hand she'd been using to pat the baby, she wiped her face. "My uncle don't take kind to strangers. Lucky he didn't catch the whiff of bacon. Cops are his least favorite visitors."

"Can we talk somewhere else?" Barnes asked. "We're trying to find the people responsible for what happened. Hoping you could help."

"Whatever help I give, is it gonna bring back my man?" Priscilla turned her baby to face them. "Is her daddy comin' home if I get you what you want?"

"No," Cahill said as he stepped back and removed his foot from the door. "But I'll make sure they pay for what they did."

The baby squirmed. Priscilla returned the little girl to her original position and began the soothing process all over again.

"You said you needed formula, right?" Barnes asked. "How about we meet you there? We'll pay for it. Buy you as much as you need. And then we'll talk. Sound like a plan?"

Priscilla said nothing as she stepped back inside. The door closed in front of them.

"Guess I shouldn't have moved my foot," Cahill said. He threw his hands up. "Guess we're back to square one. We could hit a couple of the corners the 9s used for business."

"Thinking they're probably taking a day off. Plus, I wouldn't give up on Priscilla just yet."

"Why's that?"

"Just a gut feeling."

Cahill slapped his stomach. "Well, my gut is empty. Need to get some food to sponge up the poison still swimming around in there."

Just as Cahill turned, the apartment door opened and Priscilla peeked out. "Just gonna put my baby down for a nap. I decided it's too cold for her to be out. Meet me at Jip's. Twenty minutes good?"

"We'll be there," Barnes said.

The door closed. Cahill shook his head. "And how in the hell did you know she was going to give in?"

"Woman's intuition." Barnes mimicked Cahill's cocky smile as she strode by him. "Now let's get back to the car before we freeze the rest of our respective asses off."

"No complaints here." Cahill followed behind. "Nice work getting her to come around."

"Good cop doesn't work if there's not a bad cop. Plus, we're partners, remember?"

They made their way out, Barnes avoiding the icy step from earlier. They set off for the car, retracing their steps. After giving the heater a second to warm up, Barnes maneuvered back onto the street and headed to the meet location.

16

D-Block's oppressive air hung heavily over the main space where the inmates congregated, their body odor adding to the mix. Doyle preferred the temperature-controlled hallways of the isolation wing to the confines of general population. The saving grace came by way of the interactions afforded by the cluster of prisoners milling about.

Walpole was a living, breathing testament to the grit and grime of the criminal underbelly. But Doyle also saw it for something else, the truest expression of man's desire to change his circumstances. Raised in poverty, he'd watched his father toil in a factory until lung cancer stole him away. Doyle saw his mother take up the slack, working two jobs just to keep them afloat. His parents' indomitable spirit battled against the hand they'd been dealt. Doyle saw the same tenacity in the inmates he oversaw. In spite of the differences in their situations, the resolve to rise above the choices of their past resonated within him. It was the reason he could find common ground where other guards couldn't.

Respect was the sword he wielded in his efforts to maintain the fine balance between order and chaos, an ever-present reality within the concrete fortress housing these offenders. All the good intentions in the world didn't counter the flare-ups bound to happen when this many men, each with their individual burdens, shared a common space. And on more occasions than Doyle cared to remember, he'd been driven to use force. He'd always done his best to mitigate the damage, to mend the broken connection. Sometimes the respect and trust returned almost immediately. Other times, the grudge remained. He could see it in the eyes of those inmates. Doyle was no fool; his watchful eyes constantly surveyed for any sign of threat.

"Ayo, Doyle." A tall inmate who went by Slim sauntered over. He slapped a hand on Doyle's shoulder. "How's things?"

"Same ol', ya know." Doyle smiled. He liked Slim, who seemed unfazed by the seven-year sentence he was serving.

Slim's wide grin belied the fact that he had beaten a man half to death with a lead pipe. Inside the prison, he'd been a model prisoner and earned the title of trustee, enabling him more freedom. Slim was tasked with delivering books, mopping the passageways, and a variety of other menial tasks. To an outsider, those tasks might seem beneath them, but inside, where a cell was home, any excuse to move about more freely was considered a luxury.

"Saw you're on deck for mop duty later?" Doyle asked.

"Nobody brings a shine to this turd like me." Slim pounded a fist against his chest. "You'll see when I'm gone. Place'll look like shit real quick."

"Guess we got a little time left before we need to find your replacement." Doyle knew better than to mention the actual time left on any inmate's sentence. Calling out the reality had a detrimental effect on the well-being of those incarcerated. This was an especially sensitive subject for Slim, after a recent parole review had gone poorly and eliminated any chance of a reduction in time, leaving him with three more years on the clock.

"Best get to steppin' 'cause that floor ain't gonna clean itself." Slim waved a hand at Boone, a thick inmate who had barely spoken since his arrival one year ago. He was a trustee, one who often partnered with Slim.

Boone nodded and headed for the stairwell. Slim gave a bow of his head and hustled through the meandering inmates. Doyle watched the two climb the stairs and come to a stop in front of the hallway's access door.

Doyle pressed his lapel mic. "Trustees on the landing. Open door one."

The two guards in the control station above him didn't respond. Doyle cursed under his breath. He'd told the watch commander the radios were spotty but he got the same answer he'd received when asking about the key cards not working: "We're working on it." Doyle knew that was supervisor talk for shut up and deal with it.

He waved his hands like a flagman on an airstrip. The guards weren't paying attention. Doyle could see their heads turned in conversation. He gave a frustrated effort and resigned himself to having to walk over, climb the stairs, and knock on the window. He hated doing it for two reasons: the effort annoyed him, and he'd be temporarily abandoning the floor. Typically two guards roamed during gen pop free time, but staffing had left them shorthanded.

Doyle clicked the radio one more time and was met with static again. He tweaked the dial to no avail. Just as he was about to make the trek to the stairs, a loud whistle rose from the crowd surrounding one of the chess tables. Doyle shot a glance and saw Domino withdraw his fingers from the corners of his mouth.

Domino then pointed up at the guard station, where his two-fingered blast had gained their attention. Doyle pointed to Slim and Boone, still waiting patiently by the access door. The guard above gave a nod. The door buzzed and the two trustees disappeared into the hallway. The guard then shot a questioning look at Doyle and held up his radio. Doyle gave a thumbs-down. Both men rolled their eyes, mirroring each other's frustration.

Doyle turned back to Domino. "Thanks."

The gang leader gave the slightest of nods before turning his attention back to his game. Doyle resumed his stroll of the first floor, giving enough space to the inmates enjoying their free time while maintaining enough proximity to interact or intervene when necessary.

He was at the halfway mark of his eight-hour overtime shift, and everything was smooth sailing. Doyle scanned the men, hoping the next four would pass as easily. It was then that he noticed the change. Most probably wouldn't, but Doyle wasn't most guards, and he detected a shift in the air around him.

A barely perceptible current of tension coiled like a viper in the shadows, causing his nerve endings to stand on end. Doyle stepped away from a nearby group and tucked himself behind a column. "You got eyes-on down here?" He spoke calmly into the mic. His anxiety ratcheted up a notch when he was met with the same static of his earlier transmission.

Getting Domino to be his relay wasn't an option at the moment. He was directly under the guard station, the stairs on either side equidistant from his current position. Before he went charging up, Doyle wanted to ensure the effort wasn't due to an overactive imagination. He had been working a lot of doubles over the last several months. The money was good, but that much time behind the walls wasn't good for anyone.

Doyle's keen eyes scanned the entire first floor. He moved from cluster to cluster, trying to pinpoint the source of his unease. The Irish boys, led by an inmate named Nickel, were hanging inside Nickel's cage playing a hand of cards. They seemed genuinely disinterested in the world around them. Dangerous as they were, violence was used sparingly and was nearly always due to an encroachment of their territory.

Moving on, Doyle focused on the cluster of inmates circled around the table where an intense game of chess was unfolding between Domino and one of his underlings, a heavyset prisoner named Paco Nunez who went by Gordo. The two were locked in a fierce mental battle, punctuated by the telltale clicking of the worn plastic pieces as they danced across the board. The problem didn't rest with the players, but the men surrounding the game.

He'd watched enough of these matches to recognize when something was off. Normally the onlookers would jeer and cheer each move as if watching a football game, entertainment taking on a different meaning within the gray walls. None of that was present in today's crowd. Instead of hovering over the players, the inmates were quiet. Their eyes shifted among one another and then up toward the guard station.

Doyle fought to control his breathing. Staying calm had been a hallmark of his ability to de-escalate the most volatile of situations. He'd long ago made a promise to his wife, Sal, and their four children that he'd do one thing, if nothing else: come home every night. It was in these moments, the unsettling calm before the storm, that Doyle reminded himself of that vow.

He keyed the mic one more time. Nothing. His hand slid from the radio to the extendable baton holstered behind it. He pulled it free and kept it in its collapsed position, bootlegging it behind his right thigh. Doyle felt the sweat transfer from his palm to the neoprene grip of the weapon as he stepped out from behind the pillar.

The inmates loosened their muscles. Doyle had seen enough battles go down to recognize the pre-fight warmup. They turned their furtive glances from the guard station to their immediate surroundings as Doyle tracked their looks, trying to pinpoint the target of their aggression. His heart skipped a beat when the group turned their focus to him.

In a situation like this, guards often sought refuge in the inmates they'd bonded with. But in his frantic scan for an ally, Doyle's gaze came to rest on one prisoner, sitting by himself in his cell. Roland Watt, the new kid on D-Block, was erect on his bed, his hands centered on his thighs, his placid demeanor exuding calm. Watt looked at Doyle, his eyes boring deep. A smile curled.

Doyle wanted to break eye contact, he wanted to turn and run, but something about Watt held him in place. The normal rumble of conversation faded away. Watt mouthed one word.

Checkmate.

As if on cue, the volume by the chess table picked up . Doyle broke eye contact with Watt and looked over at the disturbance. Domino's eyes flicked up, betraying no emotion as he moved his knight with lethal precision, capturing Gordo's queen in a single swift stroke. Gordo's face contorted with rage, and a snarl escaped his lips as he spat out a torrent of insults. In the blink of an eye, the tension in the room grew palpable as several of Domino's gang members materialized at his side like vultures drawn to carrion.

Doyle, sensing the imminent threat, rushed forward. With determination etched into the lines of his weathered face, he hoped to avert the chaos before it materialized. The look in Watt's eyes haunted the backdrop of his mind as he approached.

Closing the gap, Doyle felt the weight of their collective gazes sizing him up like a predator assessing its prey. But Doyle was no stranger to the machinations of this concrete jungle, and he would not be cowed.

"All right, gentlemen," Doyle said, his voice steady and calm, cutting through the cacophony of insults like a knife. "Let's all take a step back and remember that we're just playing a game here." His eyes locked onto Domino's, and for a brief moment, the two men seemed to share an unspoken understanding. Doyle felt some of the tension release. The gang leader had an ability to sway the majority and he hoped now would be one of those times.

Then it was gone. The salvation offered a moment ago vanished before Doyle's eyes as Domino spun and, with a flick of his wrist, upturned the board, sending the remaining pieces cascading to the floor.

The message was clear: the game was over, but the real battle was only just beginning. And in that pivotal moment, as the inmates surrounded him, Doyle knew that he was to become the fulcrum upon which the fate of D-Block would balance.

Harsh fluorescent lights cast a sterile glow upon the scene, as if the universe itself was a cold, indifferent observer. Without so much as a word, a pair of muscle-bound enforcers sprang into action, pouncing on Doyle like wolves going in for the kill. In the blink of an eye, he found himself at the epicenter of the storm, on the receiving end of an all-out whirlwind of violence.

His pleas for order were swallowed by the cacophony of fists, shouts, and guttural grunts. His attempts to quell the upheaval fell upon deaf ears.

His body slammed into a nearby table. The impact doubled him over, but he fought against the tidal wave of bodies to stay upright. With desperation he clawed at his chest, reaching for the lapel mic. During the assault the mic had come loose. It was now intertwined between him and one of his aggressors. As another series of vicious blows pummeled the back of his head, Doyle reached for the radio, a lifeline to the backup he so desperately needed, and ripped it from the holster. He pressed the button to transmit, the only word escaping his lips before he was swallowed by the sea of raging inmates a simple yet plaintive, "Help."

He never heard confirmation if his message was received. His head remained tucked, and he flailed his hands wildly in an attempt to deflect some of the barrage. Doyle hoped the two guards manning the station were already in motion and coming to his aid.

Surrounded by attackers, Doyle waited for a lull to find his opportunity. It came when one of the inmates struck another. A secondary fight broke out and long-standing rivalries gave way to their own brand of violence.

Doyle pushed hard, separating himself from the closest inmate. His baton had been knocked loose during the initial wave, forcing him to resort to his hands. Doyle was no expert when it came to fighting, but survival brought out an aggression he rarely showcased. He roared, exploding forward and directing his rage at the nearest inmate.

He felt his fist connect with the jawbone of the man in front of him. The punch sent the inmate into several others behind him, and the group staggered back, giving him some much-needed room to breathe and assess his situation.

Doyle's guard was up. He felt woozy and knew the damage already inflicted was bad. He tasted blood. His right eye was nearly shut, which greatly limited his field of vision. His eyes darted toward the stairwell, his lifeline. If he could just make it there, he could regain control.

Before he could get a visual on his backup, a hand gripped his shoulder and spun him in the opposite direction. With every ounce of his being, Doyle fought to reach that stairwell, his heart pounding like a drum in his chest, his breath ragged. Time slowed to a crawl, and the clash around him raged on, a maelstrom that threatened to consume him whole.

Doyle kicked at the inmate who had him in his grasp. His boot connected with the man's leg enough to free himself. In an adrenaline-driven push of pure desperation, Doyle pivoted and dashed toward the closest staircase, his soles slapping linoleum. He could feel the predatory presence of the inmates close behind, their laughter mingling with his ragged breaths.

Just as Doyle's fingertips grazed the railing, a figure stepped out from the shadows, blocking his path. Watt, the man Doyle had welcomed into the fold, stood between the horde and his salvation.

"Watt, whatever this is—whatever you think you're doing—it'll end badly," Doyle pleaded, voice shaking, his words coming in weak bursts. "Let me pass. Please."

Watt stood firm, arms crossed over his chest.

Desperation clawing at his throat, Doyle raised a balled fist.

"Is this part of your 'mutual respect' speech, Doyle?" His tone dripped with mockery.

"Doesn't have to be this way."

"Yes." Watt's smile widened, his eyes flickering past Doyle, a predator savoring the scent of fear. "It does."

The clamor of the inmates echoed off the gray walls, an unsettling symphony of chaos. As he twisted to address the approaching threat, Doyle realized the futility of his actions. A tidal wave of muscle and fury was upon him, the inmates descending like a pack of rabid dogs.

The first blow came like a bolt of lightning, the air crackling with the impact as it connected with Doyle's jaw. The metallic taste of blood filled his mouth, and the world seemed to tilt on its axis as he staggered, barely managing to keep his feet beneath him.

The world swam in and out of focus, a kaleidoscope of pain and fear as he was tossed like a ragdoll into the unforgiving steel of the stairwell. He felt his spine collide with the edge of the stairs, white-hot agony slicing through him like a thousand knives. His legs buckled, and he crumpled to the ground, the cacophony of the riot fading to a distant murmur.

Watt loomed over Doyle like a harbinger of doom, his voice a chilling whisper that caressed the dying embers of his consciousness. "Now you're about to learn what real respect looks like."

With a cold smirk, Watt strode into the fray, the throng of inmates parting before him like a tempestuous sea bowing to the command of a vengeful god.

As the last remnants of light slipped away, Doyle felt the darkness wrap around him like a shroud, the haunting echo of Watt's voice lingering. He closed his eyes and made a silent apology to his wife and children for failing to keep his promise.

17

With time on his sentence nearing its end, Kelly felt as though the passing seconds slowed to a crawl, the tedium of his out-processing paperwork adding to it. He heard the muffled conversation just outside the door, recognizing Gladstone's overbearing voice and the rookie's softer tone. He couldn't make out everything said but heard enough to get the gist. Apparently, Gladstone found some humor in making Goliath wait a little longer for his visitor. Messing with visitation was possibly one of the cruelest things to do to an inmate, regardless of the crime. The fact that Gladstone derived pleasure from such a prank spoke volumes to his character.

"You still with me?" Hopper spat into his cup. "Thought I'd lost you there for a second."

"I'm good. Just caught up in my thoughts."

"Normal. Especially at this stage." Hopper cleared the dip from his mouth in one swoop of his finger and tossed the brown clump into the cup. He then retrieved the tin of Kodiak from his pocket, slapped it three times on the outside of his thigh, took another scoop, and stuffed it into the void left by the previous. "Everybody's got a vice."

"I'd have to agree."

"What's yours?" Hopper smiled, his bottom lip protruding. "I mean— outside these walls, of course."

The question seemed simple enough, but if he were being completely honest, his vices didn't fall into the typical categories. In his time on the street, both as a cop and in the neighborhood he called home, he'd seen the grip substance abuse held and avoided falling prey to its call. But that didn't mean he wasn't driven to escape. His just happened to come in the form of sixteen-ounce leather gloves. The sweat equity he poured into each punch was his drug of choice, its euphoric release second to none. Realizing how odd this might sound to the dip-spitting guard, Kelly just offered a shrug.

"Well, whatever it is, just don't let it land you back here." Hopper's eyes grew deeper, more sincere. "I hate to see a repeater. No bigger example of the system's failure than that."

"Same for us—" Kelly caught himself. "I mean, ya know, cops. Hate poppin' the same perp doing the same crap."

"Some turds just don't stay flushed." Hopper laughed at his own joke, his chuckle exposing the black flecks dotting his teeth and gums. He then tapped the pocket where his dip was stashed and raised an eyebrow in Kelly's direction. "You sure you don't want a lip?"

"I'm good, thanks," Kelly said.

"Suit yourself. Helps take the edge off, is all." Hopper sighed as he slid the last page Kelly had signed over to the completed pile and replaced it with another. "Almost done. Couple more minutes and you're one step closer to walking out that gate."

Kelly shifted his hands. The cuffs Gladstone refused to remove rattled across the desk as he picked up the pen once more. The quiet of the room was shattered by static crackling from Hopper's portable radio. The transmission was garbled. Hopper cursed under his breath, muttering something about the terrible comms as he fiddled with the antenna and toggled the volume knob.

The sound coming through wasn't one voice, it was many, reminding Kelly of the smokers he used to fight in to make some extra cash before getting hired at the department. It was the distinct roar of a crowd, with a solitary voice rising above the cacophony. The person on the other end wasn't talking calmly, he was yelling. Kelly could only make out one word before the radio went silent. *Help!*

The door to the interview room burst open. Gladstone stood in the opening. The cocky bravado was erased, replaced by pure panic.

"What the hell's goin' on out there?" Hopper stood abruptly. His midsection girth bumped the table, sending the cup of brown spit tumbling off.

"Riot. D-Block's out of control." Gladstone's head was on a swivel, bouncing from the room to the hallway behind him. He locked eyes with Kelly. "Get your ass up! Time to move!"

Hopper stood and appeared to be weighing his options. As Kelly shuffled out into the hallway, the older guard's decision was confirmed as he took off in the opposite direction of D-Block and toward the central hub housing the prison's main guard post.

Gladstone shoved Kelly forward, nearly causing him to lose his balance.

"Easy. Pushing me isn't going to keep things under control." Kelly staggered forward and shot a glance at his escort. "Keep your cool. Level heads prevail."

Gladstone's jaw rippled and his face twisted into a snarl. He looked as though he was going to deliver a beating. "Don't need a lesson from you. I know how to handle my shit. Now get to stepping."

The alarm system let out a deafening wail, drowning out the insults dished out by his oversized escort. Hearing a loud bang from the interview room where Goliath had been taken, Kelly spun to see Gladstone's nervous eyes focusing on the door. He stepped back, allowing room for the big guard to insert himself into whatever problem was evolving inside. But Gladstone didn't move. He stood still, frozen in fear. Kelly had seen it before. Under critical stress the mind reverted to the amygdala, the brain's survival response center. Every person reacted in a different way: flight, which Hopper demonstrated, and freeze.

A loud bang, this time coming from the door itself. The wall around the frame shook. A split second later, the door swung wide, nearly colliding with Kelly, who was now grateful he'd stepped aside. The thin rookie spilled out into the hallway. Blood spread from his face to his uniform shirt, leaking profusely from the guard's broken nose.

Goliath stepped into the hallway and looked down at his prey. His cuffs were off. The beast was free.

Kelly took a step back and was now shoulder to shoulder with Gladstone. "You gonna do something?"

Gladstone seemed not to hear him. Or likely chose not to. Either way, the young guard was already at a disadvantage, one that was worsening with each passing second. Kelly's amygdala kicked in. His brain selected the third option. Fight.

"Hey, tough guy, want a shot at the title?" Kelly opened his stance, bringing himself up on his toes, his prison-issued sneakers dancing atop the linoleum. His hands were still cuffed, forcing him into an awkward version of the boxer's ready position.

Goliath turned his head slowly and eyed him as if waking from a dream. The hatred in those eyes burned a hole through Kelly's jumpsuit. He deviated course from the injured guard, redirecting his attention.

The thin guard shimmied his way backward until he found the wall. Keeping one hand clutched around his injured nose, he slid up the concrete until reaching a standing position.

Kelly was happy to see his ploy had worked. Now he had to deal with the approaching threat. Goliath moved slowly, stalking his prey. Kelly tried to stay loose. He shuffled his feet. Gladstone took a step back, his hand hovering over the baton on his waist, but he didn't draw it.

Kelly prepared for the attack, watching for the behemoth to make his move. He caught fast movement out of the corner of his eye from the hallway connecting to D-Block. The white uniforms immediately identified the two men as convicts.

Shifting himself to address the new threat while staying ready for his primary one, Kelly saw the duo's frenzied look and immediately recognized it. Crowd mentality. The wildness of an incited group spread like a virus. These two men had surely been infected.

They took their aggression out on the closest target of opportunity, the injured guard. The rookie, barely able to stand, was woefully unprepared to defend himself. Within a fraction of a second, he was dumped back to the floor, pummeled by a relentless assault of kicks and punches. The young guard curled into a fetal position, his cries for help rising above the wailing alarm.

Kelly ignored Goliath and sprinted to the crumpled guard. The first inmate never saw him coming. Without breaking stride, Kelly slammed an elbow into the back of the man's head, the impact hurling him forward. The inmate tripped over the guard's body, sending him sprawling headfirst into the concrete wall. His legs buckled and he collapsed to the ground, unconscious.

The other inmate, seeing his cohort disabled, stopped beating the guard and spun to face Kelly. His fists launched with the ferocity of a man who knew how to deliver a punch. Kelly absorbed several rapid blows to his body and head, doing his best to duck and weave his way past the assault.

He pressed forward with his fists up and his chin tucked, closing the distance to an effective range where he could offer a counterattack. Kelly saw an opportunity when the inmate reared back for a haymaker. He kicked hard, the bottom of his shoes connecting with the man's midline, just above the groin.

The strike hit the inmate while he was off balance, doubling him over. Kelly pounced. Raising his clasped hands above his head, he brought them down like a lumberjack splitting a log. He never connected with his target.

Before his hands found the inmate's exposed head, Kelly was hit by what felt like a sledgehammer. Goliath's massive fist blasted the side of his skull.

Lights flickered. The sound came in and out. Kelly was now sideways on the floor, his body stacked alongside the young guard.

Kelly fought against the dizzying effect of Goliath's sucker punch. The red of the big inmate's pant leg came into view. Kelly thrust his arms forward. The stainless steel chain of his cuffs completed the loop created by his interlocked fingers on the other side of the ankle. He pulled hard.

The worn treads of Goliath's shoe slid on the rookie's spilled blood. Like a novice ice skater, the convicted murderer glided to the left. Kelly then jerked his leg in the opposite direction, forcing him to the ground.

Kelly scrambled to his knees. The first inmate he'd knocked out was coming around. Goliath was now blocking the other one. Kelly was preparing for the next onslaught when he heard someone down the hallway shouting, "Come on!"

Kelly got to his feet, his head still ringing, his vision fluttering. He took deep breaths, trying to oxygenate his brain and clear his mind. Goliath stood. Kelly looked to his right and saw that Gladstone was no longer there. He turned to see the musclebound guard barreling toward the security door where Hopper had escaped.

Goliath growled, drawing Kelly's attention from the coward to the problem at hand.

The other inmate tugged at the big man's red sleeve. "Yo, time to go! Now or never. You hear?"

Kelly's legs weren't cooperating, and he swayed. Steady or not, no way would he leave the injured guard's side.

"This ain't over," Goliath boomed over the alarm. "Next time, you're a dead man."

"Better men than you have tried." Clarity returned. "And I'm still standing."

Kelly regretted giving into the taunt as soon as he'd opened his mouth. *Don't poke the bear*, he chastised himself. The standoff held for only a second or two, many unspoken words passing between them.

Goliath teetered for a moment and then turned to join the other two inmates racing down the hallway toward D-Block.

The wailing alarm stopped. In the ensuing silence, the only sound came in the form of a soft whimper from the guard curled at Kelly's feet.

He bent low and grabbed his shoulder. "We gotta move."

"Don't!" The rookie pulled away from Kelly's grip, eyes filled with terror. Only after surveying the area around him did he lower his defenses. "Where's Gladstone?"

Kelly's answer came in the look he shot down the hall toward the guard station. The rookie looked from the door to Kelly, confusion lining his features. "Some don't have what it takes," Kelly said.

The rookie guard's body shook. The skin not covered in blood was ghost white. Kelly recognized the shock setting in, the adrenaline bleeding away. He cursed, muttering to himself about being stupid for taking the job. His jaw was likely broken, making it nearly impossible to understand anything he said.

"You took a hell of a beating." Kelly gave a reassuring nod. "Not a lot of guys would've been able to survive that."

He tried to sit up, only managing to get halfway before grabbing his ribs on the left side and letting out a howl.

"Not sure how long we have before some other group of assholes rolls through." Kelly slid under the wounded guard's other side. "Let's get you out of here."

The rookie did his best to fight through the pain as Kelly helped him to his feet. "Thanks."

Kelly nodded, keeping his focus on balancing the guard's weight with his cuffed hands.

The guard's radio was filled with chatter. One of the officers said, "It's Doyle. They've got him. No way we can get through to him."

"Status." The voice was solemn.

"Not sure. He hasn't moved."

"Copy. Stand by for further. You're the only eyes we have on this right now. Hold your position."

"Understood."

The rest of the radio chatter faded into the background as the two pushed forward toward the door. Kelly couldn't banish the image of Doyle trapped in a cell block. And from the sound of it, he was in bad shape, or worse.

As soon as they were within a couple feet of the door, a mechanical buzzer sounded, followed by the metallic click of the lock release. The door slid open, and Kelly walked the guard inside, handing him off to Hopper and several others standing by.

Beyond the sea of corrections officers, Kelly caught sight of Gladstone. The hulking guard was leaning against the far wall, his vacant stare meeting Kelly's for a moment before he broke contact.

"Kelly, we're going to hold you in here until we get things under control," Hopper said.

Kelly had one foot in the doorway and one in the hall. He felt the tug of war, each side pulling at him. One guaranteeing his safety, the other putting that at risk for the safety of another.

"Not sure Doyle's going to have that kind of time." He looked at Hopper and gave a half-cocked smile. In one swift move, Kelly snatched the key card from the lanyard on Hopper's belt and turned to the hallway.

"What the hell do you think you're doing?"

"I'm gonna bring him back." Kelly didn't wait for a response. He was already running back down the hallway.

There was a fine line between bravery and stupidity. As Kelly prepared for his rescue mission, he wondered whether he'd just crossed it. Only time would tell, but based on what he'd heard over the radio, the clock was already ticking.

18

In the administrative hall of MCI-Cedar Junction—or Walpole, as it would always be known to him—Warden Simon Anderson sat behind the imposing mahogany desk that dominated his meticulously maintained office. His attention to detail was evident in the way the papers were stacked and the pens aligned; even the slight crease in his gray suit was perfectly ironed. It was as if the room's very air dared not disturb the order he had so carefully crafted.

The warden's keen, ice-blue eyes were drawn to the most recent addition to his workspace, an unopened box that sat on top of his desk's polished surface. It contained a snow globe, the twentieth in his collection. Each one symbolized a year of service at the helm of the notorious penitentiary, and this latest addition, still contained within its cardboard prison, represented a milestone in his career. With two more days left, he would have completed twenty years as the iron-fisted ruler of Walpole's bleak domain.

Anderson stood. His tall, lean figure moved silently across the floor to the bookcase. He traced a finger along the spine of a leather-bound book, his gaze flicking back to the box on his desk as though it held some secret he needed to unlock. He would soon hang up his warden's cap and badge, and he couldn't help but feel the weight of anticipation building within him. He could almost hear the snowflakes inside the globe, whispering a silent promise of respite and the freedom of retirement.

But, disciplined man that he was, he resisted the urge to tear open the box and unveil the symbol of his life's work. He knew the time would soon come when he would earn the right to lift that snow globe from its cardboard confines and place it amongst its brethren on the shelf.

For now, though, there were still inmates to manage, officers to command, and a prison to run. Anderson had always believed in the importance of order, control, and unwavering dedication. He would not let the alluring prospect of a future beyond these walls distract him from his duties.

He stood amidst the quiet sanctuary of his office, a stark contrast to the chaos that raged beyond its walls. The room was cast in shadows, the only source of light coming from a single lamp on his oak desk. Anderson took a deep breath and closed his eyes for a moment, relishing in the temporary solace the room provided.

Walking back to his desk, he opened the top drawer and carefully unfolded a clean white cloth. From a nearby cabinet, he pulled out a bottle of glass cleaner. The familiar sound of the spray punctuated the silence. Gaze lingering on the meticulously arranged row of nineteen globes, he reached for the first globe, cradling it gently in his palm, his thumb caressing the delicate engravings.

The sudden trill of the telephone shattered the stillness, and Anderson's features contorted with annoyance. He hesitated, unsure whether to complete his ritual or address the interruption. His decision was made for him as the prison's alarm bell let loose a deafening wail. In that instant, the globe slipped from his grasp, shattering into a million shards at his feet, the liquid splashing onto his slacks. Anger radiated from his body like a furnace, his face flushed with a mix of indignation and frustration.

Carefully, Anderson stepped around the broken glass, reaching for the receiver with a clenched fist. He growled into the mouthpiece, "What in all that's good and holy is going on? Who authorized a drill without my permission?"

The voice that responded was frantic, gasping for air, the words delivered like a hail of bullets. "No drill, sir. We're in deep trouble. A full-blown riot in D-Block!"

Anderson felt the weight of the situation press down on his chest, and the fury he'd experienced just moments before evaporated, replaced by an icy, unyielding dread. He straightened his back, his expression transforming into one of ironclad resolve. Casting a final look at the shattered fragments of his once-cherished globe, he issued a command into the receiver. "Gather all intel, and rally the response team. I'll be there shortly."

Anderson set the receiver in its cradle and stormed out of his office, abandoning the hushed refuge, heading to confront the brutal and unforgiving reality of the world beyond.

Anderson stood over the shoulder of Gary Reynolds, a five-year veteran of the prison and the most tech savvy of all his guards. He was glad to see him on duty today. "Show me the live feed."

Reynolds scrolled the dial, bringing up all seven cameras on the monitors in front of them. Black-and-white images of the inmates, loose and out of control, filled the screens. Anderson let out a sigh of frustration and leaned his weight against Reynolds's chair. "Who started it?"

"Hard to tell exactly." Reynolds rolled the dial on the console and brought the tape back to the moment before the riot kicked off.

"Who's that clustered in the middle?" Anderson didn't know the prisoners like the guards. He'd only done a short stint on the floor before getting called up to the supervisory roles. He knew the talk about having never truly served, but he dismissed the banter of those beneath him.

"That's Domino. He runs the show down there. Most moves don't happen without him knowing about or authorizing them."

"Then we need to extract him. Cut the head off, and the body will fall." Anderson gave a nod to the others in the room.

"Maybe, but we've got a bigger problem right now." Reynolds zoomed in on the bottom of the staircase leading to the guard station. "Doyle's down."

Anderson sucked in a gulp of air. He felt the room spin. A riot was bad enough, but this was worse. He fought to collect himself as he felt his subordinates' eyes burrowing holes into the back of his head. "What's his status? Is he—"

Reynolds offered a slight shrug. "Not sure. Don't think so."

"What do you mean you don't think so?" Anderson stepped back and began pacing. He felt the pinch of his necktie, the noose tightening around his throat. *Poise*, he told himself. *They'll see what you project.* He heard the words of his life coach, but under the circumstances, they only added to his state of unbalance.

"Look here." Reynolds moved the tape to a point where Doyle was standing in front of the stairwell. "If you watch carefully after he goes down, it looks as though he's still moving a little bit."

Anderson watched the scene play out. He saw Doyle face to face with an inmate he didn't recognize. The standoff only lasted a few seconds before Doyle was upended by a rush of inmates. Watching the beating turned Anderson's stomach. Seeing his guard's body slam into the stairs and the crumpled heap where he came to rest nearly brought him to tears.

"Right there—just after they step back." Reynolds tapped his index finger on the screen. "His hand moves. After that, we've got nothing. Hard to tell from the cameras if he's breathing."

Anderson had seen the laundry list of complaints regarding the outdated equipment, overlooking most to save a penny. Part of the reason the governing board loved him as warden was because he was able to stay within budget, oftentimes coming under. Right now, he was confronted with the backlash of his frugalness and could feel the mounting judgment in the men and women assembled in the control room with him.

"Where are the other guards? How come they left their man behind?" Anderson stared down at Doyle.

"He was the only one on the floor. We're short-staffed."

"What about the guards in the station?" Anderson hissed.

"They're blocked in." Reynolds brought the footage back into the live feed. Several imposing inmates were stacked on each door to the guard room.

Anderson cursed under his breath, hating himself for doing so. He'd always prided himself on his restraint in using expletives in his speech, a foreign concept for most of his staff, and one he felt set him apart.

"Do we have comms with them?" Anderson collected himself, smoothing back his hair with the palm of his hand.

"Yes, sir. Need me to reach them?"

Anderson waved his hand, his mind racing for the best course of action. He'd read every manual written about effective management, but none of the material seemed relevant. All of the wisdom he'd garnered from guide-books wasn't applicable to a full-blown prison riot.

"Damnit!" Reynolds said. "We're going to lose visual."

"What? Why?" Anderson leaned in, practically piggybacking himself onto Reynolds.

"They're going prison dark. They've barricaded the access doors with mattresses taken from their cells, blocking the windows. It'll only be a matter of time before we lose complete visual."

Anderson watched as several inmates threw wads of wet toilet paper at the surveillance cameras staged throughout the cell block. One by one, as their aim found its mark, the monitors' live feeds went dark. The last image captured—one that would forever haunt him—was Jamie Doyle, the long-time guard and one of the most well-respected corrections officers within the prison, lying broken at the foot of the stairwell.

All eyes in the control center turned to him. Anderson wracked his brain for the answer to their unspoken question: what now? How he proceeded would determine not only the fate of his trapped guard but of his own career. Legacy was forged in these moments. He knew this, and yet the decisions he needed to make to bring this ordeal under control proved to be elusive.

"We've lost the wing. I repeat, D-Block is no longer under our control." The guard from the wing's control station made no attempt to mask his panic, nearly choking on the words. "Command, do you copy?"

The room remained silent, the tension palpable. Anderson clenched his fists, the blood draining from his knuckles.

"We copy. Hold tight. We're formulating a plan," Reynolds answered.

"All right, listen up." Anderson finally spoke, his voice wavering slightly. "We need to act fast, but we can't lose our heads."

"Warden, the longer we wait, the longer it will take to bring this thing under control." Officer Hopper stepped forward. "Time is of the essence and the clock is ticking."

"You don't think I know this?" Anderson didn't give time for one of his subordinates to offer their opinion. "We can't just rush in. The sheer number of inmates would make it impossible. What we need is a foothold."

"They'll be making demands soon, I'm sure. Once things calm down." Hopper filled the bottom of his lip with a wad of chew. "Problem is Doyle. Not sure how long he's got."

"Doyle's definitely the priority. But we're going to need leverage. Right now, they've got all of it."

"What if we try to negotiate with them, sir? Maybe they'd be willing to release Doyle in exchange for some of their demands." Reynolds looked up from his chair.

"Negotiation. They've already nearly killed one of our own." Gladstone unfolded his massive forearms and pushed off the wall he'd been leaning against. "We should smash that door and crack skulls until the savages crawl back into their cages."

"Tough talk from the coward who left Lipinski for dead when you tucked tail and ran for safety." Hopper stepped forward, closing the distance between them.

"Cut the crap! No time for this," Anderson barked at his men. The commanding tone of his voice was foreign to him, though it quelled the brewing standoff.

"Brawn and big talk. When they pull the tape, you'll be scrolling the want ads lookin' for a new job," Hopper muttered as he retreated to his corner.

"You mentioned Lipinski. Where's he now?" Anderson's mind reeled. Bad enough he had one guard down, now two? He heard the flush and felt his career circling the bowl.

"He's in the infirmary. Banged up, but he'll survive," Reynolds said.

"Good." Anderson let out a long sigh. "We're going to have to establish a line of communication with the inmates. For now, let's use the station guards as a relay."

Reynolds communicated the plan to the guards on scene. They copied the order and stated they'd notify command once contact was made.

"We've got to figure out who's in charge down there. You mentioned this Domino guy—think he's our go-to?"

"He rules the roost. My guess is he's our best bet at gaining some traction with the other prisoners." Hopper spat into his cup. "They'll listen to him."

"What about the other one? The new guy. Seemed like he was part of this thing." Anderson thought of the video replay leading up to Doyle's brutal attack and the inmate blocking the guard's last-ditch effort to get to safety.

"Don't know enough to say. He's brand-new." Hopper, the only guard presenting any insight at the moment, continued, "New guys don't usually carry much clout, especially the kind capable of kicking off a riot of this magnitude. My bet's still on Domino. Maybe the Watt kid's just following orders?"

"Then I guess the play would be to try and establish a line of communication with Domino. If nothing else, it'll get the ball rolling and buy us some time while we figure this mess out." Anderson was trying to convey a sense of hope to those gathered in the prison's digital hub.

"What about ERT?" Hopper asked.

"Yes. Good point. Get me Diaz." Anderson nodded at Reynolds, who immediately sprang into action, radioing the head of the prison's Emergency Response Team.

"On her way now."

"Let's get her up to speed when she arrives." Anderson tried to give the appearance of control, but internally he was hanging by a thread.

"We've got another issue—well, two, actually." Hopper spoke to the warden but his gaze rested on Gladstone.

"What now?" Anderson rolled his neck from side to side, trying without success to reduce the strain.

"Goliath is loose. He's joined the party in D-Block."

"He's an ISO inmate. How in the world did he become part of this mess?" Anderson followed Hopper's glare to Gladstone. "One of you better start explaining."

"He wasn't in the isolation wing when this started. He was in the private visitation room down the hall. When the call went out and the alarms sounded, Goliath went on a rampage. Used Lipinski as a battering ram and busted his way out."

"And you weren't able to assist in bringing this inmate under control?"

"Ever taken a good look at him? He's called Goliath for a reason. Anyway, I was already down the hall when things went to shit." He then cocked an eyebrow at Gladstone. "Maybe you should pick things up from this point?"

Gladstone remained silent and refused to meet the judgment in Hopper's eyes.

"Guess not. Goliath tuned up Lipinski pretty bad. But the two trustees, Slim and Boone, put the finishing touches. Probably would've killed him if it wasn't for Kelly."

"You're talking about Michael Kelly?"

"Yup. He was with me filling out his walking papers. I handed him off to Gladstone after the alert went out and headed to central."

"Officer Gladstone, why am I hearing about an inmate taking up the defense for one of our brethren? During all of this, where were you?"

Gladstone teetered against the wall. Keeping his head down, he grumbled something under his breath.

"You're going to have to speak up if you've got something to say." Anderson always prided himself on composure but felt his hold slipping. The anger boiling over into his words and mannerisms was a foreign feeling, but one he found a strange pleasure in embracing. Like the flurries of his snow globes when shaken, he felt wild and free. "Open your damn mouth and tell me what happened out there!"

"There were three of them, one the size of a city bus." Gladstone was a balloon slowly deflating. "I just, I don't know, I guess I just froze."

"And another inmate had to take up your slack?"

"He didn't only take up the slack. He brought a can of whoop ass to the party. Nearly took 'em all out too, until Goliath caught him with a sucker punch." Hopper had a half-smile on his leathery face. "Tough son of a bitch, that one. Took the beating and still managed to grab Lipinski and carry him down the hall."

"And where were you during this?" Anderson's eyes were daggers puncturing deep into the soul of his largest guard. "Answer me!"

"I was here. In the guard station."

Anderson paced the small room. "When the dust settles, there'll be a full review of your actions. Until that time, you stay put. And God help you if you fail to act when called upon again. Are we clear?"

"Crystal."

"So, where is Kelly now?"

"He's out there." Hopper pointed toward the hallway. "Took my key card too."

"What's he planning to do?"

"Said he was going to save Doyle."

"Great. I've got two guards injured, one of whom is trapped in a hell-hole. I've got two more barricaded in their station. And now you're telling me I've got an inmate running around the halls playing hero?"

"Maybe he's not playing. Maybe he's an asset we can use to our advantage?" Hopper stepped closer. "Warden, think about it. He might be able to give us the eyes we need."

"Or he'll end up another body we've got to rescue. These other prisoners realize an ex-cop in a jumpsuit is loose, it'll be open season."

"Then let's hope that doesn't happen."

Anderson was alone with his thoughts. He could feel the weight of the situation bearing down on him, the responsibility for the lives of his staff and the safety of the prison. He knew that his decisions in the coming moments would define not only his career but also the lives of those under his charge. The choices he made would forever be etched into the annals of the prison's history.

The guards in the room traded uneasy looks, and Reynolds stirred in his seat. "Sir, maybe it's time to call in the state police or the National Guard? This has the potential of spinning way beyond our ability to contain it."

Anderson rubbed his temples, mulling over the suggestion. The idea of bringing in reinforcements felt like a white flag. "No, we don't need them—not yet, at least," he said. "Get me Diaz. After ERT's given me their assessment and available options, I'll make the decision on whether or not we're able to contain the problem and keep this in-house."

"Well, she better hurry because it looks like Kelly's making his move."

Hopper gestured toward one of the monitors, where Kelly was preparing to enter the second-floor hallway leading to D-Block.

Anderson bit his fingernail, a habit he'd worked hard to correct. Its return now was no shock. In fact, he was surprised he didn't bite off his fingertip.

He looked above the monitor to the television playing the local news, half-expecting to see the media hounds exposing the chaos in a breaking news segment. Anderson was grateful word hadn't reached the vultures yet. The clock was ticking on that front, and he hoped to have things under control before the story broke. The TV was muted, but he read the headline calling for the arrival of a Nor'easter bringing enough snow to put the state in lockdown. Order was besieged by chaos. Restoring things to their rightful place would take a monumental effort.

The door to the central command hub opened and Officer Evelyn Diaz strode in, her face etched with resolve. The ERT leader had a reputation for getting things done, regardless of the odds stacked against her. Anderson prayed she'd prove it true once more.

19

Barnes navigated the slippery streets, the tires crunching over the fresh layer of snow coating the slush beneath. She pulled into the back lot of Jip's Market, flakes swirling around their car like a snow globe caught in the throes of a tempest.

Cahill sighed and rubbed his temples. "I really banged myself up good last night. Next time I make a push for a night out, I'll make sure it's not a work night."

"I'll be happy if I don't see another shot glass for a very long time." Barnes cast a smile his way.

The radio played in the background; the song she was half-listening to ended. The DJ began rambling, and she reached for the dial to change the station. Barnes paused when he turned the broadcast over to the weather reporter. A woman with an annoyingly perky voice warned of a Nor'easter barreling toward the Boston area. Perfect timing. Not only was her personal life in chaos after last night's awkward encounter with Cahill, but she was also dealing with Kelly's upcoming release and the uncertain impact of his return. Add to that a blizzard, and her life was likely to be Webster's definition of a shitstorm.

Barnes chewed on her lower lip, her gaze scanning the desolate lot and coming to rest on Cahill. "You think she'll actually show up?" she asked, her voice tinged with doubt. "Maybe she blew us off. Gave us the meet location just to get us off her stoop. Wouldn't be the first time."

Cahill leaned back in his seat, a smirk playing at the corner of his mouth. "When it comes to getting an assist for her kid, no doubt she'll show."

Just as the words left his lips, they spotted Pris trudging through the snowstorm. A thick winter coat swaddled her frame, the hood pulled up to shield her face from the icy onslaught. She tugged at the edges, doing her best to fend off the biting wind while sidestepping slush-filled puddles on her way to the market.

Barnes flashed her headlights, and Pris veered toward the unmarked detective car, her boots leaving a trail of half-melted snow in her wake. She yanked the back door open, the howling wind and flurries invading the car's warmth for a moment before she slammed it shut. Shivering, she brushed the snow from her coat and rubbed her hands together in a futile attempt to regain some warmth.

Barnes cranked up the heat for their guest.

Cahill twisted around in his seat to face Pris, his expression serious. "This better be good," he warned.

Pris shot him a defiant, snarky look. "You think I would've dragged my fine ass out in this shit weather if it wasn't?"

The detectives exchanged glances, Barnes raising a brow in silent agreement. The wind howled outside, but inside the car, the air was heavy with anticipation.

Pris was eyeing both detectives, her breaths short and shallow. "What is it that you think I know that you two don't?" she asked with a hint of defiance.

Cahill shook his finger as if he were admonishing a toddler. "That's not the game, sweetheart. You're not diggin' for info, we are."

Catching a look from Barnes, her eyes silently urging him to go easy, Cahill softened his tone. "Look, Pris, we're workin' toward the same end here. We just wanna know if you've got somethin' that can put us on the straight, ya know?"

Pris hesitated for a moment, her eyes darting between the two detectives. "I might know somethin', but I ain't gonna say nothin' if you can't guarantee my safety," she finally replied, her voice barely above a whisper.

Barnes noticed the shift in Cahill's speech and mannerisms. The years as a narcotics detective working the streets, cultivating informants, and blending with the environment emanated from her partner. Being a chameleon was part of the gig. Barnes had done it when she worked prostitution stings. The longer you played the game, the harder it was to shake the personalities acquired doing it.

Cahill nodded, his voice gentle yet firm. "We'll do everything in our power to keep you safe, Pris. But you gotta help us help you."

Seeing him back in his element told Barnes two things: he could blend seamlessly with the seedier element, and he was a good detective, applying the right amount of pressure without overkill, balancing the need for justice with a genuine compassion for the victims. Seeing him in this mode raised her opinion of him.

Pris took a deep breath, steadying herself. "All right, I'll tell you what I know. But you gotta promise me you won't let nothin' happen to me."

Cahill offered a reassuring smile. "You have my word, Pris."

Pris broke eye contact with Cahill and played with a string hanging off the sleeve of her coat. "This ain't gonna come back on me, right?" Her voice was low, a deep sadness carried in the words. "My baby already done lost her daddy. Can't be leavin' her too, ya feel?"

"Nothin' you say to us is comin' back on you. We won't do you like that." Cahill looked at Barnes. "My partner and I, we understand the risk you're takin' and we respect that. No way we'd put you out."

"He's right. We do it all the time." Barnes leaned forward, pressing herself into the back of her seat as she sought to make eye contact. "No names go into reports when the information comes from a confidential source. There'll be no record we even met."

"What about testifying? Ain't you gotta bring me to trial or something?"

"Not how this'll work. You give us the information, we go and verify. We'll build our case around what we discover for ourselves." Cahill made a show of wiping his hands together. "Clean as a whistle. Scout's honor."

"You a Boy Scout?" Pris cocked her head up, eyeing his two-fingered salute.

"Nah. But I was a scout in the military."

"Guess that counts." Pris forced an uneasy smile.

Barnes and Cahill met the girl's face, each offering their own form of non-verbal encouragement.

Pris looked around, scanning the environment outside the foggy windows. Barnes recognized the nervous routine most street-savvy citizens performed before giving information to the cops.

"I don't know how Cut got mixed up with the 9s." Pris shrugged. "He was a hustler. Always lookin' to get his nut. Guess he saw an opportunity with Watt's crew. I should've talked him out of it." She cursed at herself under her breath. "Stupid ass. Now look. Tryin' to make it better for me and baby girl, left me to fend. Ain't that some shit?"

"I knew him enough to know that Cut was no dummy. Sure he made some bad choices, but I could see he had some real potential." Cahill leaned a little closer. "He was one of the ones I'd hoped had found his way out of the game."

"He did," Pris muttered.

"Then help us get the bastards who did this. Point me in the right direction so I can make sure whoever's responsible pays. Let us do that. For you and your daughter."

Pris sniffled. A tear escaped her brooding eyes. She quickly swept both her nose and cheek, adding to the dampness of her sleeve. "Thanks."

"For what?"

"For not talkin' shit about him."

"No reason to. Plus, I only speak the truth." Cahill gave a half-smile.

Barnes caught the subtle glance Cahill shot in her direction. She couldn't help but feel the comment had some double meaning, leading her mind to wander back to the previous night and the kiss that almost was.

"So like I said, he was messin' with that crew. Never told me much about it. He said it's better I didn't know. Safer, I guess." Her eyes widened slightly. "You think they'll be comin' for me?"

"I don't have any reason to believe they would. Nothing's a guarantee, but it doesn't seem like it'd be a smart move." Cahill reached for his coffee and took a sip. "From everything I've heard, Roland Watt's not stupid."

"Stupid enough to get his ass locked up." Pris spat her words.

"Fair enough," Cahill said. "We've got that Cut was playing both sides. He didn't tell you anything specific about why or what they were up to?"

"No."

Cahill sighed and looked at Barnes. She could glean from his expression that his hopes of Pris being able to provide them with a usable lead were dashed. Barnes had seen it time and again when information was offered to the police in the hope of compensation. Usually the information was useless or a total fabrication, and it was starting to look as though Pris was falling into that category. Under the circumstances, who could blame her. Barnes sympathized with the young mother.

"I may not know what they're up to or why Cut got smashed, but I know where they be hangin' at."

"Down off Talbot Street. Round the bend on Kerwin. We know the turf. Got eyes on it."

"Nah. They ghosted that spot fo' sure."

"You got another spot we should be looking?" Cahill perked up a bit and shot a glance at Barnes.

"Maybe. Don't know if they're there." Pris stopped fidgeting and looked into Cahill's eyes. "I loved my man, but damn if that fool's eyes didn't wander, 'specially after the baby. I caught him sneakin' out one night a while back."

"Figured he was creepin' on a side piece?" Cahill asked, keeping his street vernacular spot-on.

"Damn straight. I followed, figurin' I'd have to put the smack down on some trifflin' ho." Pris began posturing, bobbing her head for added effect. "But it wasn't no girl he was seeing. I mean there was a girl there, but she was with Killa."

"Where's this place at?" Cahill asked eagerly.

"Morton Street, across from Baird. Can't remember the number, but it's some nasty puke-green color. No missin' it."

"Mattapan?"

"You know it?" Pris raised an eyebrow.

"I know the neighborhood. Grew up a couple blocks away."

"Damn, who would've thought Detective Cahill came up in the hood? Murderpan ain't no joke." Pris had a newfound look of respect as she sized up the former narcotics detective.

"You sure about the address?" Barnes asked.

"Yup. Doesn't mean he's there. Just sayin' he was."

"When did you see Watt at this spot?" Barnes jotted the address into a notepad. She saw Pris give her a questioning look. "Don't worry. Your name's not anywhere in this thing. Just taking notes."

Pris gave a slow nod before answering. "It was two nights ago."

"See anyone else with Watt? Any of the other players?" Cahill asked.

"You mean 'cept for that chica he was hangin' on? Nah. Just Killa."

"This girl he was with, she from around the way?"

"Never seen her before. And she wasn't no girl. She was a grown-ass woman."

"When you say woman, what age would you guess?" Barnes asked.

"Her old ass was maybe thirty, thirty-five."

Barnes nearly let a laugh escape. Growing up in the tough neighborhoods was much like growing up in a war-torn country where life expectancy changed perspective on what it meant to be old. "Anything you can tell me about her?"

Pris shrugged. "Don't know. She looked like any other Latina I know. Black hair, tan skin, ya know? I guess she was kind of buff, though."

"Buff? You mean in shape?" Barnes asked.

Pris rolled her eyes. "Yeah. I mean, for an older chick."

Barnes waited to see if Pris had anything else to contribute. After a healthy block of silence, she determined they'd drained the well. "We really appreciate you doing this. I know talking to the police is not high on your list. But we're going to do our absolute best to find whoever's responsible for your boyfriend's death."

"Not gonna bring him back."

"No. But I've done this job long enough to know that bringing a killer to justice helps the victim's family move forward." Barnes placed a hand on the girl's knee. "And we hope to give you that."

Cahill pulled his wallet from his back pocket and thumbed through the cash. He pulled out several twenties before looking up at Pris, whose eyes were wet with tears. Groaning softly, he dug out the remainder of his cash. "There's two hundred here. It'll cover diapers and formula with some left over for you."

Pris reached for the stack of twenties. Cahill held onto it and eyed the young mother carefully. "None of this better go up your nose, you hear?"

"Been clean since the baby." Pris scowled, snatching the money. "We ain't all crackheads, ya know. Just 'cause we street don't mean we trash. Or did you forget where you came up?"

Barnes watched Cahill. He took the tongue-lashing in stride and offered nothing in the way of resistance. In fact, he smiled and nodded.

"You take care of yourself and that baby girl of yours," he said before turning in his seat.

"Get them bastards. Get 'em for my daughter." Pris folded the cash, then unzipped her jacket halfway and stuffed the money into her bra. The street-tough mother scanned the lot before opening the door. She stepped out into the cold without looking back.

Barnes watched as Pris headed toward the rear entrance to Jip's Market, disappearing into the whirling white barrier of the intensifying snowstorm descending upon the city.

"She's a tough girl," Barnes said.

"Hard-ass more like it." Cahill chuckled. "But you gotta be if you're going to survive out here."

"I guess it takes one to know one." Barnes studied her partner. During the conversation with Pris, Cahill had exposed pieces of himself she hadn't seen before. A newfound level of respect began to form.

"Maybe." He shrugged. "Sounds like we've got a place to put eyes on."

"Think we should let White know? He's supposed to be handling the hunt, remember?"

"I'd hate to waste the lieutenant's time if it turned out to be a bogus lead." Cahill had a mischievous grin. "I vote we take a little drive and see for ourselves first. Unless, of course, you're not up for driving in the snow. I'd be happy to take the wheel."

"Buckle up, buttercup." Barnes put the Caprice in drive.

The tires slipped on the slush as they headed out of the lot. Barnes quickly regained control as they navigated the city streets, now painted white in the freshly fallen snow. As the two set out toward Mattapan to investigate the address Pris had given them, she thought about the money Cahill had coughed up. In the scheme of things, two hundred dollars was a small price to pay if the information brought them one step closer to finding the killers.

20

Watt stood amidst the chaos, surrounded by the rioting prisoners. D-Block had become a living, breathing embodiment of the pent-up rage of the men who'd called the prison wing their home. In the few short hours since he'd arrived, Watt had risen to power, securing his place as the king of this concrete castle.

In the center of it all was the inmate who'd been involved in the beating of Doyle, who now lay unconscious at the foot of the stairwell, a crumpled reminder of the uprising. The inmate, a burly figure with wild eyes, was champing at the bit to finish off the guard, his bloodlust spiraling out of control.

Watt stepped forward, his voice carrying over the din. "That's enough. He's done."

The inmate turned to face Watt, his rage momentarily redirected. "Who the hell do you think you are? I don't take orders from you."

The inmate spat on the floor, just missing the tip of Watt's newly acquired prison footwear. Watt, unfazed, stepped closer, his gaze steady and unblinking. "Be easy, bro. You'd do well not to mistake my calm for weakness."

"You must think you somethin' real special. You know who I am?" The inmate beat his chest and threw his hands in the air, calling attention to the verbal sparring match.

Watt made a show of reading the number stenciled above the breast pocket. "Looks to me like your name is 19084-D."

"Oh, you a funny ass?" The mockery was evident in both his voice and mannerisms. "This one's got jokes. Aight, cool, see how them jokes be soundin' when I push the teeth down the back of your throat, bitch."

"Too bad. I thought you might be useful." Watt sized up the thickly muscled inmate, his voice low and measured. "Everything happening here, right now, serves a greater purpose. We can't lose sight of that. But you— you're not capable of seeing the bigger picture."

A crowd began to form. Watt watched as the arrival of other inmates fueled the man hellbent on turning this conversation into violence. "Kick his ass, Rocco!" someone called. "Teach this punk bitch a lesson! Show 'em how we do in the Big D." This call to arms energized the crowd.

Rocco's nostrils flared, and he clenched his fists as he took a step toward Watt, attempting to intimidate him. Watt remained composed, his confidence and poise stretching far beyond his years.

"Remember, we're all in this together," Watt continued, never breaking eye contact. "We're fighting for something bigger than ourselves. Don't let your emotions cloud your judgment. We have a chance of doing some real damage. Serves no point to waste that kind of energy on each other."

Watt directed his comments not to the man in front of him but to the gathering onlookers. Seeing the other prisoners' nods and shrugs, he was confident the message was being delivered. He just needed to punctuate it in a way this crowd would understand.

For a tense moment, Rocco stared down at Watt, his chest heaving with anger.

"I'm gonna mess you up real bad. When I'm done, I'm gonna finish up with that guard." The veins bulged in Rocco's neck as he balled his fists, preparing his attack. "Got some smart-ass shit ya wanna say before I rain the pain train down on that smug face of yours?"

"It seems we're at an impasse. Let's hope everyone gathered learns a valuable lesson from our friend Rocco here." Watt, unflinching, didn't even bother to brace himself. Instead, he looked beyond the irate man, and a slow, knowing smile formed on his lips.

Rocco hesitated for a moment before turning to look at what caught Watt's attention. Before he could react, an enormous figure strode through the crowd, which offered a wide berth to the massive beast.

Goliath's fist was already in motion, a meteor of flesh and bone sailing through the air. It landed with a devastating crunch, impacting Rocco's entire face, his nose taking the initial brunt. Rocco fell back, a red rainbow trailing behind his rapidly descending body.

Watt sidestepped the man as he plummeted to the floor. The momentum of the strike continued, sliding his limp body several feet before he came to a stop beside the unconscious guard.

Watt stood over Rocco and watched as his eyes turned vacant, their light fading. With a casual stride, he stepped over the unconscious man as if he were never a threat, and now barely a consideration. The crowd of supporters, now silenced, stepped back as Watt came closer. He ignored them and walked over to his brother, wrapping his arms around Goliath's thick chest, his hands barely making it past the flared lats. Watt closed himself off to his surroundings and allowed himself to engage the heartfelt embrace. It had been a long time since he'd been this close to his brother and he soaked in the moment, an unspoken understanding passing between them.

They separated. Watt slapped his older brother's shoulder, grinning. "Glad you could make it."

"Wouldn't miss it for the world." Goliath glanced down at the inmate he just knocked out, a hint of amusement in his eyes. "Looks like I got here just in time."

"Everything's under control." Watt pointed to two inmates standing nearby who'd watched the altercation go down. "Stick him in his cell."

The two hesitated for a moment. Their eyes drifted upward from Watt to the mountain of red standing beside him. They gave a nod, then picked up the unconscious Rocco and began shuffling away.

"Make sure he doesn't leave it again without my permission." Watt turned to his brother. "Now, with that out of the way, it's time for our next order of business."

"Yeah? What's that?" Goliath looked around. He sucked in a big breath and let it out slowly. "Damn it feels good to be in gen pop."

"It's going to feel a whole lot better soon."

"What's the play here, little brotha? I mean, shit, you went through all this to spend a little QT with me before I go to supermax?"

"Think bigger."

Watt looked up at the second-floor guard station, where one of the guards had the phone pressed to his ear. The rapid movement of his mouth and his darting eyes told Watt he was likely relaying the situation to his superiors. Watt smiled.

Goliath opened and closed his hands, sending a ripple of muscle up the red jumpsuit covering his massive forearms.

"You good?"

Goliath stopped, releasing his balled fist. Rocco's blood coated his knuckles. "I had a shot at Kelly earlier. Right there in the hallway. I could've caved his skull. I should've."

Watt considered this for a moment, knowing how deeply Goliath's bloodlust ran for the man responsible for his incarceration. He looked at the clock on the wall. Watt factored a new calculation into his plan, but for now it would have to wait. "After I get things under control, we'll see about dealing with Kelly and getting you your pound of flesh. But right now, we've got bigger issues at hand."

"Like what?" Goliath appeared temporarily satiated by Watt's words. He nodded, the fire in his eyes subsiding slightly.

Watt glanced up at the guards again, his gaze calculating. "I need to have a little conversation with the men upstairs. Grab a couple of the big boys. Have them block the doors on both sides. Can't have our guests leaving just yet."

Goliath nodded. He pushed his way into the crowd of rioting prisoners, moving with a newfound purpose as he began to rally the muscle they needed.

Watt walked to the stairs, waiting for Goliath to finish. He could feel the adrenaline coursing through his veins, the weight of the situation pressing down on him. But he knew that in moments like these, the bond between him and his brother would see them through. And with that in mind, he steeled himself for the confrontation ahead.

The control room was now a cage for its occupants. Two guards, their faces a mixture of fear and determination, stared out at the unfolding chaos. As requested, two large inmates with bulging biceps and tattoos snaking up their arms blocked the doors of the secure room. There would be no easy exit.

Watt sauntered up the stairs with a lethal calm. He was a predator, poised and deadly serious. Stopping outside the left-side door, he rapped on the shatter-resistant glass. The guards inside flinched, their eyes wide with terror.

"Come here," Watt ordered to the closest guard, raising his voice above the cacophony of the rioters continuing their rampage below.

The guard glanced at his partner for reassurance before complying with Watt's demand. "What do you want?"

"I want you and your buddy there to vacate this control room," Watt said.

"We can't do that," the guard replied, his attempt at defiance coming out flat.

Watt's gaze drifted down the staircase to Doyle. He lay sprawled on the floor, unconscious and vulnerable.

"If you don't leave this control room, I'll be forced to make sure he never regains consciousness," Watt threatened, his voice cold and unyielding. "Do you or your buddy want to have his death on your hands? You want to be the ones to tell his family that he died because you didn't want to give up your pathetic guard station?"

The guard paled, gripping his radio to relay the demand. Watt couldn't hear the reply, but after a tense silence, the two guards exchanged anxious looks, grabbed their gear, and approached the door.

"Let them walk," Watt called to the two inmates blocking the way.

They stepped aside, forming a makeshift corridor for the guards to pass through. As the guards prepared to leave, Watt added one last instruction.

"Leave your keys with my friends there."

The guards did as they were told, and one of the inmates used the keys to open the access door to the hallway. The door clanged open, and the two panicked corrections officers charged into the hallway, neither man bothering to look back at their abandoned post.

Watt controlled the grin fighting to replace the unwavering stoicism etched into his face. He signaled for the keys, and one of the inmates tossed them over. Watt caught them in midair, spinning them on his finger as he turned toward the railing overlooking the rest of the cell block.

Domino met Watt's eyes. In an unspoken sign of respect, the heralded king of D-Block turned the power over to the man with the keys. He let out a whistle that brought the roar to a hum, then pointed to Watt.

Like a king surveying his kingdom, Watt swept his eyes across the men now under his rule. "We now control the block."

Profanity-laden cheers erupted from the crowd. Inmates jumped on tables, stomping their thunderous support. Metal chimes rang out as others banged against the bars of their cells. He could see the bloodlust in their eyes; the cacophony was music to their ears. To Watt it signified the beginning of the next phase of his plan.

He raised his hands and waited until the noise subsided. "They'll be formulating a plan, but they won't be able to act. Not while we have leverage." Watt glanced at Doyle. "He stays alive. They stay out. Anyone not down with that plan can join Rocco in his cell."

Watt watched as the other inmates turned to the cell where Rocco, now awake but groggy, sat on his mattress. The two men Watt assigned to guard him continued to man their post.

"What about demands?" a voice cried out from the crowd.

"They'll try to negotiate. And we'll make our demands known." Watt looked at the eagerness in his minions' eyes. "I'll bet some of you haven't had good food in a long time." This earned a burst of supportive shouts. "That'll be our first move. After that, we'll create a list. By the time we're done, you'll think you're staying at the Ritz. Hell, people will be getting arrested just to get a bid in D-Block."

Watt turned toward the guard station, Goliath his shadow as he found the key and unlocked the door.

"You got it goin' like that, huh, little bro?"

"A lot's changed since you've been inside." Watt opened the door and stepped inside. He was greeted by cool air, the vent system pushing back the body heat infused in the air outside. "This is just the beginning."

"But on the real." Goliath leaned close. "It's only a matter of time before they bust through. Everything'll be back to norm in a split, ya feel?"

"Those guys out there, they're just pawns in a much bigger game." Watt winked. "And whatever the warden's got planned, I'm already three moves ahead."

Watt walked over to the console toward a foot-long grinder wrapped in foil. He exposed the Italian combo, releasing the scent of meats, oils, and seasoning into the small control room. Goliath's eyes widened. Watt tore off a quarter of the sandwich and tossed the rest to his brother. "I need you strong for what's to come."

Watt took a seat in the guard's chair. He looked at the list of extensions laminated on the workstation beneath the phone and found the number he was looking for. Before making the call, he took a moment to enjoy the food the guard had been kind enough to leave behind. His brother was the brawn, and Watt was the brain. Both required fuel for the task ahead.

21

Sergeant Halstead leaned back in his worn leather chair, rubbing the stubble on his chin as he scanned the case summary. The gang murder had shaken the city, and his team was responsible for putting the pieces together. With Lincoln White, head of the Boston PD's Narcotics Unit, leading the hunt for the shooters, Halstead's team had been assigned the less glamorous but equally important task of uncovering the why and how behind the gruesome crime.

The office was quiet, the hum of fluorescent lights punctuating the occasional rustle of papers. Halstead hadn't seen Barnes and Cahill, two of his seasoned detectives, since shortly after the morning briefing ended. He wondered what they had dug up so far.

As if on cue, Mainelli, the senior-most detective in his squad, and also the group curmudgeon, sauntered past his office door in the direction of the breakroom. His heavy steps and labored breathing made it impossible not to notice him.

"Mainelli," Halstead called out, raising a hand to flag him down. "Got a minute?"

Mainelli turned, annoyance carved into his face, though it was now tempered with that "What did I do now?" expression common among those called on by their supervisors.

Halstead waited patiently as Mainelli took his sweet time lumbering back to his office. The heavyset detective leaned against the doorframe, arms crossed. "You rang?"

"Any word from Barnes or Cahill?" Halstead set down the supplemental report written by one of the first patrol units on scene. He took an extra moment to line the file on top of its folder.

"Not yet."

"Any idea where they went? I haven't seen them since this morning." Halstead didn't show his annoyance. He'd dealt with suspects who required less effort. Mainelli was a good cop, but he was old school and would never volunteer anything to a supervisor. He had risen in the ranks during a time when there had been a division between those on the beat and those in the leather seat, and was conditioned to distrust any question, especially ones about his fellow cops.

"Think they were runnin' down a lead." Mainelli looked over his shoulder to see if anyone was eavesdropping.

Halstead almost chuckled at the unwarranted paranoia on display.

"Lead?" Halstead asked, his interest piqued.

"Didn't say much." Mainelli shrugged. "I think Cahill's got some old connections. Probably hitting up some of his old snitches from his days as a narc. Who knows, maybe he'll shake something loose."

Halstead nodded, his eyes narrowing in thought. "All right, keep me posted if you hear anything from them."

"Will do, Sarge," Mainelli grunted as he pushed away from the doorframe.

Halstead let out a controlled sigh, careful not to betray his worry that Barnes and Cahill weren't stepping on the toes of White and his unit. There was no telling how the hot-headed lieutenant might react if that happened.

Halstead shifted gears. "You make any headway on the evidence from the scene?"

Mainelli nodded. "I was on my way to Charles to check the status."

"You're heading the wrong way, unless Charles's office has been moved to the breakroom."

Mainelli took the ribbing in stride, offering a half-cocked smile. "Hey, no matter the case, there's always time for a cup of coffee."

"Anything else I should know?"

"Nope." Mainelli shook his head. "I'll keep you in the loop should something break. And I'll check in with Barnes to see what they've got brewing."

Halstead released him with a dismissive nod. He hadn't wanted to appear as a micromanager, and by prodding Mainelli, he had delegated while keeping his distance from crowding his team as they worked the case.

"Just don't forget to keep me in the loop," he said to the senior detective's back.

Mainelli turned back and gave an exaggerated bow. "Your wish is my command, Sarge."

With that, Mainelli followed the scent of fresh coffee lingering in the air.

Halstead's desk phone rang. He glanced at the caller ID and recognized the number as internal, belonging to Chief Ryan. He picked up the receiver, cradling it between shoulder and neck as he continued to arrange the files spread out on his desk.

"Afternoon, Chief. What can I do for you?" Halstead's voice was smooth and professional.

"Need you to swing by my office," Ryan responded, his tone uncharacteristically soft, a far cry from the normally gregarious leader of the Boston Police Department.

"When would you like me?" Halstead paused his file arrangement to give the conversation his full attention.

"Now," Ryan replied. "We've got a situation."

"On my way." Halstead hung up and exited his office, curiosity piqued by the urgency in Ryan's voice.

As he cruised through the sea of detectives, he couldn't help but notice the Homicide Unit was operating slightly below optimal numbers. With the current count at thirty-three, four-man detective squads had one sergeant assigned to oversee the investigations. Halstead's unit was down one since Kelly had been removed from the force.

Halstead, the chief, and James Sharp, head of BPD's Organized Crime Unit, were the only people in the two-thousand-man department who knew the truth—that Kelly's termination was a ruse and would hopefully lead to his infiltration of the Irish mob run by Connor Walsh. Ryan's tone and the vagueness in his message led Halstead to believe he needed to talk about Kelly.

He left his office and headed to the fourth floor, his footsteps muffled by the thick carpeting that lined the hallway. He couldn't help but feel a sense of gravity and anticipation as he neared Chief Ryan's inner sanctum. It was a space steeped in history and the weight of decisions that had shaped the city and its police department for decades.

He pushed open the heavy wooden door and stepped into the dimly lit office. The room, a testament to the chief's years on the force, was adorned with mementos of his storied career and exuded an aura of old-school toughness, like the man who occupied it.

Chief Ryan sat behind a massive oak desk, his imposing frame draped in the dark blue uniform of the Boston PD. His silver hair was cropped close to his scalp, and his piercing blue eyes seemed to bore right into Halstead's soul. The chief's face was etched with lines that spoke of a life dedicated to the pursuit of justice, and the satisfaction of putting away criminals who preyed on the city he loved.

"Sergeant Halstead," the chief began, his gravelly voice betraying the urgency of the matter at hand. "Take a seat."

Halstead settled into the worn leather chair across from Ryan, its creaks and groans echoing throughout the room. The chief leaned back in his own chair, steepling his fingers as he regarded Halstead.

Halstead's gaze shifted between Chief Ryan and Lieutenant Sharp, his heart heavy with concern. In the office's dim light, the air was thick with tension.

"What's the situation?" he asked.

Chief Ryan took a deep breath, his eyes narrowing as he began to lay out the details. "Just got off the phone with Warden Anderson at MCI-Cedar Junction. There's a rapidly escalating situation at the prison. A riot erupted, and prisoners in D-Block have seized control of that wing."

"What about Kelly?" Halstead asked, his voice tight with worry.

Ryan cast a glance toward Lieutenant Sharp, his jaw set. "His status is uncertain at the moment."

Halstead's typically stoic face furrowed in confusion. "How's that?

Kelly's in the isolation wing. Unless the riot spills out, I'm not seeing the concern. Or am I missing something?"

Sharp leaned forward, his eyes piercing through the dimly lit room. "Kelly wasn't in the ISO wing when the riot kicked off."

"Where was he?" Halstead demanded.

"He was in one of the visitation rooms, finalizing the paperwork for his discharge." Sharp's tone was somber, underscored by a hint of apprehension.

"Is he okay?" Halstead asked.

"We don't know." Ryan rubbed his hands across his face, weariness etched into his every feature. "What we do know is this: a guard was being assaulted outside of the room Kelly was in. Kelly managed to fend off the attackers and bring the guard to safety."

"Why do I feel there's more to this story?" Halstead's voice was laced with trepidation.

"You know Kelly probably better than most. You know the type of man he is, the type of cop he was." Ryan's voice wavered, betraying his own fears. "A guard in D-Block was taken hostage. The warden is still organizing his plan of action. Kelly decided to take matters into his own hands."

"He what?" Halstead's voice rose with disbelief.

"From what they told me, Kelly snatched a key card and headed toward D-Block. He informed the guards he was going to do what he could to help save the hostage," Ryan said.

Halstead shook his head, his expression taut with anxiety. "We've got to pull him out. His presence in that prison was a dangerous proposition. Under these circumstances, it's downright deadly."

Sharp interjected, his voice firm but measured, "He's as tough as they come. If anyone can come out on top, it's Kelly. I think it'd be premature to pull the plug on this thing right now."

"I'm in agreement with Lieutenant Sharp on this one," Ryan added. "We've risked a lot to see this through. If we alert the prison staff to Kelly's true purpose and tell them he's working undercover, we'll never be able to convince Walsh and his crew that Kelly's not a cop anymore. The prison has more eyes and ears than the streets. Word like that would spread in a heartbeat."

"I don't see another way," Halstead argued.

"Let's give it some time. Let Kelly do what he does best. Give him a chance to see this through."

Halstead mulled over the persuasive rebuttals offered by his higher-ups. He contemplated the weight of the human element, the personal sacrifice that Kelly had made by willingly taking on this perilous assignment against the greater good that would inevitably result from it. Halstead's thoughts shifted to Kelly, the man, the unyielding, resilient cop he'd come to know and admire. He understood Kelly well enough to recognize that there'd be no chance of persuading him to abandon this mission, not when another officer's life hung in the balance. The Kelly he knew would willingly stake everything to see justice served.

Halstead gave a solemn nod of agreement. "Let's see how our boy fares. I just hope I won't come to rue the day I endorsed this path."

22

The piercing wail of the prison's alarm was replaced by an oppressive quiet that boomed in Kelly's ears as he ghosted down the corridor. Each step was a cautious calculation, like a pawn inching its way across a chessboard. Eventually, he found himself standing at the crossroads of violence, where the melee had sprayed its fury mere moments ago.

Beneath his shoes, the linoleum whispered tales of bloodshed, a crimson testament to the brutality that had transpired. He paused, his chest heaving as he greedily sucked in a lungful of air, the bittersweet tang of iron and fear filling his nostrils.

Kelly angled his ear toward the ominous quiet, listening, dissecting. Beyond the silent veil, a low, distant rumble pulsed, a heartbeat thudding from behind the sealed jaws of D-Block.

Kelly edged toward the corner, his eyes sharp, his senses honed. He stole a glance around the bend, but the corridor was a ghost town. No echo of the monstrous Goliath or the inmates he'd battled to protect the guard from their savage onslaught.

Kelly's fingers traced the throbbing imprint of violence on his face, where the monstrous fist had hammered its brutal signature. A ridge of contusion sprawled from the hollow beneath his cheekbone, threading its painful path up the right side of his face before halting just above his eyebrow. It was a grotesque road map of the encounter, charting the trajectory of Goliath's relentless assault.

Beneath his eye, a deep gash wept crimson. His hand instinctively moved to apply pressure, trying to dam the relentless flow. His thumb kneaded the wound, encouraging clotting, forcing a hurried cauterization.

Yet in the grand scheme of scars, this fresh wound was just another chapter in the tome of his survival. Each scar was a tale etched in his flesh, a reminder of the battles fought. But this latest addition was a story in progress. The beginning had been written in pain and blood, but the ending was still a mystery.

Kelly peered down the hallway, his gaze latching onto the formidable metal door at the far end. D-Block. Through the scant rectangular window, a ballet of shifting shadows played out. Clarity eluded him; the inmates within were a blur of movement.

His strategy was not yet fully formed. He couldn't simply saunter into the lion's den. He needed a diversion, an alternate point of entry, if he was going to infiltrate the prison wing now under the inmates' control.

As a veteran of Boston's SWAT team, Kelly knew the art of observation was a potent weapon. Knowledge could be a lifeline, survival often hinging on careful reconnaissance of the target location before diving into the fray. His present predicament called for the same diligence.

Kelly moved down the hallway, his aim singular: to get within visual range of the prison wing and ascertain Doyle's position.

He'd barely made it halfway when the distinctive metallic clang of D-Block's security door reverberated throughout the hallway. Kelly would never make it back to the corridor he'd come from without being spotted.

A door to his right offering refuge amidst the chaos was a mere stone's throw away. The grating rumble and high-pitched whine of rollers straining under the weight of D-Block's heavy metal door echoed throughout the corridor.

He made a beeline for the door bearing the unassuming tag "utility." His fingers, clumsy in their haste, fumbled with the set of keys he'd managed to swipe from Officer Hopper. The first key refused to cooperate with the lock.

Out of the corner of his eye, he noticed the slow, ominous swing of the door down the hall to his left. As it yawned open, the symphony of riotous uproar flooded the hall.

Kelly plunged the second key in the keyhole, holding his breath as though the world hung in the balance. And then, like a gift from the gods, the key slid home. A swift twist and the lock surrendered.

Kelly slipped into the relative safety of the storage closet, a last-ditch sanctuary from D-Block inmates who'd traded the order of captivity for the chaos of a riot. In a heartbeat, he was cocooned in the cramped confines, the door whispering shut behind him.

Darkness swallowed every detail of his new stronghold. A solitary pinprick of light skulked beneath the door, offering paltry illumination as Kelly's eyes waged a war of adaptation against the encompassing darkness.

The echo of heavy footfalls seeped into his hideaway, each thud a Morse code of danger. His trained ear dissected the sounds. The stomps grew louder, their shadows passing by without slowing before fading into the corridor beyond.

And then, in the abyssal silence that followed, a noise prickled at the edge of his consciousness. A sound he'd missed, drowned out by the roar of his own harsh breaths moments ago.

The noise, now unobstructed, morphed into an unmistakable cadence —the rhythmic draw of someone else's breathing. In that hair-splitting instant, submerged in the pitch-dark belly of his makeshift hideaway, a cold realization dawned on Kelly.

He was not alone.

23

The chill of the deserted guard station prickled Watt's skin. In less than twenty-four hours, he had transformed from a mere prisoner to the undisputed kingpin of this concrete jungle. His gaze descended upon the scene below. The vibrant and furious riot now resembled the dying embers of a once-raging fire. Still, the undercurrent of tension remained, a wild beast waiting to be unleashed once more.

The grating sound of heavy footsteps behind him signaled Doyle's arrival, the correctional officer now a chess piece in his elaborate game of survival. Slim and Boone were dragging him into the guard station. His eyes flickered open and shut in a disoriented rhythm, a stark testament to the brutality unleashed upon him by the unruly inmates.

Inside the guard station, Watt looked from his brother to Slim and Boone, who'd proven invaluable in his rescue. Doyle lay at their feet, consciousness slipping from his grasp like quicksilver.

Watt saw opportunity in Doyle. The prison guard was his line of defense against the onslaught of guards who would inevitably descend upon them to quell the riot. A hostage would slow whatever plans were in the works. He looked down on the wounded man and hoped he stayed alive long enough to retain his usefulness.

Watt had ensured all surveillance cameras were rendered inoperative, blinding the prison's security to the situation within D-Block. This bought him a precious gift: time. Time to carefully orchestrate the next move in his audacious plan.

Watt gazed through the guard station window to the frenzied population on the first floor. He scanned the crowd of inmates until he locked onto Domino, the ink-streaked leader of the notorious East Side Locos. Until Watt's arrival, Domino held this wing of the prison under his brutal reign, his word the unchallenged law among inmates. With the guards temporarily neutralized, he needed to effectively manage the inmates, and to do that he needed Domino. It was a carefully weighed power play.

Watt signaled Domino, who stood overlooking the first-floor common space. His gang sprawled out, a volatile undercurrent of muscle and menace in the tension-filled wing. At Watt's subtle command, Domino pressed two tattoo-adorned fingers to his lips and let loose a shrill whistle that pierced the cacophonous noise of the prison like a bullet. The first whistle brought the rabble down to a dull roar, and the second one cut through the remaining chatter, rendering the room eerily silent. It was the power of fear, the respect for authority earned through ruthless dominion.

Domino then ascended the metal stairwell to the second floor. Two of his muscle-bound cohorts, faces as hard as stone and bodies marked with the insignia of their gang, shadowed his every step. At the top of the stairwell, he stood outside Watt's impromptu fortress.

Watt worried that Domino would break the deal and take the guard station for himself. It was within reason. But Watt had one advantage in the combat arena: his brother. Goliath's reputation for violence was the stuff of legend.

Watt opened the door and Domino stepped inside, his presence consuming the room. The two henchmen filled the remaining space, their presence a reminder of the volatile game Watt was playing. The door swung shut with a resounding thud.

Domino, his voice a gravelly whisper that grated the silence, broke the uneasy stillness. "So you're up here, and we're down there. You think you're the king now or something?" His tone held a note of mockery, a not-so-subtle challenge to the power dynamic that had evolved.

Watt's lips curled into a smile, a hint of amusement flashing in his eyes. "Every castle needs one."

The retort sent a ripple of anger across Domino's face, his eyes momentarily flaring with a dangerous heat. Quick to recognize the brewing storm, Watt defused the tension. "Look, I'm just passing through. This is your castle. You're the king. Consider me just one of the knights at your round table."

Domino's face relaxed, the fury receding like a fading storm. He eyed Watt suspiciously. "What now?"

Watt peered down at the restless sea of inmates. "First order of business is food. Need to keep the troops happy. How about burgers and fries? Mickey D's do the trick?"

At this, Domino's face bloomed into a rare grin. "Now you're talking."

Just as the tension in the room seemed to ease, Goliath's gruff voice echoed behind Watt. "I don't want no food. I want Kelly."

Watt paused for a moment. He knew his brother well enough to know that his tunnel vision for Kelly wouldn't rest until his quest for vengeance was satiated. He shrugged and offered a soft chuckle. "What can I say—he's got a particular taste. Maybe you could help me with that?"

Domino squared his shoulders, a subtle posturing against Watt's request. "Not sure your problem is my problem."

"Kelly's the one who landed my brother in this hellhole. And Goliath"— he nodded toward his hulking sibling—"would like to express his gratitude in person, if you catch my drift."

Domino shrugged, the air of indifference hardly masking his curiosity. "So go and get him."

Watt shook his head, his gaze steady on Domino. "Too risky. Our situation here is on a knife's edge. I can't spare a man for this. It's a Jenga tower, and one wrong move brings everything crashing down."

Domino cast a glance at his two henchmen flanking him before turning his focus back to Watt. "What's in it for me?"

"I thought you'd never ask." Watt's lips curled into a knowing smile. "Do you really think I've gone through all this trouble just so I can munch on cheeseburgers with my brother?"

"Why don't you tell me?"

"First things first." Watt momentarily ignored Domino's request and sauntered over to the guard station phone. Picking up the receiver, he studied the weathered list of internal extensions taped to the side of the console, his eyes scanning for the number he needed. He dialed the five-digit code and waited for it to connect. As soon as the line buzzed with an expectant voice on the other end, Watt launched into his demands.

"This is Roland Watt." His voice echoed through the receiver with an intensity that commanded attention. "I'm in control of D-Block. We've got a bunch of starving animals down here."

Watt paused as an indignant voice on the other end attempted to cut him off. He waited for a beat, allowing the futility of their objection to sink in, then continued, "This isn't up for debate. You tell whoever's pulling the strings that if we don't get enough cheeseburgers and fries to feed this lot in the next thirty minutes, we'll torch this place."

A stammered protest emerged from the receiver, a desperate attempt to negotiate, but Watt dismissed it with cold indifference. "And if you don't meet this demand, your friend Doyle here is going to start feeling a whole lot worse than he already does. This isn't a bluff. It's a promise."

24

Barnes and Cahill sat in their unmarked cruiser as Mattapan fell victim to the relentless snowfall's continued effort to paint the aging buildings and streets in wedding-dress white. They were in the lot of the bodega across from the address Pris had given them. It was in similar condition to the other three-family homes lining the walk. The front porch sagging under the weight of time and neglect forced the residents to the back of the building. In the twenty minutes since they'd first taken up the surveillance spot, there'd been no sign of any of the Rollin' 9s or the Hispanic woman Pris had described.

"So this is you? Where you came up?" Barnes glanced at her partner, who nodded. "Yeah? How'd you end up on the right side of the law, then?"

Cahill inhaled deeply. "I can still smell the scent of the neighborhood. My mom's cooking always seemed to fill the street. No matter how late or how much trouble I was getting myself into, that brought me home."

"Tough place to grow up, though." Barnes watched a man moving in the back of the alley between their target location and another home. She moved on after seeing the can-filled grocery cart indicative of the city's widespread homeless population. "Not judging. Just saying."

"I'm the man I am today because of it." Cahill's voice held a glimmer of nostalgia. "Every street corner, every alley, holds memories of laughter, tears, and hard lessons learned."

"You sound a lot like Kelly." Barnes saw the sting of Kelly's name on him as her thoughts continued to linger with the man she'd thought she would marry. "Sorry. Just saying, he was a product of the street."

"It's the only truth I know. No way around it, neighborhoods like these have a way of shaping you, for better or worse." He looked out at the familiar streets, his gaze distant. "I was sixteen when I saw a friend stabbed to death in the street, just like that." He snapped his fingers. "He was a dealer, and I helped him out on occasion. It was a bad crowd, but back then, it felt like the only option for someone like me."

Barnes listened, seeing that Cahill was back in that place and wanting to give him space to explore it. For her, it was an opportunity to understand her partner beyond the tough-guy exterior and cavalier one-liners. She found herself wanting to know more, and her reasoning wasn't entirely professional.

"I still remember the moment it all changed." Cahill's voice grew uncharacteristically serious. "A couple blocks from here there's a spot we all used to hang out at. Rundown little bodega, not unlike Jip's. It's where we'd meet up, find trouble—or trouble would find us."

Barnes nodded. She grew up in similar surroundings, until she was swooped up and adopted by her foster parents. Now all of it seemed like a distant memory that only visited on the rarest of occasions, usually in the form of a bad dream. She looked at the seriousness in Cahill's expression and recalled seeing the same in Kelly's when, in those rare moments, he opened the door to his past.

"Not all of my friends made the best decisions. Actually, none of us did. But my buddy, Billy Macintyre, seemed to find the worst of it." Cahill slowly shook his head, as if arguing with the surfacing memory. "He robbed a couple guys. Older dudes with a long history of violence. They didn't take kindly to it, as you can imagine. I told Billy to make it right. Give it back with interest. Maybe they'd see it as enough of an apology that they'd only offer a beating in exchange, ya know."

"I'm guessing he didn't listen?"

"Nope. Thick-headed as they come. But Billy wasn't no slouch when it came to banging it out. He'd take on the biggest of guys. Never backed down. Not once." Cahill cleared his throat. "And not when the Gallagher brothers came to collect. They put a beating on him the likes I'd never seen before. But Billy kept getting up, no matter how many times I told him to stay down. Not even when they'd finished sending their message and started walking away."

Cahill looked down the street as if half-expecting to see the ghosts of his past strolling along. Maybe, in his mind, they were.

"They were done. Billy wasn't. To this day, I still don't know what drove him to do what he did. But as the Gallaghers were heading back to their car, Billy charged at 'em. He came full tilt. Didn't even make sense he could move after the beating they'd put on him. It was like he was possessed. He took the younger brother down. Tackled him to the street. Billy smashed that kid's face off the pavement and was throwing bombs unlike any preteen I'd ever seen, then or now. I remember thinking, 'Holy shit, Billy's gonna be a freakin' legend.' The twelve-year-old who took out the Gallaghers."

Barnes could see the retelling was taking its toll on Cahill. "Look, you don't need to talk about this if you don't want."

"Nah. It's good to let this shit out every once in a while. Clears the attic." Cahill feigned a smile. "But the older Gallagher, Frankie, he lost it—went absolutely apeshit when he saw his younger brother getting bashed. Before any of us could move in to help, Frankie had a blade in his hand."

Cahill went silent. His shoulders drooped. Barnes felt compelled to comfort him but wasn't sure he wanted it. She was equally nervous any offering might be misconstrued as something else. Finding a neutral approach, she placed a hand over his and gave an encouraging squeeze.

"It looked like he was punching him—the way Frankie moved. His hand just kept going up and down. When I see it in my mind now, that's all it is. The blade is gone. It's just a brutal series of punches. I now know it's my coping mechanism. I also know it wasn't punches he was landing. By the time he was through, Billy'd been stabbed twenty-three times."

Barnes let out a gasp, the sound startling her. "Sorry." Cahill barely registered the sound or the apology. She could see he was no longer in the car with her.

"There was so much blood. It was everywhere." Cahill looked down at his hands, examining them. "I still feel it. Been on a million scenes since then as a cop. Seen bad shit overseas. But nothing stuck the way that did. He was in my arms when I felt him take his last breath. It wasn't like the movies. No last words. No message for his mother. The knife had punctured both lungs. The only sound was a wheezy gurgle. It went on for less than a minute. Then everything stopped. It was as if time itself had stopped."

"What happened to the Gallaghers?"

"They were both minors at the time. The younger one was fifteen. Did two years in juvie. Frankie was seventeen. Prosecutor got him tried as an adult. Got sentenced to seven years of big-boy jail. Only served two."

"Good behavior?"

Cahill choked out a laugh. "That'd be the day. Nope. Not for Frankie Gallagher. He was just as big an asshole in prison as he was on the street. Difference is, inside the big house, there's plenty who're more than happy to put someone like Frankie in his place. They found him dead in the laundry. I read the case report when I got on the job. He was only stabbed seven times. There were days when I used to pray he was in some kind of hell where he had to take sixteen more to make things right. Then I came to realize nothing will ever make right what happened that day."

Cahill looked away from Barnes and wiped his eyes.

"I can't imagine going through that," she said. "Must've changed everything."

"It did. I made a vow that day. Told myself I'd spend the rest of my time on this earth trying to make it right. It's why I became a cop. Figured if I saved enough lives, it would somehow eventually let me forgive myself for the one I couldn't."

"You know his death isn't your fault."

"I know. Took me a while, but I know that now." Cahill shook his head. The darkness fell away as he cleared his throat one last time. "Some days, I'm grateful it happened. Crazy as that is to say, it's true. If Billy hadn't died

—if I hadn't seen it with my own two eyes—there's a high probability I'd have continued on the same path and likely would've met a similar end."

Barnes looked at Cahill with a newfound respect. "I, for one, am glad you're here. A city like this needs more cops like you."

"Thanks." Cahill nodded. "I figure every day we get to make the conscious decision to be better, to do better. That's what keeps me going."

A metallic-gray car crept up stealthily, settling at the back of the shabby apartment building, the old brickwork appearing all the more sinister under the pallid moonlight.

"Eyes peeled," Barnes warned, her words cutting through the dense stillness. "We've got company." Her hand danced skillfully over the dashboard, the rhythmic sweep of the wipers grating through the icy crystals on the windscreen. The raw winter air had frozen everything around them, making every little movement seem more pronounced.

Their anticipation didn't last long. Within a minute, a figure cloaked in a hooded sweatshirt emerged from the shadows, his face hidden beneath a baseball cap. "I've got no visual on the face." Barnes strained her eyes, as if by some sheer force of will she would be able to see through the shadows.

An arctic gust of wind roared through the narrow alley, violently tossing off the man's hat in a game of impromptu fetch. His curse echoed in the frosty air as he scrambled to retrieve it, plucking it from a snowbank. As he dusted it off, his hat and face came into view.

"Jackpot." Cahill's whisper was laced with triumph. "He's one of our bangers."

"Shouldn't we signal White's team?" Barnes revealed little of the churning resentment within her, the thought of serving their hard-earned bounty to the detestable lieutenant a bitter pill to swallow.

Cahill turned to her, his eyes crinkling mischievously. "I say we bide our time, huh? Maybe we get a better picture before we pass the baton."

His smirk was contagious, and Barnes found herself returning it. "Couldn't agree more. We can handle this situation with finesse, unlike White."

"Sounds like we've got ourselves a plan. Besides, it's always better to do things the right way than the White way," Cahill said.

Both laughed, removing the traces of somberness that had fallen over them, their mutual disdain for White serving as a much-needed diversion. A renewed resolve settled over them, their focus sharpening on the game of cat-and-mouse they were about to play. They knew the stakes, and they were ready to roll the dice.

25

The enclosure blanketed Kelly in darkness. The hallway closet that moments ago provided a saving grace from the horde had now trapped him with the inmate lurking in the shadows behind him. Since he first recognized he was not alone, Kelly's adrenaline flooded his system, the tingling sensation spreading like wildfire through his extremities as his body prepared for battle. A lifetime of physical confrontation had long since prepared his mind.

His muscles tightened. He shifted his weight to the balls of his feet and spun. His fists were up, the autonomic response kicking in, readying him for his attacker.

The silhouette behind him, barely visible, remained motionless.

For the briefest of moments Kelly wondered if his mind had been playing tricks on him. He'd worked the night shift long enough to know the games darkness played. The apparitions were seen by any uniform who'd ever walked the beat. As the shadowed figure stood, all doubt evaporated, and the reality of his circumstances returned.

Strike first. Seize the advantage. A street fight differed greatly from the ring. The rules fell away, leaving combatants with only one—survival. Kelly knew all of this, and even though his body was coiled to strike, his mind remained coolly objective, avoiding the trappings of fear. Something in the shadowed man's movements caused him to hold his assault and reevaluate his target.

"Easy, man. Easy," the shadow whispered. "I'm not the enemy."

Kelly watched as the man slowly raised his hands in surrender. Kelly's fists loosened but remained poised to strike as he continued to monitor the man's movements, scrutinizing his target for any signs of deception. "What are you doing in here?"

"Hiding. Same as you."

"You got any weapons?" Kelly's police instincts forbid him from letting his guard down until he was able to verify all potential threats.

"Go ahead and frisk me if you want, Detective."

Kelly's defense system kicked in again. He looked over the knuckles of his left fist to the faceless man beyond. "You know who I am?"

"Pretty sure everyone 'round here does." He stepped forward. "But yeah, I know you."

Now that the inmate was closer, Kelly was able to better make out his features. He recognized him as the man he'd encountered in the mess hall earlier that day, when Kelly had to intervene and protect him from an unwarranted attack.

The tension in his shoulders dissipated. Kelly let out a long, slow exhale. He lowered his guard but kept his mind sharp. "You knew I was a detective. How?"

"Like I said, you're a celebrity 'round these parts."

"Not sure I'd put it that way."

"Oh yeah, don't get me wrong, you're not gonna be signing any autographs. Unless they use your blood for ink."

"Not you, though?"

"You and I go back a ways."

Kelly peered through the darkness. Although he could now see more clearly, he still had no recollection of the man beyond this morning. "Lots of faces crossed my path in my previous life. Do my best to keep 'em straight, but I can't place yours."

"Guess that's a good thing. Nobody wants the po-po knowin' your name, ya feel?"

"It definitely has its downside." Kelly shifted, the conversation's uncertain nature keeping him in a state of unease. "Am I the reason you're wearing the jumpsuit?"

"Nah. That came later. For guys like me, it's just a matter of time."

"So I didn't arrest you?"

"No. You collared my pops."

This just took a turn. Kelly inched back, creating space between them.

"Don't get your panties in a bunch. You good by me." He let out a light chuckle. "My dad was a good man, but he was a straight criminal. Did more time inside than out."

"What'd I put on him?"

"Boostin' cars. Caught him after a little run. Lost the wheel. Hit a street-lamp on Millet." He shook his head, the white of his teeth exposed through a tight-lipped smile. "You're quick. On his ass in a minute. Didn't even have time to bail."

"I hate paperwork. Crashes are the worst. Always better when I bring someone in for my troubles." Kelly softened his tone. "That said, putting the cuffs on isn't something I take lightly."

"Don't got to explain yourself to me. Shit, that's the game, right? If you gonna run the street, better be ready to take the heat."

"Wish everyone saw it that way."

"My dad did. He understood the rules."

"I'm still trying to place you."

"Makes sense you wouldn't remember me. I was the passenger. Only sixteen at the time."

Kelly nodded. "I'm usually pretty good with faces."

"Well, I didn't stick around too long after the crash. When things got hot, I hit the cut."

"What do you mean, things got hot?"

"You were plain clothes. Had a crew of heavy hitters. But you kept it clean. Controlled my pops. No rough stuff. Just enough to keep him from bolting. It was the other guy who did him dirty."

"Who?"

"White." He spat the word. "That son of a bitch put the work in on my pops. Busted his nose real good."

"Sorry that happened."

"You got nothin' to apologize about. Hell, if it hadn't been for you, my dad would've taken a worse beating. That's for damn sure."

The mention of White brought the memory of that night to the forefront of his mind. Kelly remembered the chase, the crash, and White's unnecessary force. "What happened to your dad was wrong, no way around it. Nothing he did that night earned what he got."

"I know. You proved that then. The way my dad tells it, you tried to pull him off. White was in it to win it, comin' at my pops like a runaway train. That is until you put him off the tracks."

"Wish I could've done more."

"You punched another cop. In my book, and my dad's, you went above and beyond provin' that point."

"I've always been a firm believer actions speak louder than words."

"How'd that work out for you?" He flicked his tongue against his teeth, making a clicking sound. "What happened to you for poppin' that other cop?"

"He was actually my supervisor."

"That's some straight up G shit right there. Bangin' heads with the boss man. Gotta have some serious consequences."

"I got a slap on the wrist. Could've gone worse for me anyways. The old guard is still alive and kicking within the PD. And White's part of that regime."

"What happened to him?"

"White? He got promoted, of course."

"That's some Grade A bullshit."

Kelly shrugged. "Sometimes to shut someone up, you got to move 'em up."

"Still bullshit."

Kelly gave a half-smile. "I'm not gonna argue that."

"If my pops were here, he'd shake your hand."

"Is he...?"

"Dead? Nah. Doin' fed time for a RICO hit. Movin' cars with powder in the tires. Just trying to make some extra scratch. Way it goes sometimes."

"Is that what landed you inside?"

"Nope. Took a hit driving a stolen. In my family, the apple don't fall far from the tree. When your dad names his son Bentley and his daughter Porsha, your path is pretty much set."

"Not always. We're not bound by our parents' mistakes. Their choices are theirs to make."

"I think you and I come from two different worlds."

Kelly thought about his biological connection to Boston's most notorious gangster. He saw no point in arguing to the contrary.

"Gotta ask. What happened? How'd you end up here?" Bentley asked.

"I punched White again."

"His face must be a magnet for your fist." Bentley gave Kelly's prison uniform a once-over. "Guess they didn't give you a slap on the wrist this time 'round?"

"Not so much. Laid him out in front of the cameras at a press conference."

No judgment in Bentley's eyes. "I'm guessin' he had it coming?"

Kelly nodded. "I can't let some things ride. Doing the right thing doesn't always look that way from the outside."

"I think if someone looks hard enough, truth has a way of proving up."

Kelly saw the truth in Bentley, the truth stretching beyond the boundaries of his current circumstances. He felt a level of respect growing for the inmate. Trust was something he'd still need to verify. "How'd you get out of D-Block?"

"I'm a trustee. I work in the library mostly. That's where I was comin' from when things broke out."

"Why hide? Why not join the party?"

Bentley rolled his eyes. "You saw how things went down in the chow line? That's with the guards a breath away. Got any idea how it would've gone without?"

"Bad."

"Bad's an understatement." He was no longer holding out his hands in surrender and had moved them to his hips. "I ain't takin' no blade in the back with less than two days on the clock. No sir."

"Looks like we're both putting this place behind us soon enough."

"Not if we end up dead first."

"I'm not planning on taking that route to freedom."

"Then best you keep your ass put in here til this little uprising gets squashed."

"Wish I could but there's a guard who needs my help."

"A guard? Needin' your help? You must be out of your mind, asking me to risk my neck for one of them."

"Never asked you to."

"You see, that's some bullshit. I ain't got a choice."

"Not sure I follow."

"I owe you. Not only for this morning but for my pops." Bentley rubbed the top of his unkempt afro and let out a frustrated sigh. "I may be a criminal, but I was raised to honor my debts."

"I thought there's no honor among thieves."

"Maybe for most. Not where I come from." Bentley swayed. "So what's the play? Who's in trouble that you feel so inclined to put your life on the line for?"

"Doyle."

"Shit. He's one of the good ones."

"They've got him captive. It's going to be a while before the other guards will be able to regain control. Doyle's situation is going to slow any tactical response." Kelly's eyes pierced the darkness. "Not sure how long he'll last."

"Then I guess we better get moving."

"I can't ask that of you."

"You didn't."

"Thanks."

"Don't go thankin' me yet. We ain't even left the closet yet." Bentley cocked his head and folded his arms across his chest, his dark skin overlaying the faded white of his jumpsuit. "Before we do, I think it's best we get you out of that red uniform. Damn thing's like a bullseye. These clowns'll be able to spot you a mile away."

"And where do you suppose I get a change of clothes?"

Bentley turned, and Kelly heard rustling. A moment later he pressed a folded uniform into Kelly's chest. "They keep spares in here for the trustees in the event one of the cleanup jobs backfires. Nobody wants a shit-covered inmate rollin' through gen pop."

Kelly made quick work of the uniform exchange. It was a little too big, forcing him to roll the sleeves and pant legs, but otherwise it was a good fit. He tossed the red into a mop bucket in the corner and turned to the door.

"What's the plan?" Bentley whispered.

"Not sure. Kind of making it up as I go." Kelly gripped the knob. "Sometimes stepping into the unknown is the only way to test yourself."

"Well, I hope it's a test we pass with flying colors. Because failure doesn't sound good for my health."

"When I open the door and ensure the coast is clear, we're going to make a break for it. Got to get away from the access door and find another way in, one that's not a guaranteed death sentence."

"I know my way around. Got an idea of where to go. Might be what you need."

"You lead. I'll follow." In those words, Kelly put his faith in an inmate he barely knew, trusting in his ability to read a person and hoping he wasn't wrong.

He opened the door a fraction of an inch and pressed himself close to the gap, listening intently for any sign of a threat. The only sound was the muffled rumble of uncaged prisoners down the hall. He reached the point of no return, and opened the door wide enough to exit the safety of the closet, exchanging it for the unknown.

Kelly held the door open, hoping it would block their view from any potential prying eyes. He stepped aside and nodded to Bentley, who entered the gauntlet. If he'd been a target prior to now, aiding a cop was sure to make Bentley a marked man.

Underneath the criminal's façade was a young man raised in a den of thieves who'd managed to learn the value of honoring a debt.

Kelly thought about his own circumstances. To everyone but the three who knew the truth, he was now an outsider, a shadow of the man he used to be. He just hoped when it all was said and done, the people who mattered most would be able to see him for the man he was.

"When I release this door, we'll have about ten seconds of cover before we'll be exposed to anyone looking out." Kelly propped the door wide with his heel and bent his knees in a sprinter's stance.

"Try to keep up." Bentley flashed a smile as he shook his arms loose and bounced on his toes. He turned his back to Kelly and faced down the hall to the T-intersection, their finish line. Without looking back, he gave a thumbs up. A split second later, Bentley was down the hall.

Kelly watched the car thief disappear around the corner, then took a deep breath, released his foothold on the door, and broke into a dead sprint. He thought of Barnes and the morning runs she'd dragged him on. Her face in his mind fueled the fire inside him, propelling him forward.

Just as he reached the intersection, he heard the closet door slamming shut. Kelly ducked around the corner and crashed into Bentley, who caught his arm, bringing his momentum to a halt and keeping him on his feet.

His heart rate was jumping, and after taking a second to catch his breath, Kelly held up a finger. Hearing no indication they'd been seen, he looked to his guide. "Where to?"

Bentley looked down the hall to the door where the guards had fled earlier before turning in the opposite direction. "ISO. We can use the yard tunnel and enter the hall that leads to the first-floor access door to D-Block."

"Guess you know your way around."

"Like the back of my hand. Pays to play the game. It's how I became a trustee. It's how I survived this hellhole."

"I'll be sure to put in a word when this is all said and done."

"Let's not go celebratin' things yet. Still got some ways to go."

Kelly nodded. They picked up the pace as they trotted past Kelly's cell. Now that he was outside and roaming free, the space he'd been confined to for the better part of the last three months seemed a whole lot smaller.

Ignoring the isolation wing inmates' muffled screams as they begged for their release, they reached the next checkpoint, the access door to the lower-level tunnel that led to the yard.

Bentley stepped aside, allowing Kelly to work his magic on the door. He looked back down the hall and shook his head. "Of all the stupid things I've ever done, this definitely tops my list."

"Maybe you'll look back and say it was your bravest."

"That's if we live to talk about it."

Kelly pressed the key card against the access panel, breathing a sigh of relief when the light went from red to green. That meant the guards either hadn't disabled it or were allowing him to continue. The why didn't matter right now, though.

He pulled the door open. Bentley slipped past and resumed his lead, Kelly on his heels. The door closed behind them, and then a buzz and metallic click indicated the locking mechanism had been activated.

The pleas of the ISO inmates faded, and as they descended the stairwell a new sound filled the dank, cool air: the thunderous churn of D-Block's rampaging inmates reverberating through the walls.

Kelly pushed against the fear building inside him as he considered the gravity of the situation. Adding Bentley to the mix meant he had three lives to protect. Right now, the priority was Doyle. Getting to him would be hard. Getting him out would be next to impossible.

26

Barnes and Cahill found themselves holed up in an unmarked, frost-ridden Caprice. Parked in the desolate, snow-cloaked district of Mattapan, they staked out a nondescript apartment complex where they'd seen one of the Rollin' 9s gang members a mere thirty minutes ago.

Hushed murmurs played against the harsh backdrop of the elements pounding on the vehicle's exterior. Barnes felt her patience begin to ripple with unease, giving way to gnawing anxiety. Doubts surfaced. Had they missed something critical? She started to question whether or not they'd missed the banger's departure.

They had toyed with the idea of contacting White. Technically, the take-downs were to be carried out by his unit. Both agreed they would give it another half hour before handing it off.

A black van emerged from the blanket of white and eased into the back lot of the apartment complex.

The van's doors opened and a trio of men stepped out. Barnes watched as one of the men hauled another out by the arm, his body limp. She squinted through the icy window, then glanced at Cahill, who was using the binoculars.

"That's our crew. Looks like the party's all here." Cahill set the binoculars on his lap.

"We've got them locked down. It's probably time to call it in."

Let's wait a minute," he proposed. "We could circle around to the back, stake out the rear. If they decide to bolt, we'll be ready to intercept."

Barnes took a moment to consider his proposal. What was the harm in waiting a few minutes? She nodded, and just as she was about to slip the car into drive, a figure materialized in her periphery, approaching the passenger side of their vehicle. Barnes instinctively placed her hand on the butt of her pistol. "Got a walker creeping up on your side."

Cahill pulled the handle and reclined his seat in an effort to dip from view.

Barnes did the same. Using the side mirror, she watched as a preteen boy wearing a puffy coat drifted alongside the car.

"Lookout?" Barnes asked, her voice barely a whisper.

Cahill shrugged. "Could be? Kids around these parts are always hustling, trying to climb the ladder, hoping to catch the eye of these gangs."

The boy trudged past their vehicle, seemingly oblivious to their presence. His gaze was fixed ahead, but just as he passed their window, Barnes caught a subtle shift in his eyes, a brief flicker in their direction. He continued his journey across the snow-encrusted sidewalk before pivoting and trudging toward the apartment building they were surveilling.

The color drained from Cahill's face. A string of profanities spilled from his lips as realization dawned. "No doubt about it. We've been made."

Inside the dimly lit apartment, three hardened members of the infamous Rollin' 9s gang were gathered around a battered kitchen table. The raw stench of fear was a cruel contrast to the homey backdrop. In the living room, their wounded lay on a threadbare couch, his face a grim mask of pain as he nursed a gunshot wound that was twelve hours old.

As the storm raged outside, a volatile discussion was unfolding within the grimy walls. They spoke in hushed tones about their precious cargo: the drones. The Polish crew had delivered as promised. The news about the all-terrain vehicles was equally positive, revving up the group's morale; they were fully operational and ready for action.

Their conversation shifted to the figure sprawled on the couch, his labored breathing punctuating the grim reality.

"What's the plan? We can't just walk him into a hospital," the junior man in the group said.

"Ain't like we got a doctor on the payroll. Options are limited." Watt's second-in-command looked at the members seated around the table.

"If we don't, he's a goner," the junior man replied, his voice hushed.

The third man proposed a solution. "We do a dump-and-run. Toss him at the ER entrance and bolt. It wouldn't be the first time."

The de facto leader balled his fist. "It's different this time. Every badge in the city's out for our blood. Watt told us to lie low until it's time to shake things up. Almost time."

The gang members were on edge, the tension mounting with each passing moment, but an unexpected knock at the door sent them into over-drive. Instinctively, every hand in the room gravitated toward concealed weapons, the collective breath held in silent anticipation.

A second knock followed, then a youthful voice cut through the tense silence. "It's me, Dante Coleman. Got something for you."

The junior man was directed to answer the door. He rose from his chair, slinking silently across the sparse room. He peered through the peephole and nodded at his companions before releasing the deadbolt and pulling the door open. Dante was ushered quickly inside, the door secured behind him with a solid, reassuring click.

The gang member towered over Dante, his imposing figure barring the boy from venturing deeper into the apartment. "Well, spit it out, fool. This look like a birthday party?"

Despite his obvious nerves, Dante maintained a bold front. He informed them of the detectives he'd spotted across the street.

A wave of tense curses erupted from the table, the air suddenly laced with frustration and fear. "We got detectives scoping out our hideout. We're toast. We'll never make it out undetected. No chance in hell we'll pull this off." The junior man started to pace around the room.

The wounded gang member on the couch grunted, hauling himself into a seated position. Each drawn-out breath was an agonizing testament to his dwindling life force. With gritted teeth, he offered a desperate plan. "I'll lead them off your tail. Once I'm on the move, get to the warehouse and grab the ATVs. Finish what we started. No backing out now."

The gang members exchanged a series of meaningful looks, silently debating the proposal. The mutual agreement came unspoken; it was the best, perhaps the only, option they had.

A bitter smile curled the wounded man's lips, his determination burning brighter than ever. "They'll have to kill me. Ain't no way I'm goin' back to the pen."

The weight of the decision hung heavily in the room. They understood the fatal implications, the inevitable end.

The senior man locked and loaded one of the handguns, then handed it to his wounded friend. "We'll see this through. Catch you on the flip side, brother."

27

In the prison's nerve center, Warden Anderson and his band of corrections officers were planted firmly in front of the surveillance screens, their eyes darting across the grainy footage that was fast becoming their only window into D-Block.

The screens flickered, then went dark. They were blind now, the prison's eyes and ears in D-Block violently gouged out. The inmates had coated the lenses with a mixture of food and filth, improvised paint that left the system helpless.

The guards were left to sift through the recordings made before the cameras went dark, each frame a hunt for the puppet masters amidst the chaos. These men weren't just participating in the riot, they were orchestrating it, choreographing this brutal ballet with a grim determination that chilled Anderson to his core.

A suggestion floated in the room like a ghost: cut the power. A flick of a switch, and the roar of chaos would be swallowed by an ocean of darkness. But Doyle was in there, alone and vulnerable, his life hanging by a thread. A standard riot response, so easy to implement from the outside, could easily snuff out that last thread, pushing Doyle from critical to the abyss. They shivered at the thought, the specter of death hanging heavily in the room.

The thick metal doors swung open and in strode Evelyn Diaz, commander of the prison's Emergency Response Team. She was an imposing figure, a storm cloud against the bleak gray backdrop of the control room. Her sharp eyes surveyed the room, piercing through the tension like a hot knife through butter, before finally landing on Anderson.

"Seems like my crew just got a front-row invite to the soirée," she drawled, her voice laden with icy confidence. A grin curled her lips, not quite reaching her eyes. It was cocky, a flash of white against her tanned skin that matched the swagger she exuded, a tangible aura that flowed around her like electricity. "Hope our gracious hosts are fond of unexpected party tricks."

Her words hung in the air, the promise of action a tonic to the helplessness that had infected the control room. Her confidence was contagious, a spark of hope amidst the engulfing darkness. And Anderson, although unsure of what the night would hold, found himself grasping onto that spark.

Diaz was rapidly briefed on the ticking time bomb that was D-Block, and the surveillance footage played a savage symphony of violence. The imagery was clear: Doyle, ambushed, outnumbered, his body flung against the unforgiving metal staircase. His lower back bore the brunt of the impact, a sickening crunch that reverberated throughout the room. Then, motionless. Whether he was unconscious or worse, they couldn't ascertain. The security camera's once-omniscient eye was now just a lifeless husk.

The maestro of this anarchy was none other than the prison's newest guest, Roland Watt. A few minutes had passed since Anderson's conversation with Watt. He was a puppeteer pulling strings, his inmate enforcers his obedient marionettes. The guards in the station had been overthrown, their authority trampled under Watt's iron will.

The thought of the inmate turned ringleader controlling the guard tower disturbed him greatly. Anderson was losing control but knew the importance of maintaining its illusion. He felt the expectant looks from the corrections officers huddled around him and the uncertainty they held. His authority was being challenged and the next decision he made was likely the most important of his career to date. It would be his legacy.

Watt had made a chilling assurance. Doyle, he promised, would not be subjected to any further harm, provided his demands were satisfied. A sinister barter—a life for compliance. Watt's first demand had already been voiced, the words hanging in the air like a guillotine blade poised to fall. Diaz knew the game of power and survival had begun, the stakes dangerously high, and each passing second came with a price that could prove too steep to pay.

Watt's demand—a request for McDonald's, a feast of burgers and fries large enough to satiate the rioting horde thrice over. And Anderson had complied. He'd seen enough standoffs to know that even a bizarre demand could buy them precious, life-saving time.

The food was on its way, a massive order that would likely overwhelm even the bustling kitchen of a McDonald's. Outside, the guards tasked with the pickup wrestled with nature's own rebellion, a fierce snowstorm that blanketed the city, turning roads into icy labyrinths and visibility into a game of roulette.

Diaz, seeing an opportunity in the delay, turned to Anderson. Her words were sharp and pointed, slicing through the tense air. "This gives us time to prepare my team."

Anderson, on his part, spoke of reinforcements—the State Police's SWAT team, the National Guard. An army was on its way, their mutual aid request met with promises of swift response. But to Diaz, this seemed like unnecessary stalling. She was not one to wait, especially when lives hung in the balance.

With a hard stare and a voice edged with steel, she countered, "Sitting idle while you have a ready tactical team here is a critical mistake, Anderson. If Doyle bleeds out while we wait for backup, his blood will be on your hands."

The room grew deathly silent, all eyes darting between Anderson and Diaz. The warden swallowed hard, the weight of the entire prison seeming to bear down on him. He could feel the icy touch of potential regret, the chilling possibility of Doyle's blood on his hands. It gnawed at him, doubt creeping in and casting its shadow over every decision. Finally, with a sigh that seemed to leach the tension from the room, he nodded to Diaz, conceding to her relentless determination.

"Go ahead, Diaz. You and your team have the green light. Let me know when you've put your response team's plan together."

"Already have it," she said without a moment's hesitation.

Anderson gave her a curious look. "Let's hear it."

Diaz laid out her tactical plan with a cool precision that belied the violent chaos raging beyond the walls. A team of four was all she asked for, herself rounding off the count to five.

Anderson blinked at her, visibly taken aback by the modest number. "Only five?" he questioned, skepticism lacing his words. His experience as warden had never extended to the front lines of such a crisis, and it showed.

Diaz offered him a glance that was dismissive yet assured. "Five's all we need," she said, her voice calm and certain. She explained her tactic, the ingenious ruse she intended to pull off. Her team would pose as simple delivery men, making good on the prisoners' first demand. She argued that a larger, overtly tactical response would only arouse suspicion, potentially escalating the situation further. With a resignation that sat heavily on his shoulders, Anderson conceded to Diaz's expertise.

Emboldened by his acquiescence, Diaz delved into the intricacies of her plan. Her team would enter through the second-floor access door to D-Block, the one closest to the guard station where Doyle was held captive. The first team member, protected by a sturdy ballistic shield, would muscle through any initial resistance.

The following duo would push a cart laden with fast food toward the guard station door, their movement shielded by the first operator. Diaz herself would follow closely, the fourth member of her tactical entourage. The final team member had the dual responsibility of securing the access door to the main hallway while keeping a watchful eye on their rear.

Upon reaching the guard station, their true intent would unfold. Flash-bangs and gas grenades would explode into life, their disorienting chaos providing the perfect smokescreen for the team to seize control. And once they had control, they'd make the extraction, whisking Doyle away from the rioters' dangerous grip.

Every word Diaz uttered was laced with the steely resolve that had seen her through countless operations and would see her through this one too. There was no room for error, no margin for doubt. It was a daring plan, as precise as a surgeon's knife, and the look on her face told him she was ready to cut through the chaos.

Doubt crept in. Anderson's need for control, the meticulous nature of his very existence, compelled him to consider and reconsider any decision, oftentimes leaving him in a mental stalemate, something this situation couldn't afford. As Anderson reviewed the tactical blueprint Diaz laid out for the prison's Emergency Response Team, he began to second-guess her plan and the audacious, almost cavalier approach.

"What's to stop Watt and the other inmates from gaining the upper hand?" Anderson felt the newest addition to the worry lines already etched into his forehead. He hoped this would be the last before his time as warden was through, but as the last several hours proved, nothing was a guarantee. He felt his ticking clock to retirement slowing to a halt until he could find a resolution to the unfolding crisis. "The last thing I need right now is five additional hostages to complicate things. What's the assurance you can give me that this won't happen?"

"There's no crystal ball, no way to see the end of an operation that hasn't been initiated. But I can tell you I've got no plans of giving myself or any member of my team to these savages." Diaz met his worry with calm resolve. "As far as assurances go, we'll have the advantage. My team will be armed with less-lethal shotguns. But I'm a realist and know that inmates, especially ones as volatile as these, could potentially overpower us. That's why I'll need your authorization for a lethal force option, should the situation dictate. Do I have it?"

This was the question Anderson had hoped to evade. He hesitated, his unease palpable, before nodding reluctantly. "Only as a last resort," he managed to utter, his voice strained.

"Hopefully it won't call for it." Diaz didn't flinch. "I'll be in control of the lethal option," she said, her tone setting in stone what she might need to do.

With a sigh that echoed around the tension-filled room, Anderson gave his final approval for the plan. As if on cue, another guard announced the arrival of the food, the opening gambit of their high-stakes operation.

Anderson looked at Diaz, his words falling heavily in the room. "Get your team ready to move."

A third guard, his attention glued to the still-functional exterior cameras, issued a quiet but urgent warning. "Better make it quick," he said, beckoning Anderson over.

On the screen, a distressing scene was unfolding. Kelly, the ex-cop he'd been housing for the last three months, was being led down the isolation wing hallway by an inmate named Bentley. As they halted in front of the secure door leading to the tunnel passageway, he stared at their figures flickering on the screen.

The guard monitoring the camera system glanced at Anderson. "Warden, we're going to lose visual on them if they enter that stairwell. The tunnel's got no live feed. Cameras have been on the fritz all week. Went dark earlier today, I'm guessing due to the storm."

Anderson almost broke character, fighting the urge to blurt the litany of expletives running through his mind. Instead, he opted for silence.

"We could send a couple guards from B-Wing to try and intercept them?"

"No. We can't afford to deviate any officers from their current posts. We're short-staffed as it is and we don't need to be weakening our strength with the units still under our control." Anderson clenched his jaw, his teeth grinding out the frustration permeating his mind. "We'll focus on the plan in place. Once Diaz and her team have dealt with the uprising and returned Doyle to safety, we can corral these two."

"Maybe we don't look at them so much as loose cannons but more as a backup option," Hopper asserted, speaking up for the first time since Diaz arrived.

"These men aren't backup, they're inmates, plain and simple."

"Well, Kelly sure as hell proved otherwise earlier." Hopper directed his words at the warden, but his eyes were dead set on Gladstone, who was still licking his wounded ego in the corner.

A tense moment of silence passed between Anderson and Hopper, both of equal time in service but different career paths and levels of authority. Anderson knew better than to continue this argument any further with his senior-most guard; the devotion garnered by Hopper's experience on the ground floor outweighed his, if not by rank then by respect. He held tight the little swagger he had with the men and women in the room and wouldn't risk losing it in a battle of words when there were much bigger problems at stake.

A brittle joke shattered the heavy silence, one of the guards ribbing Diaz about Kelly and Bentley's "fashionably late" arrival to the riot. Diaz didn't laugh, her face a mask of grim determination. Instead, she shot back, "Bad form to show up at a party without a gift."

Her hand brushed against the semi-automatic pistol holstered on her thigh, her fingers grazing its cold, lethal surface. A shark-like smile played on her lips, her dark eyes flashing a promise of retribution.

Anderson put his faith in the hope that Diaz and the members of her team were about to bring the party to an abrupt, chilling end.

28

The raw, sour stench of mildew struck their senses. Even with the cold air flooding the tunnel system, years of leaky piping had lined the walls and edges of the concrete walkway in the grime and mold of neglect. It was a potent reminder of the desolation that thrummed in the very marrow of this underground labyrinth, the bones of the prison on full display.

Bentley continued to honor his role as tour guide, leading Kelly down the dimly lit corridor. "Lock onto my every step, Kelly. Stray here, and you might as well sign your own death warrant. No tellin' who's roamin' free. Don't want to catch any surprises. Doubtful any will be of the friendly sort."

"I'm not planning on leaving your side. As long as you keep me on the right track, I'll be on your six." Kelly slipped as he navigated the slick steps, grabbing hold of the rusty railing for support. Cold air combined with moisture in the tunnel, coating the stairwell in a thin layer of ice.

Kelly righted himself and continued his journey, staying tight on Bentley's heels like a SWAT operator on entry. The bone-damp air pierced through the scant protection of his prison garb, gnawing at his skin as though it were trying to freeze the pulse within his veins.

They reached the bottom. The concrete flooring wasn't much better than the stairs, and Kelly found himself pushing his feet along like a skater taking to the ice for the first time.

Bentley wasn't faring much better, using the piping along the wall as a guiderail. "Not much further. Just up ahead on the left."

Kelly looked down the passage and saw a red hue cast by a frost-coated bulb. It was only twenty feet beyond them, but the slow going made it feel three times farther.

When they reached the checkpoint, Kelly and Bentley took a moment to give their leg muscles a chance to recover. They leaned against the wall outside the inconspicuous iron door, its scarred, oxidized surface bearing the ravages of time and neglect. Kelly had traversed the hall many times over the course of his stay while being escorted out to the yard and had never noticed the door, or considered it worth noticing, before now.

"You sure this leads us to D-Block?"

"It leads to the hallway that connects with it." Bentley shot him a look. "You still don't trust me?"

It was a loaded question, Kelly knew. His answer tread lightly across their delicate alliance. "Just preparing for what comes next. Trust's got nothing to do with it."

Bentley jostled the keyring and held it up to the dim light as he looked for the correct key. He picked one out of the mix and tried it on the lock. It failed. Kelly waited as Bentley repeated the process three more times before finding the right fit.

"Ready to see what's behind door number one?" Bentley, doing his best gameshow host impression, raised an eyebrow at Kelly.

"Ready as I'll ever be." Kelly opened and closed his hands, readying his only weapons for the unknown.

With a hard tug, Bentley pulled the door open, revealing the bright light of the hallway beyond. "This is it. We cross through and it's a straight shot to D-Block. Just down the right. Door'll be on the left."

"Got it."

"Um, I'll get you there, but not planning on going in." Bentley hesitated. "I know I owe you, but—"

Kelly waved a hand and shook his head. "Don't have to explain. You've already gone above and beyond. Your debt is paid in full. It's me who now owes you."

Bentley exhaled, his breath crystalizing into a plume in front of him. "Let's just call it even."

"I'll take the lead." Kelly stepped in front of Bentley and took point. "Just make sure you've got the key ready to hand off so I can get into the cell block."

They entered the hallway, their eyes adjusting to the injection of brightness. Kelly was still squinting when he heard footsteps on the linoleum approaching from his right, and fast.

Kelly turned to see a pair of convicts hurtling toward him. He recognized them as the same two trustees he'd battled in the hallway earlier, the bigger one's gait impeded by the damage Kelly had inflicted.

Their faces were twisted into sadistic delight. In the split second before they closed the gap, Kelly called on his lifetime of training and exploded into action. He balled his fists, turning them into instruments of precision as he prepared to fend off his attackers.

But they closed the distance quickly, and the taller, thinner inmate landed a blow to the side of Kelly's face, finding the same spot where Goliath had delivered his devastating sucker punch. The punch had a dizzying effect, spinning him sideways.

Kelly's head slammed into the metal frame of the open door, bright light flashing across his eyes as the hard steel collided with his skull. Woozy, he managed to keep himself upright, but he was unsteady on his feet and totally unprepared for the onslaught.

Both inmates swarmed him. Their fists pummeled him, smashing into his head and body. Kelly did his best to fight back but his efforts were met with limited success. He switched into defense mode, tucking his arms tight and doing his best to cover his head and body from the relentless attack.

Kelly noticed their punching power was waning. His rope-a-dope tactic appeared to be wearing down the two inmates. He was waiting for the moment to launch his counterattack when he was struck from behind, letting one slip past his defenses. It was a punishing blow from a heavy, blunt object. The impact swept the ground from beneath Kelly, and he crashed onto the unforgiving floor. His vision speckled with dancing stars, his world pitching and rolling like a ship in a storm.

Rough hands seized him, dragging him across the floor. Blood emptied from wounds unseen, leaving red smeared in his wake. Kelly's consciousness wavered, teetering on the precipice of darkness, his reality a cacophony of agonizing sensations and bewildering disorientation threatening to pull him into the abyss.

Through the veil of his rapidly blurring vision, Kelly caught sight of a figure retreating through the doorway. Even in the shadows, he recognized the man as Bentley, now disappearing into the cloak of darkness. As Kelly's vision faded in and out, he noticed Bentley pause. There was a moment of hesitation as he glanced back, a flicker of something—regret? pity?— dancing briefly in his eyes. Bentley's lips moved, mouthing two words, "I'm sorry."

Kelly was hauled away, his limp body dragged toward the roar of inmates. D-Block's fire of rage blazed, and Kelly knew he'd just become the pig for their roast.

29

The gray haze of an expiring winter day descended heavily over the city of Boston. Detectives Barnes and Cahill were still nestled deep into the threadbare upholstery of their nondescript, unmarked car. The biting winter chill whistled around them.

As they waited, a figure abruptly materialized from the rear of the dilapidated building. His gait was unsteady, betraying his attempts to mask an injury. Even through the dim veil of the dying day, Barnes and Cahill identified him. He wore the signature brand of the Rollin' 9s, the tattooed serpentine emblem unmistakable. He clambered into a waiting van and tore away from the scene, his tires screaming against the frosted asphalt, biting through the deepening shroud of white.

A silent communication passed between Barnes and Cahill, their gazes locking in unspoken agreement of the adrenaline-fueled chase that was about to ensue.

The van roared through Boston's frost-encrusted streets, flinging a shower of ice crystals in its wake as Barnes gripped the wheel, navigating the winter-ravaged terrain in pursuit. Cahill sat transfixed on their quarry.

The elements seemed to conspire against them, but Barnes refused to give in. She saw that the operator of the van was unable to do the same, losing his battle with the slick, icy streets. The van pirouetted wildly before plowing first into a bank and then a telephone pole. The impact reverberated through the neighborhood, but the blizzard greedily swallowed the sound, leaving a chilling silence in its wake.

Barnes pumped the brakes and skidded to a stop. Silence fell over them, a dance they'd done many times before. Both set their focus on the van, keeping careful watch for the driver as they exited their vehicle and advanced cautiously with their guns drawn.

Upon reaching the back of the van, Barnes and Cahill used hand and arm signals to communicate their coordinated approach. They split, with Barnes moving along the passenger side and Cahill approaching the driver's door.

Inside the mangled van, the gang banger slumped motionless against the steering wheel. His life force was ebbing away, draining into the frigid night.

Cahill removed a glove, biting it at the tip and pulling it free while keeping his gun hand trained on the unmoving driver. Barnes kept the front sight of her Glock centered on the wheelman's head, taking an angle that ensured Cahill wasn't in the backdrop. She covered him as Cahill slowly reached through the shattered window. His hand connected with the man's blood-spattered neck.

Cahill pressed hard, searching for a pulse, then looked up at Barnes. "Faint but still kicking."

Just as Cahill released his fingers, the driver exploded into a flurry of movement, thrusting his right hand down into the space between his seat and the center console.

"Gun!" Cahill boomed.

For Barnes, time slowed. Pulling the trigger, regardless of the threat, took a level of commitment few could honestly answer. But she knew the answer. She'd been here before, knowing the line between life and death was in her hands. The pad of her index finger held the trigger at the break point, controlling the fall of the Reaper's scythe.

She watched as the driver, in his weakened state, fought for purchase on the gun. The butt was in view now. Barnes held her breath in anticipation of the shot, but before she could take it, she realized the backdrop was no longer clear.

Cahill had holstered his sidearm and launched himself inside the shattered window. Using his left hand, he grabbed the banger's arm while his right hand clutched the curls atop his head. In a move of speed and force, Cahill jerked the would-be gunman forward. The weakened driver offered little resistance as his head slammed against the steering wheel, his nose colliding with a sickening crunch. Blood poured from his nose, adding to the red already painting the vehicle's interior.

Barnes continued to hold her Glock at the ready, her finger still resting on the trigger break. In her mind's eye she'd already seen the round leave her gun and obliterate the driver's skull. It took a moment for her mind to adjust the image to the one before her. She let out the breath she'd been holding as she took in Cahill's quick thinking that thwarted the gang member's attempt at forcing her hand. The blow to his head had caused him to release the gun.

She darted around to the other side to assist.

Together they yanked him out, his body limp, like a broken doll. They brought him to the ground, quickly cuffed him, and propped him up, using the wheel well as support.

Blood seeped onto the pristine canvas of snow beneath him, tainting it with the harsh reality of their world. His breaths came in shallow, ragged gasps, a clear sign death was hovering ominously close. His weak hand clawed the snow, searching for the gun that wasn't there, a final act of defiance in his fading strength.

"It's over," she uttered, her voice nearly lost in the howling wind.

"It ain't over. Just gettin' started. You'll see." The dying man's last-ditch display of loyalty to his felonious brethren.

Cahill leaned close, examining the gunshot wound. "Terrible patch job. He's been on a slow bleed for a long while. Surprised he lasted this long." He looked up at Barnes and shook his head.

Barnes squatted close to the driver, kneeling in the bloodstained snow. "You're dying. You understand that? You've got a chance to do the right thing. Consider this your penance. Make this right and tell us where the others are. Tell us what the plan is." She sought the dying declaration, the confession requiring no Miranda warning and one that stood up in court. It paid dividends in past cases and she hoped the same would prove true now.

The banger smiled weakly, his teeth coated in blood, as he offered a response in the form of his middle finger, which dangled in front of Barnes's face. The message was received loud and clear—whatever the 9s were up to, they wouldn't learn it from this man.

"We roll hard. We'll pull your card. Ain't no lie. We can't die. 'Cause nine lives is what we got. Until the tenth bullet is shot." He threw up a nine-finger sign, repping his crew one last time. "9s for life, bitch." A convulsive cough wracked his body, spewing fresh blood onto the snow. And then, with a final shudder, he was still.

Barnes stood amidst the chaotic aftermath of their frenzied pursuit, her gloved hands resting defiantly on her hips. Her gaze swept over the man lying lifeless on the snow-laden ground.

As the relentless snowfall continued, additional reinforcements poured in, the glimmering blues and reds of patrol units casting an ethereal glow over the crime scene. Yellow tape was unfurled, marking the sphere of their investigation.

From the heart of the swirling snowflakes, a figure emerged—Lieutenant Lincoln White. He stormed through the frigid landscape with the wrath of an approaching storm all his own. He made no attempt to mask the rage etched in his hard-set features, his eyes blazing with a fury rarely seen. White's veins pulsated in his temples as he squared off against Barnes and Cahill.

"You've just butchered our golden opportunity at reining in the Rollin' 9s!" he bellowed, his voice slicing through the howling wind and catching the attention of the patrolmen nearby. "You assumed you were donning the capes of heroes, but all I see are reckless renegades!"

Detective Sergeant Halstead arrived just as White's verbal barrage reached its peak. He strode into the eye of the storm, demanding attention and halting White's tirade mid-phrase. Halstead's steel-gray eyes locked onto White's, a silent exchange flickering between them.

"These detectives were doing their job, Lieutenant." Halstead's voice cut through the icy air, steady and unflappable. "They made a judgment call based on the intel at hand. You, of all people, should appreciate how circumstances can pivot in a heartbeat in the field."

White's fury simmered under Halstead's unrelenting gaze, his tirade momentarily stunted. He muttered something under his breath before spinning on his heel and turning away, his broad figure fading back into the swirling white. A tense silence lingered in the frost-bitten air.

"Thanks for lookin' out, Sarge," Cahill said.

Halstead held up his hand, deflecting the compliment, his face unreadable, his attention focused on the two detectives before him. "You two better have a damn good reason to justify that chase. And an even better one as to why I wasn't kept in the loop. White isn't about to sweep this under the rug, and if I'm going to be able to back your play, you need to put it all on the table."

Before either could formulate a response, a patrolman summoned them over. He stood in the falling snow, guarding a crumpled piece of paper a few feet from the back end of the van.

"What do you have?" Barnes asked, looking down at the finding.

"Looks like a hand-sketched map," he said. He bent down and retrieved the paper from its frosty bed, carefully brushing away the icy crystals clinging to the surface. "You think this could be related to the shootout?"

"Not sure." Cahill shrugged. "Looks like some building. Maybe it's related to last night's shooting gallery?"

Barnes sidled up to him, her gaze flitting across the scribbled lines and cryptic symbols. Her heart skipped a beat when she recognized it. "That's not just any building, it's a penitentiary."

Cahill pivoted the paper, his eyebrows knitting together as he deciphered the crude drawing. "No shit." The veil had been lifted and the reality of the blueprint unraveled before him.

Barnes wasn't sure of the reason, but she was certain of the location. "Looks like the Rollin' 9s have a target in mind."

"Ideas?" Halstead looked at Barnes.

"Well, their leader just took up residence. If I had to guess, looking at this diagram, I'd say they were planning on breaking him out."

"Where are the rest of the 9s now?" Halstead asked.

"Don't know. I'm guessing they popped smoke and disappeared." Cahill shot a glance in the direction of the crashed van and the tarp now covering the dead man. "I think that kid made us."

"What kid?"

"When Barnes and I were running surveillance on a possible hideout, a young kid passed by. Pretty sure he was playing lookout. The van was a decoy."

Cahill kicked the snow off his boot. "Guess we should've stayed put."

"Let's not waste time with the would've, should've, could've game. No way to make that call with what we had at the time."

Halstead uncharacteristically cursed under his breath. "There's another problem."

"What kind of problem?" Barnes could see a ripple of concern stretching across her normally stoic sergeant's face.

"There's a riot at the prison. Inmates have taken over one of the cell blocks."

"You think this is all related?" Cahill's voice was muffled as he tried to warm his hands with his breath.

"Anything's on the table at this point." Halstead remained tense as he directed his attention at Barnes. "There's more. Kelly is in the thick of it."

"What? How?" A wave of panic flooded her. "He's in isolation. He shouldn't be anywhere near the general population."

"The takeover happened while he was completing his out-processing paperwork."

"It still doesn't make sense."

"Several of the guards were attacked. Kelly assisted in fending off the attack and getting them to safety." Halstead paused. "A prison guard within the cell block was badly injured and taken hostage. Kelly couldn't walk away."

Barnes felt the weight of Halstead's words pressing her deeper into the snow-covered ground. "What does he expect to do against a group of rioting prisoners?"

"You know him better than any of us. If Kelly can find a way, he will."

"That's some real hero shit," Cahill said.

"When?" Barnes had an accusatory edge to her voice.

"A few hours ago."

"Hours? Why are you just telling us now?"

"Communication with the prison has been spotty at best. They're still working to contain the riot."

"And what about Kelly?"

"For now, he's on his own."

"Sounds like we're way behind the power curve on this one." Barnes felt the redness of her cheeks, the anger bubbling just beneath the surface. She didn't know where to direct it. Kelly for getting himself mixed up in all this. Halstead for holding back. Or the Rollin' 9s who were turning this city upside down.

"You two start heading to Walpole. I'll have White and his crew run the streets and see if we can get a lock on these guys. Maybe we can get lucky and stop them before they take their next step." With that, Halstead headed off in White's direction.

Cahill shook his head. "This mess has turned into a real shitshow."

"That's the understatement of the year." Barnes cocked an eyebrow. "But we've got an advantage."

"Yeah, what's that?"

"They don't know we know their plan."

"Then I guess we best get a move on." Cahill walked to the driver's side of the Caprice. "My turn to drive."

30

The cell block was much like the back alleys of Boston, dark corners where reputation was the currency each man used when carving out his own tiny kingdom. As Kelly's vision cleared, two things surprised him: he wasn't dead, and he was secured inside a cell, cut off from the other inmates. These were unexpected developments, and though grateful to be alive, he was left to question the why.

He sat against the cool concrete wall and quickly discovered he wasn't alone. Kelly, a battered knight, was seated at the round table of the Irish mob. As he took stock of the damage from the less-than-cordial welcome to general population, his eyes took in the cocksure swagger of Nickel, a man who'd built his reputation through violence. He'd been one of Connor Walsh's top enforcers, a job now held by Kelly's best friend, Bobby McDonough.

Nickel gained the nickname after supposedly killing a man who'd shorted him five cents on a debt. The truth often didn't match its legend, but one thing was certain—Nickel was a cold-hearted killer. His murderous past defined him, and the look in his eyes told Kelly his time inside had done little to curb it.

Nickel was a man of few words, but his presence spoke volumes. He laughed in Kelly's direction, the sound echoing in the cell, cold and hollow.

Kelly tensed his muscles and tried to stand to face this new threat, but his body refused to cooperate and he slumped back to the concrete floor with a grunt.

"Looks as though you should've slipped when you dipped," Nickel taunted, amusement lighting his eyes. His loyal crew, a group comprised of former Walsh lackeys, joined in the laughter.

"Could've been worse." Kelly shrugged off the verbal jab. "Being able to take a punch is as important as being able to give one."

"You read that on a fortune cookie somewhere?" Nickel rolled his eyes. "Because you're anything but safe in here. And if those savage assholes on the other side of those bars are given the chance, they'll be having pig for dinner."

"Maybe so." Kelly bristled at the thought. "I'm more interested in my odds inside this cell."

Nickel shifted on his bunk, the rusted frame creaking. "If you're asking me whether my guys are gonna be adding to the damage on your face, the answer is no. Unless you give me a reason otherwise."

"Why the pass?" Kelly asked.

"Simple. Your father." Nickel rubbed a hand across his chin. He took a moment to evaluate their new guest. "Don't look so shocked. Word travels fast, on the street and inside these walls."

As grateful as Kelly was for the temporary moratorium of violence, he hated the reason for it. Every day since learning the truth of his conception, he'd wished he could transfuse the bloodline connecting him to Walsh. "I'm not looking for any favors."

"The favor's not for you. It's out of respect for Walsh." Nickel went still, a ripple of tension running along the wiry Irishman's forearm as he clenched his fist. "I'd hate to have to explain why I wasn't able to honor that, so don't go forcing my hand."

The not-so-veiled threat was received, and with the line in the sand established, Kelly had no intention of crossing it. His attention shifted to the inmates running rampant outside the cell. The riot was chaos personified, the rules of society replaced with the primal law of survival. Nickel's warning was not an empty one; the dangers beyond the bars were real. Kelly had made many enemies in his time as a cop—it came with the territory. Seeing the faces of those who had placed his name high on their list unnerved him. The steel bars of his confinement were the only things standing between him and their uncontained thirst for blood.

His gaze returned to Nickel. "It won't be long before the guards take back the prison. These things never last."

Nickel shrugged. "Don't matter to us. We ain't goin' nowhere."

A movement outside the cell caught Kelly's attention. Out of the corner of his eye, he saw the cell block door open. He watched as Bentley slipped inside, noticed by only a few of the inmates closest to him. His prison sherpa, who left him in the passage, had returned to D-Block.

Bentley's decision to re-enter the chaos perplexed Kelly, who questioned the man's loyalty and his reason for returning. The answer came a moment later as he flashed the keyring he'd used earlier. The gesture was quick, meant only for Kelly's eyes, before Bentley stuffed them in the front pocket of his jumpsuit. The debt he had sworn to repay was apparently still being honored. And with it came the possibility of Kelly escaping his current circumstances. Doing that would require some careful planning and extra muscle.

Kelly waved a finger, staving off Bentley momentarily as he turned back to Nickel. A new plan had begun to percolate in his mind as he looked at the hardened men loitering in the cell with him. He moved closer to Nickel and quietly proposed a deal, an alliance formed in desperation. Kelly understood the need for power within prison walls and saw it as leverage in convincing the mob enforcer of the mutual benefit his assistance would provide. He needed to clear a path to the guard station if he wanted any chance of saving Doyle. Kelly's best and only chance of doing so came from Nickel and his men.

After listening to Kelly's plan, Nickel looked skeptical. "I said we wouldn't hurt you. Didn't say we'd help you. Especially with that wild-ass plan you concocted all to help out a guard. No thanks."

"What if you saw this more as an opportunity?"

"An opportunity to get ourselves killed. You, definitely. Us, maybe." Nickel cocked an eyebrow. "So, tell me what I'm missing."

"Like I said, you and I both know that this riot won't last. When it's all said and done, the prison's going to be seeking the influencers. New leadership to replace those who'll be rounded up and isolated."

"That's why being locked in here works out. No problem from us."

"True. But what if you looked at the flip side." Kelly saw he had their attention. "A group of inmates putting themselves at risk while trying to rescue a wounded corrections officer—that's the kind of shit they give awards for."

"Do we look like the type of guys lookin' for a medal?"

Kelly shook his head. "Maybe not. But I'm sure it wouldn't hurt to have a couple favors come your way. The guards will remember what you did today. Might make the years left on the clock a little easier."

A couple of the guys in the back whispered their opinions among themselves. Nickel remained quiet, his face pensive, while he contemplated the offer. He looked at Kelly and then to the rioters beyond the bars. "Seems like a big risk for a lot of maybes."

"What about Domino?" Kelly asked.

"What about him?"

"From what I've seen and heard, he's the block's ruler." Kelly watched as his words stirred something in Nickel. "Domino and his goons are controlling the ground floor. I need you to clear a path through them. It's an opportunity to knock him off his throne. You could be the next king of the cage."

Nickel turned to his men. A round table discussion was silently carried out in a series of non-verbal exchanges, most of which were slow nods.

Kelly decided to pour a little gasoline onto the fire, hoping not to get burned in the process. "That is unless you and your guys don't think you could take him?"

Nickel spun to face Kelly, fire in his eyes. "We'll cut through 'em like a warm knife through butter. That isn't the problem. Getting out of this cell is. Guess you haven't noticed, but me and my boys are stuck inside here just like you. And unless you're some kind of magician, I don't see how you're supposed to pull that off."

"Abracadabra." Kelly turned his head and gestured to Bentley, signaling him over. "I've got a way out of this cell, so you'll get your shot. Question is, will you take it?"

Nickel looked at Kelly for a long moment. He hushed his men's snide remarks with a sharp look, then turned back to Kelly, his interest evident. "Ready when you are."

Amid the chaos, with uncertainty hanging in the air, an alliance was forged. Like a living chessboard, Kelly had amassed his army. In the back of his mind, a thought gnawed at him, and he couldn't help but wonder if this moment with Nickel would translate beyond the prison walls and serve to further his efforts to infiltrate Walsh's crew. He tabled it for now. First, he had to survive the next phase of his plan. He knew it was a gamble, but in times like these, survival was a matter of strategy, not luck. And he was ready to play the game.

Kelly watched as Bentley moved toward the cell door. Before the key could be inserted, the door to the second-floor guard station opened and Roland Watt stepped onto the landing. Bentley paused, keys dangling alongside his thigh.

Most of the inmates quieted, though some continued their banter. Domino gave the command for silence, and immediately a hush fell over the group.

Watt smiled as he looked out on his subjects. "You asked for food, and I give you a feast."

Kelly followed Watt's hand as it swung toward the access door to the right of the guard station. He could see the prison's Emergency Response Team geared up and stacked outside the door to the cell block. From Kelly's previous experience as a member of BPD's SWAT team, he knew that in critical incident situations like this, protocol dictated it was safest for tactical teams to serve as the relay for any exchanges. He also knew that tactical teams used these as opportunities to gather intelligence, and in some cases, to initiate an assault.

Kelly shot a glance at Bentley, who was still inching closer to the cell door, and gave a subtle shake of his head. The message was received; Bentley halted a few feet away.

"Your bellies will soon be full of all the Mickey D's you can shovel into your mouths." Watt's words brought the rioters into a frenzied state. A look of amusement spread across his face as he turned and retreated into the guard station.

Nickel leaned close to Kelly and whispered, "This part of your big plan?"

Kelly shook his head. It looked as though his heroics wouldn't be needed; the tactical unit's arrival meant the end of the siege might be close at hand. Maybe Watt had negotiated for the food in exchange for Doyle. If that was the case, Kelly would just have to wait it out in the safety of this cell. On the upside, Bentley wouldn't be in any further danger, and Kelly might be able to use the opportunity to build some rapport with Nickel and further strengthen his ruse within Walsh's crew.

There was a downside. Kelly had been on plenty of tactical operations in the past. Not all were successful, and some were downright disasters. He hoped this was not one of those cases, but something nagged at him, a piece out of place he just couldn't seem to put his finger on. And then the answer hit him like the sucker punch delivered by Goliath: it was the look of confidence in Watt's eyes when he saw the tactical element arrive, almost as if he'd been waiting for them.

Kelly would have his answer soon enough. A loud voice boomed from beyond the access door, ordering the inmates via megaphone to step back from the landing and clear a path to the guard station. The two large inmates serving as doormen looked toward the guard station, nodded, and stepped onto the staircase, giving the tactical element a wide berth.

Then Kelly heard a loud clang as the access door receded along its track. The two ERT operators in front had less-lethal shotguns at the ready. They swiveled with the weapons as they stepped into the cell block, their muzzles sweeping their immediate surroundings. The ERT team member closest to the guard station kept his shotgun leveled at the door. The other posted himself at the top of the staircase, aiming down at the two inmates standing at the halfway point.

The third to enter the landing carried a ballistic shield and took a position alongside his teammate on the stairs. The shield bearer raised his right arm and, with a precise chopping motion, directed the remaining members of the team toward the guard station.

The fourth to enter was pushing a large cart stacked high with bags of McDonald's. The scent of the food wafted down into the main space, causing an excited uproar from the hungry prisoners. Kelly caught wind, and although he wasn't a fan of fast food, the adrenaline and physical demands of the day had left him depleted, and he couldn't help but feel the pang of hunger rumble in his gut.

The fifth and final member of the team was shorter than the rest. A messy bun of black hair peeked out from beneath the ballistic helmet. She gave commands, directing the team forward as they converged on the guard station.

The team stacked outside the door. The female officer commanded Watt and the other inmates inside the guard station to back up against the far wall. Seconds slowly ticked by. Kelly could feel the tension in the air as the inmates looked on in excitement and worry.

Then he saw the silent "tap up" given, initiating the team's next move. The door to the guard station opened, and before he could let out the breath he'd been holding, all five members of the prison's Emergency Response Team disappeared inside.

As the door closed, Kelly heard the team belting out commands: "Hands! Get on the ground! Don't move!" The words were immediately followed by three concussive booms. The first two came with an explosion of light. The third released a cloud of smoke that blotted out any visibility through the windows. Blasts from the less-lethal shotguns rang out. Screaming and crashing echoed from within the enclosed space.

The dynamic entry stunned the onlookers into an uncharacteristic silence. Kelly was sure each of the inmates knew deep down that the riot, and the freedom that came with it, was destined to be short-lived. The next few moments would dictate whether the tactic had worked to save Doyle. Then the guards would begin the long process of restoring order to chaos.

"Guess that's that," Nickel hissed.

"Time will tell." Kelly heard the clock in his head continue to tick off the seconds as he waited for the smoke to clear.

Kelly had used a lot of his luck to get this far. He wondered how much he had left, and prayed he wouldn't be forced to find out.

31

From the temporary safety of Nickel's cell, Kelly heard the shuffling of boots and trained his eyes on the guard station, taking in the scene unfolding before him.

Kelly's breath hitched as the Emergency Response Team emerged from the guard station, their imposing figures a stark contrast against the grimy industrial backdrop of the prison. Their tactical gear clung to them like a second skin, their faces obscured by balaclavas and the gas masks donned as a counter to the gas grenade deployed during the raid. The prisoners on the first floor, a sea of white jumpsuits and hardened faces, slowly coalesced into a loose crowd, their raucous voices merging into a low, ominous rumble.

The point man leading the ERT team communicated without speaking, pointing a gloved finger toward the frenzied inmates. He seemed to be singling out Domino. The prison leader gave a single nod before turning to his loyal followers. They formed a formidable human barricade between the ERT members preparing to go down the stairs and the inmates waiting to devour them. Kelly observed the unfolding dynamics with a strange amalgam of awe and confusion. But as the ERT began their cautious descent down the staircase, the final piece of the puzzle fell into place.

The last member of the team was a behemoth of a man whose body stretched the fabric of his tactical armor to its limits. His hulking frame didn't match that of any of the response team members who'd entered the guard station minutes ago. The hints of his red prison jumpsuit peeking out from beneath his gear served as the final confirmation. Goliath, the prison's proverbial titan, was now taking up the rear flank.

Kelly's sharp eyes flicked to the second person in line, whom he recognized as the female ERT leader, moving in step with the others. She was unarmed and Kelly wondered if she'd been taken as a hostage to replace Doyle, who was conspicuously absent, perhaps a casualty of what now appeared to be a disastrous rescue attempt. Kelly's mind raced as he connected the dots of Watt's twisted chess game.

A surge of adrenaline coursed through his veins, the jolt of clarity sparking a decision. He knew what needed to be done. The next move was his, and the time was now. His heart pounded, ticking down the precious seconds. Steeled by years of experience and driven by the exigency of the moment, Kelly prepared himself for the risk he was about to take.

"Whatever the hell their plan was, looks like it went to shit," Nickel commented, his voice as rough as gravel. "Unless Goliath there suddenly decided to play for the other team."

"Hell in a handbasket." Kelly cracked his knuckles and worked a kink out of his right shoulder. He suppressed the pain of the earlier beating, allowing for the adrenaline of the moment to serve as the numbing agent. "Looks like I'm going to need that help after all."

Watt had once again proven his mastery of deception, but his final plan remained a mystery to Kelly. But he was a seasoned player in this game of cat-and-mouse and knew he had to follow. Before he could, though, he had another task at hand. The actual members of the ERT team were still trapped in the guard station, their lives hanging in the balance. Doyle was hopefully still among them, his status worrisome.

He locked eyes with Bentley, a silent communication transmitted in the fraction of a heartbeat. A subtle nod of his head, the merest twitch of his chin toward the cold iron bars of the cell door, and Bentley took the final steps forward.

Beyond, in the main space of D-Block, Domino and his henchmen fought to keep the swirling tide of prisoners at bay, their beefy arms pushing and shoving with all the brutal force they could muster. The tension in the cell block was electric, a live wire poised to spark off at any moment. The other prisoners had seemed confused by Domino's sudden allegiance to the tactical unit. That had given way to anger, and the crowd surged as the procession of dark uniforms made its way to the exit door. One by one, the ERT imposters disappeared through the door into the hallway beyond. When Domino tried to fall in behind, Goliath turned to face him. Without warning, his massive hand shot out like a wrecking ball, colliding with Domino's chest with bone-jarring force. Domino staggered backward, catching himself against his men. The reigning king of D-Block's crown fell, his dominance shattered as the other inmates bore witness.

Goliath disappeared into the hallway. The cell door's metallic clang echoed, serving as a grim punctuation to Watt's broken promise. Domino's hold over the prisoners was now in question, opening himself and his men to the uprising taking shape.

Meanwhile, Bentley slipped the key into the lock, and Kelly took advantage of the window of opportunity. In the escalating pandemonium, the prisoners seemed to momentarily forget his presence.

Kelly locked on his objective as he mentally plotted a trajectory through the human obstacle course. He whispered to Nickel, "I just need you to clear a path so I can get up to that guard station."

"Better be worth it," came Nickel's gravelly response, his menacing scowl connecting to the tattoos covering his neck.

"I'll take that as a yes." Kelly inched toward the cell door.

Nickel followed close behind, his neck rolling from side to side, his fist slamming into his open palm, a promise of the violence to come. "Follow us."

Bentley slid the cell door open. The sigh of metal on metal was swallowed whole by the prisoners' rising cacophony. Only those in the immediate vicinity shifted their attention, their bloodshot eyes narrowing as Kelly stepped forward.

Like a coiled spring, Nickel and his crew surged past Kelly and out into the maelstrom. They barreled through inmates with the ferocity of a runaway freight train, carving a path through the writhing sea of bodies.

Kelly fell into step behind them, mimicking a seasoned running back trailing his offensive line. Around him, the air was thick with violence. Kelly's head was on a swivel, scanning the surroundings for potential threats as he homed in on the stairwell leading to the guard station. Bentley was a reassuring shadow at his side, joining him on the brutal path they were navigating. This was the point of no return, a leap of faith with no promise of a safe landing.

When Kelly reached the stairs, he saw that his protective detail was losing control, and fast. Nickel and his boys were doing their job, but the chaos was spreading faster than they could contain. The riot surged below them as he and Bentley ran up the stairs. The air was thick with the sour tang of sweat and fear, laced with the sharp scent of blood.

Suddenly, a lone voice rose above the pandemonium. "Kelly!" His name echoed through the concrete corridors like a gunshot. It was a call to arms to the inmates unaware of his presence in the fray. Their eyes swiveled upward, gazes locking onto him.

Kelly's heart kicked up a gear, adrenaline pouring into his veins. The shield of invisibility had been lost. They were exposed. Vulnerable. He quickened his pace, the stairs clanging under his heavy steps, Bentley at his heels.

He shot a glance at Nickel. The enforcer and his men were entrenched in a battle against the human tide of rage and desperation.

From the corner of his eye, he noticed a blur of movement. A long, sinewy figure clad in a prison uniform sprang from a tabletop like Jordan launching from the three-point line. He seized the railing near the midway point of the stairwell, swinging himself up and over. The inmate was unfamiliar to Kelly, but based on the burning intensity in his gaze, Kelly assumed they'd crossed paths before. He recognized that look as one of murderous intent.

Bentley fumbled with the keys outside of the guard station while Kelly prepared for the approaching threat. They jangled as Bentley tested them one by one against the lock.

Kelly squared his shoulders, his posture steady. He had the high ground and planned to use it to his advantage.

The attacker sprang onto the landing. His intentions were clear, but his movements were unpolished and lacked finesse. The anger fueling his aggression left him off-balance and clumsy.

The first punch thrown was a wild haymaker, its trajectory telegraphed by the uncontrolled nature of the attacker. The unrefined movement gave Kelly the opportunity he needed. With swift, practiced precision, he slipped the blow. His counter came in the form of a devastating body shot that landed with a sickening crunch. The man bellowed and clutched his side before doubling over in agony.

Kelly didn't hesitate and wasted no time in seizing the moment. He delivered a swift knee strike to his attacker's head, sending him reeling backward. Dazed, the inmate teetered on the edge of the landing.

Kelly caught him by the collar, saving him from a potentially fatal fall, but the inmate still posed a threat. To neutralize it, he delivered a ruthless left hook to the man's temple, rendering him unconscious.

With a sigh of relief, Kelly dropped the unconscious man onto the landing, shoving his limp body out of the way. He felt a tug on his shoulder and instinctively spun around, his fist cocked and ready for another fight. Bentley threw his hands up. Kelly let his muscles relax, tension fading as he looked beyond him to the open door to the guard station.

They slipped inside, the door closing behind them with a soft click. The raucous roar from the cell block was muffled. Despite the imminent danger, they had a moment of reprieve, a chance to catch their breath before they crossed into the danger zone.

The first order of business was Doyle and the other guards strewn about the station.

32

The chill of the Nor'easter gnawed at the edges of the Chevy Caprice, its fury whipping up dense sheets of white that made the blacktop road seem like a distant memory. The usual cacophony of city life was replaced by the harsh whisper of the wind and the grating crunch of tires against the snow-laden road.

Detective Kristen Barnes sat rigid in the passenger seat, her hands clutching the leather upholstery so tightly her knuckles had turned white. Her eyes were riveted on the barely visible road ahead, her foot involuntarily pumping an imaginary brake with each swerve. Her heart pounded in sync with the windshield wipers battling the ceaseless snow.

Despite the dire circumstances, Cahill seemed unaffected; in fact, he seemed to be downright enjoying himself. He laughed at each slip of the wheels as if taunting the slick road's attempts to kill them.

"Not sure this car was built for that," Barnes managed, her voice betraying her fear.

"You've never watched NASCAR, have you? It's never the car, it's always the driver." Cahill laughed again, although his eyes never left the road. He wrestled with the wheel as they hit a thick drift of snow kicked up by the plows. The Caprice held the road as they barreled toward the looming penitentiary.

"Well, I'm not sure I'm built for this," Barnes replied, her tone half-hearted.

"That's why I'm driving."

Barnes would likely never admit it, but she felt an uncharacteristic sense of safety in his presence. The partnership had shifted on its axis in the last twenty-four hours. She wasn't sure what it meant. The innocent, or not-so-innocent, drunken kiss had awakened an unexpected torrent of emotions, stirring within her a fresh perspective of the man beside her. She'd begun to wonder about the possibility of something more. Each time the thought crept in, Kelly's face would appear. Two versions of the man she loved came into view. The one she'd thought she would spend the rest of her life with. And the one who had made it clear to her that ship had sailed. But she dared not let her thoughts meander too far down that path. The harsh reality of their current mission wasn't lost on her. Their destination was the prison holding Kelly.

Barnes's cell phone rested on her thigh under her hand. The number she had been dialing for the past thirty minutes taunted her. Her mounting frustration was released in a grunt as she made another attempt to connect and was met with the same monotone recording with its series of prompts. Without allowing the lifeless robotic voice to complete the welcome greeting, Barnes tapped number three on the dial pad, which redirected her to the line reserved for law enforcement. After the tenth annoying ring, she ended the call.

"No joy," she said.

"Storm's pretty bad." Cahill, playing the optimist, shrugged. "Could be the line's out."

"Then that's one more problem to add to the mix. Or it could be we're already too late."

"You're definitely not drinking from the half-full cup."

Barnes rolled her eyes and tossed the phone into the cupholder.

The screen lit up as the phone began vibrating against the coffee-stained plastic. Barnes glanced at the caller ID. Mainelli. She answered with an edge to her voice. "Tell me you got something? I'm batting zeros in getting someone from the prison to answer."

"I believe so," Mainelli replied, less snarky than usual. "Had to do some serious digging, but I think I've got a lead on that address you wanted me to look into."

"What address?" Barnes asked, her mind blanking.

"The one from Mattapan," Mainelli supplied. "You told me to look into the info you got off Cahill's snitch. Some girl Watt might be connected with."

"Right, of course. Almost forgot. Go ahead with it."

"The apartment's leased to an Evelyn Diaz," Mainelli revealed.

"Got a record?"

"Clean as a whistle."

Barnes cursed under her breath. She put the call on speaker.

"Did I hear you right, Diaz doesn't have a history?" Cahill shook his head. "Damn. Figured that intel was a slam dunk."

"I didn't say it wasn't. I just said she wasn't a criminal." Mainelli paused. "But she does work with them."

"I'm not in the mood for riddles," Barnes said.

Mainelli continued without addressing the attitude in Barnes's tone. "I thought it was a coincidence at first, but then, when Halstead told me about the map found at the crash site—"

The Caprice veered sideways after encountering a slick spot on the road. The cellphone shot off her thigh and onto the floorboard. Cahill steered into the skid and brought the unmarked under control. Barnes retrieved the phone from the damp floormat. "You still there?"

"I'm here. I was saying, Diaz works in corrections. Want to guess where?"

A curse slipped past Barnes's lips as she exchanged a knowing look with Cahill. "Let me guess, Walpole?"

"Bingo. I guess your cowboy heroics paid off." Mainelli's sardonic nature returned. "White is still fuming, but that makes it even better."

"Do us a favor and try to get in touch with the warden, or anyone at the prison for that matter. No luck on our end. Line seems to be down. We don't know what timeline we're up against, but we need to warn them—get them up to speed on everything."

"Consider it done."

"And Mainelli..."

"Yeah?"

"Nice work." Barnes ended the call before the gruff senior detective could dismiss the compliment.

The car decelerated, and Barnes, momentarily grateful for the respite from Cahill's driving, took a deep, cleansing breath. She quickly understood why he'd dropped his speed. Up ahead, a kaleidoscope of red and blue lights bounced off the white landscape.

As they crept closer, Barnes could make out a trail of crimson taillights slithering down the highway like a column of fire ants, ending at a hulking tractor-trailer lying on its side.

"Looks like we've hit a roadblock," Barnes mumbled.

Cahill seemed undeterred. "We'll see about that." He flipped the switch beneath the ignition, activating the emergency lights. As he pushed along the buried shoulder, Cahill chirped the siren.

The Caprice came to a halt just shy of the barricade of road flares outlining the crash site. A trooper, his face hidden behind a gloved hand fending off the stinging snowfall, trudged over to their vehicle. Cahill lowered the window and a gust of icy wind barreled in, showering them in fresh snow. The trooper's massive frame blocked the worst of the storm as he leaned into the window.

"Boston Homicide, trying to get to Walpole," Cahill announced, pulling up his collar against the biting cold while flashing his credentials.

The trooper shook his head, snowflakes flying from his hat. "Sorry. Not going to happen. At least not for a while. Road's closed. Hell, pretty much all of 'em are at this point."

"This isn't a routine call." Barnes leaned over the center console. "The prison's under siege, and we've got reason to believe there's a breakout planned. It may even be underway as we speak."

"You notify the prison?"

"Tried. Can't get through," Cahill replied, his frustration clear.

The trooper glanced back at the overturned semi. "You aren't going to make it in that thing," he said, assessing the Caprice. "Give me a second. I'll see what I can do."

Cahill closed the window and cranked up the heater. "Great. Now we've got to wait while a 'big hat' goes and runs it through his superiors. I'm about to punch this thing and take our chances off-road."

"Give him a chance. Who knows, maybe he'll be able to reach the prison."

The trooper made his way back to them a couple minutes later and stood outside Cahill's door. "Like I said before, no way you're making it in that thing." Cahill opened his mouth to protest, but the trooper cut him off before he could speak. "That's why you're going to park it over there on the side of the road. We're going to be taking my vehicle."

Barnes and Cahill looked out through the slurry-coated windshield at the blue and gray Humvee the trooper was pointing at. Then they turned to each other and shrugged.

"The name's Ramirez, by the way." Trooper Ramirez trudged off, not waiting for a response, and disappeared into the swirling snow.

"Guess we're getting an escort from the Staties." Cahill chuckled.

"Seems like it's the only option."

"Been a while since I've bounced around in a Humvee. Should be fun."

"You and I have a different definition of fun." Barnes rolled her eyes as she bundled up her coat. "At least I get a break from your driving."

"Hey, we're still alive, aren't we?" Cahill feigned offense as he pulled off the road and parked where Ramirez had directed him.

They climbed into the Humvee. Ramirez greeted them with a smile and wildness in his eyes. Great, Barnes thought to herself, another Masshole with a badge.

With a deftness that belied its size, the Humvee rolled out. The snow underneath the tires crunched and groaned, giving way to the relentless pursuit of the armored behemoth. The flashing lights reflected off the falling snow as they put the crash behind them.

The headlights illuminated the highway sign. Through blotches of snow clinging to its metallic surface, Barnes read: *State Prison, 12 Miles.* She tried to calculate the time it would take under these conditions, knowing every second counted and hoping they weren't too late.

33

Kelly surveyed the scene inside the guard station. It resembled a war zone after a battle. Watt and his crew had taken away the team's leader, leaving the remaining four members of the Emergency Response Team inside. They were scattered around the room, handcuffed and gagged, their eyes wide and terrified. The trauma of the unexpected and overwhelming force used in the takeover was etched into their faces.

Among the helpless guards, one figure stood out, his body sprawled against the cold, unforgiving gray wall near the station's nerve center. Compelled by the sight of the kindhearted guard, Kelly bypassed the others, making a beeline for Doyle.

His fingers tracing along Doyle's neck, Kelly moved carefully, not knowing the extent of his injuries. The bruises and blood made his features nearly unrecognizable. Kelly pushed back against the rage welling inside him as he searched for a pulse.

The seconds stretched like minutes until, finally, there it was—the faintest whisper of a pulse, fluttering weakly against his fingertips. He let out a sigh of relief.

"Doyle. Can you hear me?" Kelly's voice was shaky, a combination of nerves and adrenaline. Doyle's response came in the form of a weakly uttered groan, indecipherable yet a sign that the seasoned corrections officer still had a little fight left in him. Between rounds of Kelly's final and toughest bout in his first Golden Gloves Championship, Pops had told him something that he applied to his life beyond the ring many times since: "Willpower is the strength no opponent can see. Its power can turn the tide of any battle, no matter the odds." Kelly hoped it would apply here.

"Hang on, Doyle. I'm getting you out of here, no matter what."

The only illumination inside the guard station came by way of the emergency lights and the glass windows overlooking the cell block. Kelly gave a gentle but reassuring squeeze of Doyle's hand before leaving his side and navigating his way to the nearest guard.

The guard didn't make eye contact with Kelly; instead, his gaze was transfixed on the prison jumpsuit. The guard's body went rigid as Kelly squatted low and moved closer, and he flinched and reared back against the metal cabinet behind him. Kelly inched forward, slowly reaching out with his hand toward the gag covering the guard's mouth.

"Easy now." Kelly's voice was barely a whisper, as though taming a wild stallion. "I'm not with the men who did this. We may not look like it"—Kelly shot a thumb in Bentley's direction—"but we're the good guys. And right now, we're the best thing you've got to a lifeline. You understand?"

The guard responded with a labored, apprehensive nod as Kelly dislodged the repugnant gag, a sock pulled from the bootless man. He spat on the floor, expelling the vile taste. "Thanks."

With the first guard freed, Bentley jumped in to assist the remaining guards, who had been bound at the wrists by thick plastic zip ties. Kelly pulled a folding knife clipped inside the guard's pocket and freed his hands, then continued the process until the rest were free. As the men stood unsteadily, the brutal aftermath of the surprise assault became horrifically apparent. Each guard had received a beating, but two bore the brunt of the attack. Kelly was certain these injuries were Goliath's work.

One of the guards limped over to the control console, stabbing the keys with blood-crusted fingers. He slammed his fist against the keyboard and swore. "We've got no comms with command. No way of letting them know what happened in here."

"What about the cameras?" Kelly asked. "Maybe someone saw it go down. Saw them leave out the other side. There'd be no mistaking Goliath."

The guard shook his head and pointed to the static-filled screens on the four mounted display monitors. "What you're seeing is what they see. They're in the blind."

"When they don't hear back from your team, they'll mobilize another." Kelly based his assertion on his years of SWAT experience. His optimism was immediately dashed when he saw the guard's sour expression.

"Skeleton crew. They'll do their best to organize a response, but it won't be ERT. We were it." The guard pushed his hand through his sweaty mop of hair. "Plus, that candy-ass warden of ours isn't going to be mobilizing shit. Not if we failed to bring home the bacon."

"Then I guess that leaves it to us." Kelly gave the group of battered guards another once-over.

A chilling silence settled over the room. Kelly's gaze swept around, taking in the men surrounding him. They were built strong, full of muscle and grit. Now, under the harsh reality of their situation, their confidence was all but lost.

"Situation's critical. It's do or die time, gentlemen." Kelly asserted his command of the ragtag group. "We need to prioritize our actions. That means getting Doyle the hell out of here and in the hands of medical. He's on borrowed time."

"I don't think we'll be able to carry him out like that," the smallest guard in the group challenged. "He's in bad shape. We might do more harm than good."

"I understand that. Under optimal circumstances we'd try to stabilize and wait for the medical team to respond. But like your man said, that's not going to happen, at least not anytime soon." Kelly cut his gaze around the room, searching for something, anything, they could use as a makeshift backboard. His eyes landed on a supply cabinet against the far wall. He crossed the room and began wrenching the door open with a metallic screech.

"Give me a hand here." Kelly separated the door and tossed it on the floor. "We'll use this door to stabilize Doyle's back for extraction."

"Even if we stabilize him for transport, what's the plan for those two?" The smaller guard gestured toward the inmate enforcer team blocking access to the exit.

"When faced with an obstacle, you've got a couple choices. Go around, go over, or run through it. We're taking the latter."

"And how do you expect us to do that? We're not exactly operating at a hundred percent," the thicker guard said. "Plus, we've got Doyle."

Kelly looked past the guard, his eyes settling on an unexpected weapon: a cart piled high with McDonald's. "Seems we've got ourselves a gurney. All we need to do now is clear a path."

A tense hush blanketed the room as the guards exchanged looks. Doyle let out a loud whimper, his breaths spiraling into erratic, tortured gasps. There was no further debate. Their friend's dire state didn't allow it. The guards were forced into action.

Some of the men swept food from the cart in a whirlwind of motion while others wrestled the heavy cabinet door free, placing it beside Doyle with grunts of exertion.

"Nice and easy, boys. On three, everybody lift," the guard closest to Kelly said.

They moved as one as they lifted Doyle's prone form, with Bentley shoulder-to-shoulder with the guards, humanity seeing past the uniforms each wore.

After placing Doyle on the cabinet door, two of the guards used their belts to fasten him to it, then hoisted him onto the food cart. The smaller guard positioned himself behind the makeshift gurney while the other three prepared to clear the roadblock. The lead guard, the biggest and strongest of the men present, picked up the shield and held it tight against his chest. The remaining pair squared up behind him, lowering in a ready stance.

"The moment this door opens, we're carving our way through those dipshits." The lead guard banged his shield like a Spartan warrior preparing for battle.

"Speed is our friend here. We catch them off guard, we take the advantage," Kelly said. "Once they clear a path, Bentley's going to open the access door." Bentley nodded and held up the key. "After everyone's safely in the corridor, I'll make sure it's shut."

"Are you out of your mind?" Bentley blurted. His eyes widened. "These savages will eat you alive."

"I've got this. Get Doyle to safety."

"You stayin', then I'm by your side." Bentley puffed out his chest.

"Not this time." Kelly's words held a finality to them. "This next part, I've got to do on my own."

"You stay alive, Michael Kelly, ya feel me?" Bentley jostled the keyring in his hand, getting the manual access key ready. "I'll catch you on the flip."

Kelly turned and squared himself to the door. He felt the silent doubts plaguing every mind in the room as he looked toward the danger looming just beyond the door.

"You need to stick with us," a guard insisted. "Bentley's right. They'll be gunning for you. Staying in here is a death sentence."

Kelly shook his head. "I don't plan to stick around. I'm going after Watt."

"That's a suicide mission." Shock painted the guard's features. "You've done enough. Hell, you've done more than enough. There's nothing left to prove."

"It's not about proving. It's about finishing. And I've got another round left in this fight." Kelly offered a weak attempt at a smile, hoping it masked his fear. "Plus, he's still got one of your own."

"Diaz? She's not a hostage," the guard scoffed, almost spitting her name. "She's with them."

"You're telling me she's part of all this?"

"Wouldn't have believed it ten minutes ago. But the truth came out the minute we stepped inside this guard station. Never saw it coming."

The revelation sent a ripple of icy realization down Kelly's spine. It added up. Watt needed more than just leverage for his escape—he needed an insider. The sheer scale of Watt's masterplan made Kelly question if he could outmaneuver the gang leader. He forced away the doubt creeping in.

"Then it's even more important I go after him, if for no other reason than to slow them down until you're able to send backup."

"I don't like it."

"You don't have to. Not your burden to carry."

Just then, Doyle let out another whimper, this time weaker. His breathing became more labored. The guard took notice and shook his head at Kelly. "I see there's no convincing you otherwise. I hope you've got a shit ton of luck, 'cause you're gonna need it."

"I'm Irish. We've got luck to spare," Kelly said, the bravado falling short as the weight of the situation pressed down on him.

"As soon as we're all in the clear, I'll make sure I alert them to your situation. Backup won't be far behind."

The two hulking inmates formed a human barricade separating the group from the access door leading out of D-Block and into the relative safety of the prison. Kelly's hand curled around the doorknob, and with a twist and a shove, the door flew open. He immediately pressed his body against the door, clearing a path for the charging guards and the cart following on their heels.

Powered by the wrath of retribution, the lead guard slammed full force into the first inmate, his heavy ballistic shield crashing into the large man's chest and striking under his chin, sending him backward into the inmate standing behind him. The other two guards pushed the back of their shield-wielding leader, adding their energy to the mix.

In the mayhem, Bentley did his part, unlocking and wrenching the access door open so the smaller guard could shoot the gurney through the gap. The two inmates had been laid out by the three-man team, their bodies stacked awkwardly near the stairs. The guards then made a break for the open door. The one carrying the shield looked back at Kelly and made one more silent plea for him to follow before turning and joining his men as they spirited Doyle away.

Bentley flung the keys toward Kelly. "Remember, Kelly, we're bidding this hellhole goodbye tomorrow. Don't go gettin' yourself killed."

Kelly snatched the keys from the air. From the corner of his eye, he saw the downed inmates begin to stir. Bentley retreated into the hallway, pulling the door closed behind him. The metallic thud reverberated across the landing, sealing him inside.

The escape had caught the attention of the inmates below. Kelly made quick work of retreating inside the guard station. One of the inmates who'd been toppled during the skirmish was at the window, hammering his fist against it. Kelly disregarded him and took a moment to prepare for the next phase of his ever-evolving plan.

The inmates continued their relentless pounding on the door, adding threats of unspeakable violence. Kelly ignored their taunts and focused on the stairwell that would lead him to Watt. This time, he could no longer count on the element of surprise. Kelly stood at the door. He rolled his shoulders, loosening his muscles for the fight ahead.

He knew that opening the door would signify the point of no return. Kelly gripped the knob. Somewhere in his mind he heard the bell ring. The final round had begun.

34

Watt walked closely behind Evelyn Diaz, his guide in this labyrinthine prison. Their shadows danced along the damp walls lining the corridor as they headed to the tunnel that would be their final walk to freedom.

Watt stopped in his tracks at the sight of a surveillance camera tucked in the corner like a mechanical spider. "You said they wouldn't be able to see us. No cameras, remember?"

"It's all good. Half the cameras in this place are crap, haven't worked in months."

"And the ones that are?" Watt tucked himself against the wall. "You sure they aren't watching our every move?"

Diaz slowed her pace, her boots screeching against the grimy floor. She turned her head, meeting Watt's gaze with a hardened look of conviction. "I told you, baby, I took care of it. I've shut them down. Every camera between here and freedom. And as for the other tunnel, it's as surveillance-free as a desert highway. Anyone ever tell you that you worry too much?"

"It's what's kept me alive. I know some people who didn't worry enough. They're all resting six deep now."

Watt eased off the wall and continued following Diaz. They approached the door, an unremarkable slab of cold, dull metal that belied its promise of escape. As Diaz worked a key loose from the lanyard attached to her belt, he looked back down the hall. D-Block's cacophony continued to filter out. He listened carefully for a moment and noticed the volume was rising. He wondered what bit of viciousness had roused the frenzy. He was happy to be clear of the barbarians. Watt preferred the controlled chaos of the streets where he reigned supreme. Shedding the prison's stink from his nostrils couldn't come quick enough.

Diaz slipped the key into the doorknob. "Relax. Everything is falling into place. This is your plan, remember? You're always three steps ahead and we're two steps from the end."

Watt merely nodded. Plans, even the most meticulously orchestrated ones, were fraught with unseen dangers. His rise to prominence in the treacherous criminal underworld was testament to this insight. He never allowed complacency to dull his vigilance, never ignored the dread lurking in the shadows of success.

"I can see you're still not convinced." Diaz held the key in place and cut her eyes to Watt. "The response team is incapacitated in the station room. The warden won't make a move tactically without me. They'll be crippled. Even if they come up with a plan of action, we'll be long gone before it ever gets off the ground."

"Your end's not my biggest worry. My crew better not miss the mark. Timing is everything. Getting out of here hinges on it."

"Tick tock, baby." Diaz turned the key. A heartbeat later, the door groaned open.

Watt braced himself as a gust of icy air blasted from the gaping maw of the tunnel, slicing through his thin clothing not protected by the borrowed body armor.

"This route is our lifeline to the yard," Diaz said, her voice bouncing off the tunnel's frosted walls. "Our very own secret passage. It's only used by maintenance or by the ISO ward prisoners."

A low grunt echoed through the space as Goliath stepped through the threshold.

Watt shifted his gaze to Slim and Boone, the prison trustees he'd manipulated by feeding their commissary accounts over the past several months. Their roles were crucial to Goliath's escape. Every chess master knew how to use their pawns, and these two were nearing the end of service to their king. One more task remained.

With a swift flick of his wrist, Watt sent a less-lethal shotgun skimming toward Slim, who caught it midair. A brief nod at Goliath cued him to follow suit, and he tossed his weapon to Boone.

"You two, guard this door till we breach the yard," Watt instructed, his voice battling against the backdrop of the tunnel's whispering wind. "Ensure nothing interferes with our departure."

The two inmates exchanged a glance, uncertainty clouding their eyes. Slim voiced their collective apprehension. "You ain't intending to abandon us, are you?"

Watt's face hardened like a sheet of ice. "Are you questioning my integrity? Doubt the loyalty I hold for the men who risked everything for my brother? Have you forgotten the dollars that filled your commissary account? Or your mother, Slim, shivering in her cold apartment before I stepped in?"

Slim's gaze dropped to the icy floor, his reluctance diminishing under Watt's fury. "We just don't want to get left behind. After this stunt, we ain't ever gonna see the light again."

"I'm requesting your assistance at this door," Watt continued, disregarding the man's attempt at softening his tone. "Trust is something I think I've earned. To question it now would be a mistake."

Slim gave a brisk nod, Boone following suit. The two men stood erect and took up their post near the door.

"Understood, boss," Slim said. "Nobody's slipping by us."

Satisfied, Watt flashed a predatory grin. "When we reach the yard's exit, you'll know. Freedom will be just a stone's throw away."

What Watt kept veiled from his pawns was a grim fact: the escape vehicles were equipped to carry three passengers, and three alone. These were simple men, capable of only seeing their next step. By the time they realized their misfortune, Watt would have moved on.

His brother stood adjacent to Diaz, the titan's silhouette looming large in the dimness. His gaze was hardened and focused, riveted on the tunnel before them—the road to their salvation. It had been the briefest of stays, but Watt already craved the intoxicating thrill of freedom. "I promised you, didn't I? Swore I'd never let the bastards take you to that hellhole. No way they're sticking you in that supermax."

A smile crawled across Goliath's face, rippling his thick jawline. "You always did have the smarts. Guess that's why they call you the king."

"Hold off on the toasts," Watt cautioned. "We've still got the guard towers to deal with. Shouldn't be an issue if the rest of the crew does their job. If not, all this will be for nothing."

"Then we best get moving," Diaz said, her voice tight with controlled adrenaline. She continued forward, her footfalls resonating against the tunnel's clammy floor.

As they moved out, Goliath veered closer to Watt. "You really think this is gonna work?"

"Do you think I'd ever set foot inside this prison if I didn't?"

Goliath's throat rumbled. "You never put yourself into somethin' you couldn't get yourself out of. Guess that's why you ain't never seen the inside of a cell."

Watt cracked a sly grin. "Always three moves ahead, big brother. Always."

35

Kelly paused with his hand on the knob. From inside the guard station, he peered down the stairwell, the whole world narrowing to the chaos below. In the fluorescent glow of the cell block, he scrutinized the unruly swarm of inmates like a hawk eyeing a snake pit. Watt had escaped, leaving behind disorder that was escalating by the second.

Domino stood like a monolith in the epicenter of the turmoil, trying desperately to reclaim the dominion he'd foolishly ceded to the backstabbing Watt. His reign had been weakened, corroded from within by his ill-judged allegiance.

Sporadic explosions of violence bloomed across the cell block's concrete floor, now coated with fresh blood. If Kelly ever tried to pick the worst imaginable situation in which to die, this would rank near the top of that list. It was Shark Week without the cage.

Kelly frantically looked for a lifeline in the tumult. A blockade of flesh and testosterone barred the staircase. The largest, most menacing cluster of inmates formed an impenetrable wall between Kelly and his salvation.

His nostrils flared as the scent of burgers and fries wafted toward him from the bags littering the floor. The pungent smell was both mouthwatering and maddening, meddling with his cognitive gears, derailing his train of thought.

And then it struck him like a bolt from the blue.

Flashbangs.

In his SWAT days, they were the perfect means of disorientation, a stunning blitz of light and sound. In this scenario, with the tantalizing aroma of food in the air, the burgers might serve a similar end. A diversion. A distraction. Amid this human zoo where hunger was constant, food could be the perfect flashbang. Kelly had a newfound hope, a daring plan taking shape in the recesses of his survival-tuned mind.

The landing was a desolate, concrete vacuum, devoid of human life, silent but for the echo of distant chaos. The inmate he had momentarily incapacitated had shaken off the haze of unconsciousness and plunged back into the pandemonium below, unleashing his animalistic instincts on any inmate within arm's reach.

Kelly found himself staring at the trove of grease-stained bags. He grabbed as many as he could manage and shuffled, arms full, to the door.

As he eased it open, the sharp cry of the steel hinges announced his exit. Instantly, a cacophony of shouts and clashes spilled forth, so tangible he could almost taste the raw ferocity in the air. The safety of the guard station was behind him now as he stepped onto the landing and launched the first bag into the fray. It arced through the air, landing a distance away from the spiraling staircase.

For a moment, the closest inmates stopped, their attention hijacked by the flying object. They glanced up, their primal gazes tracing the trajectory of the bag and its precious cargo, then followed the descent. Their focus shifted instantly to the food. The distraction was effective, the bait taken.

The subsequent bags cut through the air in quick succession, drawing even more inmates away from the stairwell. The scent of the burgers was impossible to ignore. It summoned them, luring them away from the stairwell.

The diversion ignited a new frenzy. Like a spark on a gasoline trail, an explosion of violence erupted around the landed bags. Feral growls and savage roars echoed off the concrete walls as each inmate battled not for dominance but for his share of the feast.

A small cluster of inmates managed to stay within a dangerous proximity to the staircase, creating a potential blockade to Kelly's desperate escape route. Among them was Domino, who, by some uncanny sixth sense, seemed quietly attuned to Kelly's intent. His eyes were riveted on Kelly with an unsettling intuition.

On the other side of the chaos, Nickel was in the thick of the pandemonium, swinging wildly at any convict unfortunate enough to cross his path. His fists were blurs, every strike a demonstration of his fierce determination to claim the status of D-Block's newly crowned ruler. Sweat and blood peppered the floor beneath him as he ground his way to absolute dominance.

Kelly's arsenal of food grenades had been exhausted. Time was running out for him. The tide of chaos had peaked with his distraction and was now beginning to ebb, leaving him vulnerable. It was a game of life and death and every second counted.

In the briefest of moments, the image of his daughter flashed across his mind. He held onto it as long as he could, and before it disappeared, he made a solemn vow to see her again. Kelly propelled himself forward. His shoes pounded the metal steps as he descended at breakneck speed, sliding recklessly down the cold steel rails and bypassing several steps at a time. The concrete rushed up to greet him as he hit the ground floor with a bone-jarring impact. The stinging resonated up his spine and served as a grim welcome to the battlefield.

His breaths came in sharp gasps, mingling with the acrid tang of fear and aggression in the air. His every sense was firing on overdrive as he rose, muscles coiled in readiness. His enemies closed in on him from all sides.

The doorway loomed ahead, but first, he had to fight through the gauntlet of threats. His fingers clenched into fists, knuckles white with the strain, ready to carve his path to freedom.

Domino materialized from the crowd, a vicious sneer stretching the taut skin of his face, warping his mouth into a cruel snarl. With unstoppable determination, he bulldozed his way through the sea of hardened inmates who obstructed his path. He was fixated on one man and one man only —Kelly.

Kelly instinctively braced for the impending storm. He slipped into a modified boxer's stance, the well-honed reflexes from countless bouts guiding his muscles. His eyes flickered around, scanning the periphery and seeking out any opportunists lying in wait, ready to strike when he least expected.

Two menacing figures were bearing down on him, inching closer with every passing second. It was a pincer movement, a well-practiced tactic used by the predators of the cellblock. They moved like a pack of raptors, using Domino to draw Kelly's attention to maximize the effectiveness of their combined attack.

Kelly retreated a step. It was a quick but calculated move, providing him with enough room to maneuver. Light feet and fast hands were his best assets. And he planned to utilize them to the best of his ability.

Steadying his mind, he took a deep, fortifying breath. He'd been in fights before, and on more than one occasion, against multiple opponents. The key was positioning, keeping each aggressor in line with the others, like dominoes waiting to be toppled. The efficacy of this strategy was dependent on how effectively he could corral them into a single-file formation. It was a game of control and maneuvering, turning a group's strength into its weakness.

But this was no ordinary fight. He was surrounded by men who wouldn't hesitate to stab him in the back. Setting up his attackers was going to be the real challenge.

Domino lurched forward, his clenched fist a promise of violence. The king of D-Block was now on a collision course with Kelly.

In the strange fluctuations of time that occurred in battle, Kelly's attention was momentarily drawn to the intricate blend of tattoos and scars marking his knuckles. Domino's devastating punch cut through the air. Kelly brought his guard tight, pulling his arms protectively around his head. He dipped low, the blow skimming off his left forearm. The deflected punch grazed the top of his head, minimizing the potential damage.

Kelly counter-attacked, his body moving like a well-oiled machine. His fists shot out in a rapid-fire combination—two hooks designed to bruise and break the ribs, followed by an uppercut. Kelly's body blows found their mark.

Domino winced but didn't yield. He kept himself from doubling over and thus avoided Kelly's uppercut, his head jerking backward, evading the blow meant to finish him.

Domino connected with a heavy-handed hook that landed on the side of Kelly's jaw. The impact snapped his neck to the side and sent a shockwave down his spine, the intensity nearly dropping him to his knees. Kelly staggered, his foot slipped, and his balance faltered, opening a window for attack.

From his peripheral vision, he saw one of the raptors moving in from his left. In a whirlwind of movement, the inmate swooped in, snatching Kelly into an immobilizing bear hug. His arms were crushed against his sides, rendering them useless.

Domino advanced. This time, his right hand was riding low, almost at his hip. It was a strange stance, but the reason quickly became clear. Kelly saw a shiv, the crude tool of violence, its sharpened plastic tip edging closer. A few inches of the makeshift blade protruded from the improvised tape handle, enough to drive plenty deep into his flesh.

Kelly had seen the effects of such a weapon on more than one occasion. He also knew the worst typically came when the fragile blade broke off inside the victim, a cruelly intentional act that turned a quick stab wound into a complicated medical emergency. His stomach twisted at the thought of it.

Adrenaline coursed through Kelly's veins as he quickly strategized, his mind racing as fast as his heart was pounding. He had to act fast. His arms were trapped, but his legs were free. He flexed his thighs, feeling the solid muscle under his prison uniform. That would be his best shot. But the inmate holding him was no pushover. His grip was vise-like, holding firm against Kelly's struggling body.

The pressure on Kelly's diaphragm was suffocating, each breath becoming a battle all its own. He kept his focus on the biggest threat: the prison-made knife and the man wielding it. This fight was far from over, and he wasn't planning on being a victim. Not now. Not ever.

As Domino stalked toward Kelly, he could feel the brute's hot, humid breath rolling over his shoulder, assaulting his senses. As he processed this, a secondary strategy started forming in his mind. Relying on instinct and a dash of luck, he braced himself.

Kelly tucked his chin down, and with a swift, forceful jerk, he threw his head backward. His skull connected with a jarring thud against the man's cheekbone. The grip didn't entirely release but the hold faltered, slackening just enough for Kelly to shift his center of gravity. He dropped his weight, sinking lower before throwing his body backward with an explosive thrust.

The combined force of Kelly's attack and his sudden backward launch toppled the massive inmate. He crashed backward, his broad back colliding with the metal railing, his grip around Kelly released. A rush of cool, crisp air flooded his lungs.

Domino lunged forward, the crude shiv slicing through the air. Free of the man holding him, Kelly was able to sidestep the attack, spinning out of the way in a swift, deft movement. The blade swished harmlessly by, missing its mark.

Kelly regained his poise, steadied his feet, and prepared himself for the next round. Domino's miss was his opportunity. Kelly was back in the fight.

Rotating his forearms inward, Kelly defended his veins by exposing the backside of his arms to his attacker. Domino repositioned himself and prepared for his next strike.

Kelly braced himself. Just as Domino began to spring forward, an unexpected whirl of motion to the right drew his attention. Kelly looked on as a human hurricane suddenly unfurled, landing a rapid-fire onslaught of punches on the unprepared gang leader.

Domino faltered, knocked off balance before he could redirect his weapon to this new threat. Then, out of nowhere, another man emerged, a muscle-bound freight train that bulldozed into Domino with the force of a professional linebacker.

The impact jarred the shiv loose from Domino's grip. The deadly weapon clattered onto the floor, and Kelly, seizing the opportunity, swiftly booted it out of reach, sending it skittering across the floor, lost amidst the chaos.

Nickel stepped forward, delivering a brutal blackout-inducing kick to the fallen gang leader. Then, with an air of swagger, he pivoted to face Kelly, a smug half-smile gracing his face. "Ain't you got a score to settle? Best be on your way, boyo."

Two of Nickel's henchmen moved in, bodies like wrecking balls, clearing a path to the door. Kelly acknowledged the newly crowned king of

D-Block with a nod of appreciation before he maneuvered to the access door. He made quick work with the key, and with a hard pull of the handle, he was through the gauntlet and into the hallway.

In the moment of peace that came with closing the door, Kelly wondered briefly if this bout of shared combat would build favor within Walsh's crew. The thought was fleeting, however, as he had more immediate problems to deal with.

Right now, Watt and his brother were the only things that mattered. The race was on, the tunnel to the yard the only foreseeable option for their escape.

Cool air crept through the narrow cracks of the door leading to the tunnel, a refreshing respite from the muggy, oppressive atmosphere of the hallway. As he readied himself for what lay beyond, Kelly thought of an old saying: *luck favors the prepared.*

As he gripped the cold doorknob and took his next step into the unknown, Kelly hoped his jar still held enough of that luck to see him through to the end.

36

Watt followed Diaz down the cold, damp tunnel. Goliath lumbered a few steps behind. His older brother's slow gait was a sign of his extended stay in the prison. Watt had seen it before from those in his neighborhood who'd served hard time. The gray walls became a haven, a second home, and once outside them, they often sought to return to them. It reminded Watt of his purpose in orchestrating his brother's escape.

They had reached the halfway mark of the subterranean route when a harsh, grating noise echoed from behind them. Watt turned and scanned the path, his eyes flicking over the detail-starved darkness.

Light cascaded into the tunnel from their entry point as the metal door they'd used swung open. The violent force of it caught Boone off guard, slamming into him and sending him sprawling out of its merciless path.

Slim stepped forward with the less-lethal shotgun at the ready. He swung the muzzle up toward the fast-moving target, but his motion was interrupted. A hand struck out from beyond the gloomy threshold and grabbed hold of the long barrel.

The intruder delivered a swift kick that caught Slim square in the chest, the blow knocking the lanky inmate back. The shotgun was stripped from his hand and sent clattering across the tunnel floor.

Boone regained his footing on unsteady legs, but his recovery came a heartbeat too late. Watt looked on as the attacker scooped Slim's shotgun from the floor in a blur of movement. With brutal finality, the butt end of the weapon connected with the side of Boone's head. A sickening thud echoed down the dank tunnel and he crumpled, dropping into a helpless heap alongside Slim.

The cascade of pale light filtering through the open door illuminated the unfolding drama, and Watt could now make out the assailant. As Kelly stood over the toppled pawns, a realization dawned on Watt. He'd underestimated the former cop's resolve and, in doing so, allowed his opponent to open the board and gain ground.

Kelly swiftly retrieved zip ties from the ERT vest strapped to Slim's chest and bound both men at the wrists and ankles, just as they'd done to the guards earlier. He then propped Boone up and tucked himself behind the groggy inmate, using him as both cover and hostage. With one arm Kelly raised the captured shotgun, aiming it down the tunnel toward Watt while the other wrapped tightly around Boone's chest . He stood, then began a slow, deliberate advance. "Watt, it's over! No way you're getting out of here."

Watt absorbed Kelly's words, measuring them against the meticulously devised escape plan lodged in his mind. "You're good, I'll give you that. But I'm better. You've played a good game. If you plan to live to play another round, I suggest you walk away."

"Not gonna happen. Quitting's not in my wheelhouse." Kelly continued his advance.

"Then it looks like your luck's run out." He turned to Diaz and extended his hand. "Hand me the ratchet."

Diaz hesitated only for a moment before reaching inside her waistband and pulling out a sleek semi-automatic pistol. She handed the gun over.

"Those bean bag rounds you've got won't save you. Not against this." Watt brought the handgun up and looked down the sights at Kelly. He hadn't intended on taking another life during this escape, but the best players adapted to the circumstances. Just as he prepared to unleash the first volley of shots, Goliath's bear-like paw landed heavily on Watt's shoulder.

"Let me handle this," his older brother requested.

Watt's grip on the gun remained unwavering, his gaze steady. "Not worth it. We're too close."

Goliath shook his head with conviction. "I've got some unfinished business. And trust me on this—I plan on finishing it here and now."

The determination burning in his brother's eyes conveyed a finality that Watt had seen many times before, and he knew there was no convincing him otherwise. With an exasperated sigh, Watt relented. "Make it quick."

Goliath's lips twitched into what could loosely be described as a smile. "Just 'cause it's quick don't mean it ain't gonna be painful."

His brother's titanic figure swallowed Kelly from view, blocking the shot he had. Watt called out to him, his voice a blend of brotherly concern and warrior's farewell. "I'll see you in the yard."

Goliath didn't reply with words. Instead, his response was a deep, resonating rumble, an animalistic growl that reverberated off the rusted metal pipes lining the tunnel walls. The low grumble morphed into a deafening roar as Goliath broke into a run.

Watt and Diaz picked up their pace, moving toward the tunnel exit connecting them to the yard. As they closed in on the door, a bone-jarring blast erupted from behind them. Watt spun. His eyes widened at the sight of his brother absorbing the full force of a beanbag round to the shoulder. The blow caused Goliath to stagger but did little else to deter his relentless charge.

A torrent of conflicting emotions surged within Watt, triggering an almost instinctual hesitation. He was compelled to turn back, to aid his beleaguered brother. But his strategic mind usurped his initial guttural reaction, calculating the risks and weighing the consequences.

Another blast missed its mark and ricocheted harmlessly off the tunnel wall as Goliath crashed into Kelly and Boone, who'd been his shield. The force of the collision sent the shotgun spiraling into the gloom. Goliath now had the advantage.

Kelly lay sprawled on the concrete floor beneath his brother's feet. Goliath cast a fleeting glance back at Watt. Their eyes locked and Watt gave a nod of approval. He swiveled on his heel, turning his back to his brother's raging vengeance. Diaz remained at his side as he strode the remaining distance to the door.

Diaz unlocked it, and carefully edged open the door just wide enough to catch a glimpse of the world beyond. What greeted them was a relentless barrage of snow that whipped their faces with icy ferocity.

Through the swirling tempest, Watt squinted toward the guard towers silhouetted against the frozen backdrop. Despite the storm, he could see that they were still manned. He cursed.

"Maybe the storm was too much. Or maybe they're just delayed." Diaz's voice was barely a whisper over the howling wind.

Watt only half heard the comment. His mind ran a frantic marathon, hunting for alternative solutions. Nothing came. As critical seconds passed, Watt scanned the area beyond the fence. His confidence began to falter when, amidst the squall, he discerned a dark shape followed by three others. As the wind momentarily abated, the fading light of day offered a glimmer of hope.

The four small shadows moved toward the courtyard from the forest beyond the razor-edged fence. A slow, knowing smile spread across Watt's face. He was acutely aware that the guards in the towers remained oblivious to the storm of a different nature about to be unleashed upon them.

Watt turned to Diaz. "Looks like the cavalry's arrived. You ready?"

With a curt nod, she moved to position herself in front of Watt as they'd rehearsed. His hand snaked around her neck, expertly applying pressure— not enough to strangle her, but enough to convince the watchful guards. He pressed the gun against the soft curve of her temple, and they stepped out from the tunnel into the snowy courtyard.

"Almost there. Then we're home free. By this time tomorrow we'll be far away from here. A new life is just around the corner."

They ventured further into the courtyard, their feet crunching on the fresh snow. The snipers in the three guard towers exploded into action as they took their position, aiming long-barreled rifles down at Watt. Commands blared from the PA system, dominating the white silence with harsh orders of surrender.

His meticulous planning had accounted for this. In fact, it hinged on this exact type of response from the prison's final line of defense. Their undivided attention was fixed on him, their gazes not straying, blind to the approaching drones.

Watt could almost taste victory on his tongue—this ruthless game of chess was nearing its end, and he was about to call checkmate.

37

Kelly lay flat on his back on the tunnel floor as he watched the access door to the yard close behind Watt and Diaz. He couldn't focus on the escaping duo. His present situation demanded his full attention. The collision with Goliath was accompanied by a devasting impact that sent Kelly reeling backward, his world tipping into a disorienting spin as he hit the ground. The only saving grace, and the reason he was able to retain consciousness, was that Goliath's shoulder plowed into Boone, his human shield, which provided a buffer. But even the barrier of flesh and bone did little to ebb the violence.

As Boone once again returned to his combat-induced dream state, the kinetic force of Goliath's charge sent his elbow into Kelly's sternum like a wrecking ball, driving the air from his lungs and forcing the shotgun from his grasp.

His world now swirled in a disoriented haze as he frantically scanned his surroundings, searching the damp floor for his weapon only to find it was out of reach.

Goliath towered above him, a mountain of menace poised to unleash his lethal intentions. Kelly recognized the look. He'd seen it once before, on the night they had first crossed paths years back. The difference then came in the glimmer of opportunity provided in the form of his partner. But in this hellish moment, there was no one to rely on but himself.

As the weight of the confrontation bore down upon him, a burning question flared in the recesses of his mind. A question that had haunted him ever since that night. Could he have emerged victorious without assistance? He would soon know the answer. Fate had conspired to offer him the opportunity to test himself once more, and Kelly would discover whether he possessed the strength, the grit, to triumph against insurmountable odds. *Willpower is the strength no opponent can see.* Facing off against Goliath, Kelly heard his mentor's words as if he were by his side now. Maybe he was. Maybe he wasn't alone after all.

Kelly knew the stakes. Defeat meant death. Surrender was not an option.

In the arena of combat, action always trumped reaction, leaving no room for hesitation, no alternative but to face this giant head-on. Victory was the only path forward.

Goliath's meaty hand tossed Boone aside like a ragdoll and latched onto Kelly's jumpsuit. He tugged the fabric taut against his chest, the prison uniform constricting around him. With a display of brute strength, Goliath hoisted Kelly off the ground as if he were a mere child. Time slowed and their faces locked in horrifying intimacy, the fiery unspoken exchange mingling in the charged air between them. And then the moment passed. With an unyielding force, Goliath slammed him back down.

The impact reverberated through Kelly's body, a seismic shockwave that rattled his bones and sent tremors down his spine. The sheer weight behind the punishing blow threatened to shatter his resolve. His survival instincts combined with years of training caused him to reflexively tuck his chin a split second before he hit the ground, sparing the back of his skull from the bone-crushing impact. His consciousness teetered on the precipice, but through sheer will he staved off the darkness.

Goliath released the stretched fabric of his jumpsuit and straddled Kelly's body. Desperation surged through Kelly's veins as he thrashed against the behemoth, a futile attempt to free himself from the weight pressing down on him. Blow after blow rained down. Kelly absorbed the first wave, swiveling his head to avoid the full force of the attack. He writhed, managing to free his hands, and fired his counter-offensive. He made contact, but the supine position robbed Kelly of the leverage necessary to deliver a decisive blow.

Goliath absorbed the punches, then fastened his hands near the collar of Kelly's uniform. Constricting the cotton tight around his neck, the beast once again wrenched Kelly off the ground.

He hung in the air for an agonizing moment, his clothing constricting his airway and cutting the flow of blood and oxygen along the jugular. Blackout was seconds away. In a desperate bid to break free from Goliath's suffocating grip, Kelly twisted his body with a surge of primal strength. He kicked outward, the bottom of his foot connecting with the tender flesh of Goliath's inner knee.

Goliath's leg buckled. The iron-clad grip released as he succumbed to the pain. He was now off balance.

Seizing the opportunity, Kelly stomped down on the same knee. He felt the pop. Goliath roared in agony and dropped to his hyperextended knee that was bent in grotesque opposition to its natural alignment, leaving Kelly to stand tall.

Shaking off the beating, he brought his fists up and lowered his head.

Goliath cocked his head up at Kelly as if trying to make sense of the sudden turning of the tide. He released his knee but remained hunched as he attempted to shift his weight.

Without an ounce of hesitation, Kelly unleashed a devastating over-hand right. His knuckles connected with the side of Goliath's head with a thunderclap.

Kelly's sinewy shoulder became a slingshot, and his fist the rock. His knuckles found their mark, crushing against Goliath's exposed temple. The giant fell, collapsing to the unforgiving ground. The once-indomitable beast lay motionless. Pops's swords had proven true once more.

Kelly stood tall, taking the briefest of moments to savor the victory. The answer to his haunting question had finally been answered. Wasting no time, Kelly quickly grabbed two pairs of flex cuffs and secured Goliath to a nearby pipe, then did the same for Boone and Slim, who had regained consciousness in time to see Goliath's end. Neither man offered further resistance.

With the three inmates secured, Kelly shifted his attention to the door leading to the yard held ajar by a snow drift. Through the veil of white, he saw two figures moving in tandem toward the heart of the prison yard.

Kelly retrieved the less-lethal shotgun from the ground, its weight a familiar reassurance in his hands, then loaded the final round into the chamber and moved down the tunnel.

He had eliminated the brawn of the operation. Now, he was left to face off against its brain.

38

Watt stood in the center of the prison's desolate recreation yard. Diaz was held firm against his body, shielding him from both the wind and the rifles in the hands of the guards above. A fresh layer of snow covered the ground, a deceivingly pure canvas upon which their fate hung by a delicate thread. The frigid air seeped into his bones.

Diaz continued to play her role as captive. She did as they'd planned, keeping her arms raised to prevent the gunmen from getting a clear shot at Watt's head. He kept the gun's cold barrel pressed against her temple.

The blizzard's fury momentarily quelled, offering a temporary reprieve from the relentless wind and driving snow. A calm settled over the yard, the world around them seeming to hold its breath as if nature itself recognized the gravity of the situation unfolding.

The snipers' commands, repetitious and continuous, reverberated through the towers' speakers. "Drop your weapon! Surrender now! Deadly force will be used against you if you do not comply!"

Watt stood without acknowledging them, failing to even lift his gaze. He knew this would be part of it. Diaz had laid out the protocols in full during their many nights spent rehearsing this very moment. His failure to speak or react would compound the decision to fire. She also warned that the delay caused by his lack of response would only last so long. He felt the ticking of that clock counting off the seconds in metronomic fashion.

The squadron of four drones glided through the wintry haze, rapidly closing the gap between the wooded forest and the fence. Watt's eyes darted between the advancing drones and the oblivious guards. Their focus remained fixated on the hostage situation at hand. He leaned closer to Diaz, his lips barely brushing against her ear. "It's almost over. We're minutes away from freedom."

"I trust you, baby. Let's finish this." Her teeth chattered between words.

The final phase of his plan was unfolding yet there was still no sign of Goliath. He prayed his brother's need for vengeance hadn't compromised the sole purpose of Watt's mission. With each passing second, his worry compounded. A churning anger clawed at his gut, his frustration aimed squarely at himself for not stopping his brother.

"Where the hell is he?" Watt followed the question with an uncharacteristic string of profanity.

Diaz shifted slightly. "He'll be here. Just hold on a little longer."

"Time's up."

Then, out of the corner of his eye, Watt caught movement from within the dark recesses of the tunnel, and a surge of relief coursed through him. The dissipating worry was quickly replaced with confusion as the silhouette emerged, bathed in the muted light that was dancing atop the snowy landscape.

It was not Goliath.

Locked in a chilling gaze, Watt found himself face to face with Kelly. The shotgun was in Kelly's hand and aimed in his direction. Watt's position of advantage had evaporated.

Watt's mind whirled as he recalculated the odds and sought to overcome this unforeseen and unexpected wrinkle in his masterplan. Watt's body shifted slightly, a calculated move to complicate any potential shot Kelly might attempt while keeping Diaz in front of the snipers' scopes.

It was Kelly's voice that pierced through the howling wind. "It's over!"

Watt kept his gaze fixed on Kelly, his peripheral vision catching glimpses of the approaching drones. A defiant smirk played on his lips. "It's never over, Kelly. Haven't you figured out by now that I'm always one move ahead?"

"Then why do you look so nervous." Kelly inched closer. The shotgun barrel remained fixed on Watt.

Watt tightened his grip around Diaz's neck. Her body reacted, a cough escaping her lips as she squirmed within his grasp. "Got to make it look good. Stay calm. We have the leverage."

Diaz's head bobbed slowly but Watt felt the tension radiating from her body. His grip remained firm, his eyes never straying from Kelly.

He watched the drones from the corner of his eye. The four shadows broke from their tight formation, each one charting a different preplanned target. "Get ready for the boom," he whispered into his captive's ear.

A split second later, three synchronized explosions rocked the courtyard as the payloads unleashed on each of the guard towers. Time suspended for a heartbeat as Watt, transfixed by the mayhem, looked on as the snipers and their rifles disappeared into the crumbling structures. Screams of agony bounced off the prison walls.

The incapacitation of the guards provided Watt with a fleeting window of opportunity. He knew the element of surprise would soon dissipate, replaced by a renewed fury, a relentless pursuit to restore order.

Watt shielded himself as the fourth drone exploded and ripped a hole in the yard's fence. The access door to their escape had been opened.

"We need to go! Now!" He tugged Diaz along with him as they sprinted through the courtyard.

The snipers' screams were consumed by the howl of wind as the storm's fury returned.

Every step forward was an act of defiance, a rebellion against the prison's suffocating grip. The path ahead was once again shrouded in the blizzard's relentless assault.

As he approached the gaping hole, Watt slowed. He cut his eyes to the tunnel doorway, hoping against reason that his brother would miraculously appear. The driving force behind this escapade had been to liberate Goliath from prison before his transfer to the impenetrable confines of the supermax. Disappointment coursed through his veins. Failure was not something he'd often endured, and its presence now fueled a burning rage inside him, the fires of which clouded his vision and painted the surrounding white a murderous red.

Only one outlet could possibly satiate the anger boiling over within him. Kelly, the man responsible for his brother's incarceration, had now ensured it would continue. He'd derailed his master plan. With the sniper threat neutralized, Watt calculated the additional time it provided. Just enough to even the score. His focus sharpened, his attention homing in on Kelly.

Watt released the barrel of the gun from Diaz and redirected its aim toward Kelly.

His finger tightened around the trigger. Time seemed to stretch, suspended between retribution and redemption.

With the pawns no longer in his control, it was now up to the king to claim his victory. The bullet left his gun with a deafening roar. Kelly disappeared from view behind the blinding flash of the muzzle blast.

39

The drone attack had caught Kelly off guard, with the fourth causing him to duck and cover near the cage area used by the ISO wing prisoners. He watched as Watt dragged Diaz toward the opening forged in the fence line. With the tower guards out of commission, he was left with two choices: let Watt and Diaz escape and hope they were picked up by the manhunt sure to follow, or intervene and put a stop to this madness here and now.

For Kelly, there was only one choice he could live with. He steadied his hand and, gripping the less-lethal shotgun, stepped out to make his final play. Kelly watched as Watt and Diaz closed in on their escape. He took aim at the moving target, knowing his best opportunity would come if he hit Watt in the legs with the hope the impact might knock him off his feet. A target in motion required the right amount of lead, firing in anticipation of where he would be rather than where he was. Tough under normal situations, tougher now with blinding white stinging his eyes and obscuring his point of aim.

Kelly was surprised to see Watt slow his gait as he neared his gateway to freedom, and even more so when he stopped altogether. His shot was now lost to Diaz, her body twisted in front of Watt as he turned back to the tunnel area. A moment later, Watt redirected his attention to Kelly.

Without warning, Watt released the gun pressed into Diaz's temple and thrust it in his direction.

Action and reaction. In the underworld of violence and survival, Kelly understood a cardinal rule: the initiator always had the upper hand. The microsecond it took for a bullet to leave the chamber could mean the difference between life and death. And today, Kelly refused to be on the Reaper's roster.

As Watt's finger squeezed the trigger, Kelly was already a blur of motion, ducking low and throwing himself behind the sturdy cage. The gunshot ripped through the icy silence, the bullet splitting the air around him as he took cover.

The heavy bag in the middle of the cage was his shield, the hundred pounds of solid bulk that he had thrashed daily since his arrival at Walpole serving him one more time.

He knew the anatomy of these bags like the back of his hand, having crafted many himself over the years. Ten sandbags, each weighing ten pounds, stacked in the center and surrounded by layers of padding. An unusual but perhaps life-saving armor. If he lived to see another day, he'd have quite the tale for Pops. Another instance in Kelly's life where the lessons learned in the ring extended far into the reaches beyond.

Watt thankfully did what most novice shooters do. He lowered his gun and looked downrange to see if his bullet had hit its mark. This gave Kelly an extra second to limit his exposure. The bulky security of the heavy bag served well as a barrier to the next volley. Bullets ricocheted off the cage, with several pelting the heavy bag. The rounds shredded the canvas exterior, but none managed to find their way through to Kelly.

Kelly tried to count the number of shots Watt had taken, but between the reverberation of sound within the courtyard and the adrenaline dump at being the intended target, he found the mental math an impossibility. With the second wave of bullets receding, Kelly took several deep breaths to steady his nerves.

Sand began spilling from the bag, the tiny grains dusting the white snow. He was grateful the shower was earthy brown instead of the dark red of his own blood. The thought ignited a fresh wave of adrenaline that coursed through his veins. He was not out of danger yet, and every second counted.

Kelly instinctively moved, positioning himself for the next attack as he waited for his opportunity to retaliate. But instead of the menacing crack of the gun, a low rumble echoed across the prison yard. It was the unmistakable roar of engines, a sound that spurred a glimmer of hope within Kelly.

He shot a glance to his right, keeping Watt in his periphery. He squinted against the flurries disturbing his view as his mind conjured the image of reinforcements, prison guards swooping in to control the chaos. The swirling snow thinned out enough for him to locate the source, painting a starkly different picture and erasing any illusion of rescue.

Breaking from the shadowy cloak of the tree line, a trio of ATVs surged into view, their silhouettes slicing through the snowy landscape. They charged with reckless abandon toward the prison yard, each second diminishing the quarter mile that stood between them and Watt.

"Looks like my ride's here." Watt's voice cut through the icy air. "We'll have to finish our little dance another time. Don't worry, I'm really good at paying people back in full. Since you've destroyed my brother's chance at life, I figure it's only fair I return the favor. Kelly, you got a brother? Maybe a son or daughter?" Watt's words hung in the air, as chilling as the cold winds whipping around them. "Don't feel the need to answer. I'll find out. And when I do, we'll settle up."

The threat sank its cold claws into Kelly. Images of his brother Brayden and his daughter flashed in his mind, another point in his life where his choices, and the path he'd taken, directly impacted those who mattered most. In the span of twenty-four harrowing hours, Watt had shown himself to be a man of action, a relentless force capable of turning threats into reality.

Kelly estimated he had less than sixty seconds before Watt's backup breached the fence. He could almost hear the countdown ticking in his head.

Stealing a glance from behind the bag, he found Watt's focus riveted on his rescue party. Using the opportunity, Kelly stepped out from his protective barricade while maintaining a wide berth to stay out of his adversaries' line of sight. Stealth and surprise were his only allies now.

Kelly inched closer to Watt, the distance between them rapidly shrinking to less than thirty feet. Weathering the icy flurries that stung his eyes, he raised the shotgun. One solitary round rested in the belly of the weapon.

His goal was simple: level the playing field, render Watt weaponless. Watt's gun was now laxly at his side, a pendulum swinging against his right thigh. A well-aimed beanbag round to his wrist might be sufficient to jolt the weapon free.

But at thirty feet, against a canvas of howling winds and flurries, threading such a needle was akin to a Herculean task. Undeterred by the odds, Kelly sought to bridge the gap, attempting to negate the punishing elements that toyed with his aim.

His effort was cut short as Watt swiveled around. Not in Kelly's direction, but in another. The sudden movement disrupted the precarious aim Kelly had, robbing him of his target.

Watt was riveted not on Kelly but rather on a spectacle unfolding beyond the prison walls. The ATVs were a mere half-minute from breaking into the prison's sanctum. It was then that Kelly spotted the distraction that had seized Watt's attention. A dark blue Humvee was charging through the wintry labyrinth, plowing snowdrifts aside with an indomitable force.

As the vehicle drew closer, the frost-tinged light revealed more details. Stenciled on the pale blue metal of the driver's side door was a familiar emblem: the stark white insignia of the Massachusetts State Police.

The Humvee was on a collision path with the incoming ATVs. With reinforcements on the way, the game had changed.

40

Barnes sat in the back of the Humvee, the scene unfolding in front of her through the snow-laced windshield. They'd arrived at the prison just in time. In fact, their timing couldn't have been better. She watched as the trio of four-wheelers snaked their way downhill, the terrain causing them to skid in a serpentine pattern, kicking up snow into a white mist all around them.

Ramirez had made relatively quick work of the remaining leg of their journey. Just before pulling up to the prison's main entrance, Cahill had noticed the trio of ATVs explode from the tree line. There was no questioning who was operating them or what their intentions were. The crude drawing on the map they'd found matched what they saw. The decision to intercept had been jointly agreed upon after she, Cahill, and Ramirez determined they were the only ones capable of reacting to the situation in time.

"Didn't think an ATV would be able to handle these conditions?" Barnes asked, as much to herself as the others in the Humvee.

"Depends. Fitted with tracks, they're almost as good as a snowmobile." Cahill turned to face her.

"Learn that in the Army?"

"Spent most of my winters in Vermont. Things you learn when freezing your ass off in the mountains." He gave her a half-smile and chuckled. "But these fools apparently didn't check the weather. Tracks or not, those city boys are going to find out navigating in these drifts is a lot harder than it looks."

"Guess their plan didn't account for Mother Nature," Barnes said.

"She can be a real bitch." Trooper Ramirez's deep voice carried over the roar of the Hummer's engine. "And don't forget, proper handling defaults to the operator. From where I sit, these boys skipped a few lessons."

"Then maybe it's time we give them a crash course." Barnes gave him a wink.

"I like this one." Ramirez threw a thumb back in Barnes's direction and then shot a glance over at Cahill, who was manning the front passenger seat. "Looks like you've got yourself a good partner."

"Better than good," Cahill said. "She's the best."

Even in the cold penetrating the Humvee's interior, Barnes felt warmth spreading across her cheeks. Cahill's comment seemed to carry a personal connotation, but she questioned whether she was reading him correctly. Another question danced in the recesses of her mind, too, one she refused to answer. If it was personal, how did she feel about it? She was grateful for the unfolding chaos that quieted any further inner conflict.

Trooper Ramirez was a wild maverick who pushed the Hummer's limits as they went off-road, charging through the monstrous snow drifts that rose around them.

Through the storm, she caught a fleeting glimpse of Kelly standing in the prison's courtyard holding a shotgun. Watt and a female guard, presumably Diaz, were near the fencing, engaged in what looked like a standoff. Seeing Kelly in the jumpsuit was strange. What wasn't strange was that even though he no longer wore the badge, he continued his endless pursuit of justice. It reminded her of the man he was and solidified any wavering doubt brought on by the months of separation, answering once and for all her feelings for him. In that moment, frozen in time, she had never loved him more.

"Kelly looks like Clint Eastwood about to make his last stand." Cahill's tone held an equal dose of pride and worry.

Ramirez gunned the engine. "Well, let's be sure he's not alone when he makes it."

"What's the plan?" Barnes asked.

Ramirez was nonchalant, a reckless grin stretching across his face. "I haven't had one since I jumped in the Hummer. But from where I sit, there's not much of a choice."

Cahill cocked an eyebrow in the trooper's direction. "Ramming speed?"

"Aye-aye, Skipper." Ramirez leaned into the steering wheel. "They're either going to stop or get stopped."

Barnes's lips curled into a wicked smile. "Either way sounds good to me."

Watt stood with his gaze fixed on the Hummer. He wanted to call out to his soldiers, to warn them of the imminent attack, but it was a frivolous thought. His voice would never penetrate the storm and roar of engines. His loyal gang was blind to the massive vehicle barreling toward them.

A metallic crash echoed across the courtyard as the Hummer slammed into the closest ATV. The impact catapulted it into the nearest one, setting off a terrifying chain reaction that turned the snow-covered field beyond the courtyard into a war zone. In the blink of an eye, the first two ATVs were totaled, twisted wrecks of their former selves. Only the third ATV continued forward. Thankfully, the Hummer responsible was now lodged within the wreckage.

Guards swarmed into the courtyard through the access doors. An older, slightly pudgy guard with a large wad of dip protruding from his lower lip was leading the charge. No less-lethal options in the hands of these men. Not this time. Watt knew, without a doubt, the green light had been given. Lethal force was now in play.

He still had one option to leverage, one chance to hold them at bay just long enough to make his escape. Watt pulled Diaz tight and returned the gun's aim to the side of her head, pressing the cold barrel against her temple. The courtyard held its breath.

The dip-spitting guard came up alongside Kelly.

"No one's died, Watt. You can still walk away from this. We can work this out."

Watt shook his head. "Never planned on sticking around. Prison's not for me."

He took a step back, his boot brushing the torn edge of the fence. The roar of the third ATV's engine drowned out any further communication as it skidded to a halt just a few feet away from where Watt stood.

He caught the action taking place in the wreckage of the crashed ATVs. Watt watched in anger as Barnes and Cahill, the detectives who'd interrogated him the other day, descended in a whirlwind on the injured members of his crew. Any resistance was quickly quelled as they were placed into custody.

The guards continued to shout as they stood at the ready with weapons drawn.

Watt's next move was inevitable and one he had already factored into his plan's long game. He decided to deploy it now as a preemptive countermeasure.

Diaz was his ticket to freedom. This was part of the plan he'd never shared with her. Like the others, she was another pawn in his game. And now she'd make her final sacrifice.

His voice as cold as the icy air surrounding them, he leaned close and whispered in her ear, "This is the part where we say our goodbyes."

She twisted, her eyes wide, searching for answers in his. "What are you talking about? You said I was your queen."

"It's said that all pawns are just queens-in-waiting. You just happen to be a queen who's always been my pawn."

The gun moved from her temple. She struggled to rip herself free, but Watt held firm. The gunshot blasted through the wintry air. Diaz clutched onto Watt for a moment before crumpling to the snow, the white melting as her warm blood emptied from her body.

The gunshot shattered the standoff. Kelly looked at Hopper standing next to him, surprise mirrored in their expressions. His eyes worked down the line of deputies. In the split-second struggle between Watt and Diaz, he assumed a corrections officer with an itchy finger had pulled the trigger. The deadpan look on each guard's face quickly put an end to that train of thought.

"Son of a bitch popped Diaz," Hopper growled.

Kelly knew the other members of the Emergency Response Team had updated the chain of command, alerting them to Diaz's involvement in the escape plan. Regardless, the years of service had forged a bond between Diaz and the other guards that would not easily break.

Watt was using this shock-and-awe tactic to gain the advantage. He was already through the gate and only a few short steps from the awaiting ATV.

Kelly sprang into action and took off in a dead sprint, Hopper and the other guards on his heels.

Seeing the rush of men heading his way, Watt unloaded his gun, firing indiscriminately in their direction.

Bullets snapped the cold air around Kelly and the others. They dove for safety, scattering into the piled snow of the courtyard. As quickly as the hail of gunfire erupted, it ended, the click of the gun punctuating the fact that Watt had spent the entire contents of the magazine.

His shots were poorly placed, and none found their mark. Watt tossed the empty weapon into the snow at his feet and straddled the ATV, taking a seat behind the driver.

"I've got a clear shot," one of the younger guards called out.

Hopper was quick to intervene, waving off the junior man. "He's unarmed with his back to us. Lethal force is no longer authorized."

The younger guard's cursing was caught up in the wind. A cry rose above the storm. Diaz let out a tormented scream as she began writhing on the ground. The guards rushed to her aid. The bullet had struck her upper thigh, which continued to bleed profusely.

Better to wound than to kill. It drew elements away from the fight to triage the victim. Kelly saw the move's effectiveness as the deputies broke from their pursuit of Watt to focus on saving Diaz's life.

Kelly was bound by a different purpose. He stepped over Diaz as he exited through the hole in the fence created by the drone explosion and charged through the deep snow. He gave chase, the ATV rapidly widening the gap between them.

Kelly stopped and raised the shotgun. He controlled his breathing and took aim down the long barrel, refusing to allow the torrent of snow to steal his last opportunity to put an end to this ordeal. Watt looked back and smiled.

One shot. Make it count. The ATV was nearly thirty yards away when he pulled the trigger. The recoil jarred his shoulder. His aim hadn't been for Watt. Instead, Kelly fired at the driver.

The round struck somewhere in the man's upper torso. His body jolted upward and he jerked the handlebar, sending the ATV into a violent spin. He was unable to correct the skid. The vehicle rolled over and came to a dead stop, launching a plume of crystalline powder into the air.

The driver lay pinned under the wreckage. Watt, catapulted from the back of the ATV, sailed through the air and landed in a deep snow drift fifteen feet away.

Kelly closed the gap in a heartbeat. Watt lunged at him with fist balled, but the gang leader was slow, impeded by the dense snow surrounding him. His movements were sluggish, making it easy for Kelly to sidestep the attack. He countered with a powerful hook to Watt's jawline, and he tumbled backward and became a snow angel without wings.

Dazed, Watt looked up at Kelly through eyes dancing on the cusp of unconsciousness. The Rollin' 9s had fallen, and their king was now dethroned.

As law enforcement and correctional officers descended on the scene, Kelly leaned in, his voice just loud enough to carry over the biting wind.

"Checkmate."

41

The arctic wind tore through the ghostly field, gnawing into every crevice of the disaster-stricken landscape. The wreckage of ATVs lay strewn about, a kaleidoscope of debris scattered by the steel of the Humvee's devastating blitz.

Watt was recaptured and brought back into the gray walls of the prison alongside Boone and Slim, his misguided accomplices. Goliath was returned to isolation to await his transfer to supermax.

The members of the Rollin' 9s who'd assisted in the attempted breakout were placed into custody. One by one, they were loaded into the fleet of Massachusetts State Police vehicles that had converged on the scene.

Trooper Ramirez maneuvered the last of the dejected gang members into a cruiser. His powerful slam of the door shook free a dusting of snow from the vehicle's roof. The swirling flakes of the fading Nor'easter caught the throbbing pulse of red and blue lights.

The storm made its exit with a whimper rather than a roar. As it died down, the early darkness of late winter descended. The reign of terror ended with the dying light of day.

Watt was merely the latest name added to the growing roster of criminals in Kelly's life, each one baying for their pound of flesh, each one a reminder of the peril his job invited. To reach out and touch those he loved, they would have to go through him first. And if this day had taught them anything, it was that breaking through Kelly's will was a challenge many had tried but few had achieved.

And now, with the threat neutralized, Kelly found his focus drawn to the duo that had emerged as his saviors in the eleventh hour—Barnes and Cahill.

His heart clenched at the sight of Barnes. A rush of emotions surged within him. Every instinct screamed at him to break the distance, to pull her into a comforting embrace, to confess the depth of his feelings. He yearned to free himself from the shackles of his subterfuge and reveal the true purpose behind his cold dismissal of her.

Yet he battled it back with the same determination he'd summoned to overcome Goliath, perhaps even more. It was a war within him, a clash between his duty and his heart, a fierce duel between his commitment to the undercover assignment and the profound love he harbored for the woman he'd once planned to make his wife. And still did.

A groan slipped past his lips, its bitterness carrying his unsaid words into the ether. His face remained impassive, a battle-scarred mask that betrayed nothing of the storm raging beneath.

Barnes trudged through the snow to where he stood. Cahill followed but maintained a respectful distance.

"Mike, I—I'm glad you're safe. When I heard about the standoff at the prison, I needed to be here, but..." Barnes's words trailed off.

Kelly managed a wry smile. "You couldn't have timed it better. Not sure how this thing would've played out if you didn't make it when you did."

Her emerald eyes glistened, the edges shimmering. She looked to be on the verge of tears. Whether from the icy gusts or the unspoken feelings each were holding back, Kelly couldn't discern.

"How've you been holding up?" Kelly could've kicked himself. After three months of incarceration and separation, was that all he could muster? Why didn't he just talk about the weather? It would've been on par with the weak attempt he'd made.

"Getting by, I suppose." She shrugged.

He noticed that, in the uncomfortable silence between them, Barnes looked to Cahill. An unspoken understanding flickered between the two, a shared secret, a camaraderie that seemed unfamiliar to Kelly. He dismissed the thought, chalking it up to his months of isolation, as Barnes shifted her attention back to him.

"You're out tomorrow." She sighed.

Kelly nodded. "Let's hope the next day unwinds faster and calmer than this one."

She gave a soft chuckle. "Need a ride?"

The question lingered between them, heavy with unspoken possibilities. A moment's hesitation was all it took for Kelly to weigh the implications. To accept her offer would be to set them both on divergent paths— her clinging to a fragile thread of hope, him embarking on a journey to finish his assignment and take down the Irish mob from the inside. It would never work. Not until he'd set things right.

He shook his head, forcing the muscles in his neck to defy the gravitational pull of his heart. "Thanks. I'm good. Bobby's got me covered."

The flicker of hope in her eyes died out, replaced by an all-consuming sadness that seemed to seep into her very being. It hit him harder than Goliath's punches ever could. He swallowed down the sharp edges of his own pain. "I'll see you soon."

Barnes wiped at a clump of snow clinging to her jacket. "I hope so."

He hoped so too, more fervently than he'd ever hoped for anything. With that, Barnes gifted him a feeble smile, turned her back, and walked away until she was swallowed by the Hummer's shadow.

Cahill lingered for a moment before speaking. "Hell of a thing you did back there. Some real John Wayne shit."

"Didn't have a choice."

"Sure you did. You could have let him go. Wait for someone else to pick up the pieces."

"I guess." Kelly shrugged.

"Even now you don't see it as an option." Cahill gave a shake of his head. "They don't make 'em like you anymore."

"Sure they do." Kelly leveled a gaze at the squad's junior detective. "You and I are cut from the same cloth."

"Thanks. Means a lot coming from you."

"Barnes too. She's as tough as they come with the brains to match.

Enough of the old school mixed with the new." Kelly stared after her, but a wall of white barred his view. He wondered if she was looking back at him. "You two make a pretty good team."

Cahill gave a sheepish nod. "I think so."

It looked as though Cahill wanted to say something else, but the words never came. The adrenaline dump's magic from earlier had worn off, and the abuse Kelly's body had taken over the past several hours began crashing down on him. The pain coupled with the cold cutting through the fabric of his jumpsuit. He rubbed his arms for warmth. "I best get back inside. Gotta get my beauty sleep. Big day tomorrow."

"Right. Bet it'll feel good to put this place behind you."

"No truer words." Kelly slapped Cahill on the shoulder. "Be safe out there. Do me a favor and keep an eye on Barnes. Partners always got to watch each other's backs."

"She's in good hands." Cahill stuck out his hand.

They exchanged a firm handshake, then turned and headed off in opposite directions. Cahill returned to the frenzy of law enforcement officers working the scene. Kelly walked back through the hole in the fence and into the courtyard, where he was greeted by Hopper.

"Friends of yours?" Hopper jutted his chin in the direction of Cahill.

Kelly gave a subtle nod. "Good cops. Better people."

Hopper tilted his head, his eyes sparkling with a hint of curiosity. "Might be none of my business, but it appears you and the lady cop might have had something... deeper?"

Kelly was impressed with the senior guard's keen eye. "Whatever was there, it's gone now."

"Things always look different from the inside. Give it some time once you're away from these walls. Whatever you had might not be as far gone as you think." Hopper threw his hands up and chuckled to himself. "But what the hell do I know."

"You're a good man, Hopper."

"Nah, I'm just a man. Same as you. Part sinner. Part saint. Good is a relative term." Black spit shot from Hopper's mouth, staining the white powder at his feet. "And no place is a better showcase of that than a prison. Bentley had made some bad choices in life that landed him here. But look at the good he did when given the opportunity. I think it speaks to his true character."

"Maybe when he gets out of here, he'll find a way to carry that forward."

"Speaking of getting out, you have a heap of paperwork that needs signing before I can get you out that front door tomorrow morning. Unless you're planning to extend your visit here?"

"Not a chance." With that, Kelly followed Hopper back into the prison. Upon reaching the door, he mustered every ounce of his strength not to cast a final glance over his shoulder at Barnes.

42

The Homicide Unit no longer thrummed with the electric buzz of earlier. The manhunt was over, and the unit began its return to homeostasis. The ebb and flow of adrenaline-fueled pursuit and the tedious paperwork was a hallmark of any police department. Boston was no different.

Nor was the clicking of keyboards and low-volume conversations between fatigued investigators. It was well past the hour when most detectives had resigned their battles with caffeine and paperwork, leaving the department's starkly utilitarian space to the ghosts of unsolved cases.

Barnes, fueled by caffeine, sat hunched within her cubicle fortress, resigning herself to her battle with the remaining paperwork. Cahill had departed an hour ago. Her bloodshot eyes strained and her keystrokes slowed. The energy to shape this mess to her standards had evaporated.

Her attempt to formulate the events of the past twenty-four hours into a cohesive police report was eluding her. It wasn't just the fatigue; Barnes was distracted. Her mind continued to spiral back to Kelly.

Seeing him again stirred something within her, disrupting the well-practiced autopilot she had slipped into after his departure from the PD and her life.

Barnes forced the thoughts from her mind and returned to the stack of paperwork, repeating the vicious cycle once more. Distracted by her thoughts and the task at hand, she hadn't noticed Sergeant Halstead standing alongside her cubicle partition.

"Why don't you give it a rest for tonight." His voice was gentle while holding an edge of command.

"I just wanted to get as much down on paper as I could before cutting out." Barnes pushed back from her desk and looked up at her direct supervisor.

"The paperwork can wait. State Police are taking the initial arrest on the Rollin' 9s' members scooped up at the prison. We'll be filing our arrest warrants at a later date. You've got time. Take a moment to breathe."

She rolled her neck, extracting a series of pops and momentarily alleviating some of the pent-up tension that had taken up residence within her. "I'm good."

"No. You're not. I can see it plain as day, even if you can't." Halstead dipped his head and lowered his voice. "I know you're going through a lot. And I'm not just referring to the case."

"I've got this." It was a weak response, weaker in delivery.

"I know. But I also know when a cop needs to step back and put some distance between themselves and a case. So I'm not asking. Consider this an order. Pack it up and head home."

Barnes contemplated offering up another challenge, but she saw the unwavering resolution in her boss's eyes and knew any further protest would be futile.

With a sigh that echoed her internal surrender, Barnes pushed back and rose, her body suddenly aware of the weariness overtaking her. "Thanks," she muttered.

"Just doing my job as supervisor," Halstead responded before retreating into the landscape of partitioned solitude.

Barnes reached for her jacket and keys, then turned to Halstead. "Might think about taking some of your own medicine."

A rare smile played on his usually impassive features. "Maybe you're right."

Barnes exited the Homicide Unit. She made her way down the hallway, steering clear of the elevators and opting for the stairway instead. The door to the Narcotics Unit opened as she passed by.

Lincoln White materialized in the doorway, an unwelcome surprise ending to a long day. Barnes sidestepped him, attempting to circumvent any interaction with the man solely responsible for driving Kelly's termination and catalyzing the demise of their relationship.

White's face sported a half-smile, a smug twist of his lips that gave him an air of cockiness he wore with regularity. "I was just on my way to your office. Got a little info on those drones they used."

Barnes crossed her arms, her posture taut. "I'm all ears."

"No need for the attitude. Just figured you might want to know that one of the Rollin' 9s turned state's witness in an attempt to reduce his charges."

Barnes nodded. She wasn't surprised to hear one of them flipped. Even the most ruthless criminals turned canary when faced with serious jail time. The trick was the value of their song—the information had to implicate a bigger fish in the criminal pond.

"Well, this turd is giving up their connection. And you're not going to believe who he's fingering." White cocked an eyebrow.

"Let me take a wild guess. Walsh?" Barnes ventured. It seemed like a logical leap. Weaponized drones fit the Irish mob's innovative ruthlessness.

White shook his head, his grin widening. "The Rakowskis."

Barnes felt her chest tighten. The Rakowski family, a rival mob faction, had faded into the city's underbelly after she and Kelly had dismantled their trafficking network. The Polish mobsters, particularly their matriarch, were woven intricately into the tapestry of Barnes's personal vendettas.

During their investigation, Barnes had been ensnared by their ruthless tactics, held captive, and stowed in a car trunk. She knew who was responsible for ordering her kidnapping. But without the evidence to back it, the head of the Rakowski family eluded justice. The burning desire for another shot at them had been simmering in her, awaiting the spark that would ignite it into action. The mere prospect of personally slapping the cuffs on the Polish mobsters filled her with a renewed sense of purpose.

Without uttering a word of thanks, she made for the stairwell, leaving White in her wake. Before descending, she threw over her shoulder, "Keep me posted. I'd like a piece of this one if it shakes out."

White, using the paperwork he was clutching, gave a tipping of the hat gesture before heading off in the opposite direction, toward her unit.

She descended the stairs, a newfound lightness in her step, her mind drifting to the prospect of taking down the Rakowskis. She only wished she could share this news with Kelly. Barnes pushed the thought to the periphery of her consciousness as she stepped into the cold night air.

43

Kelly sat in the quiet solitude of his cell, the final minutes of his sentence winding down. It was time to say goodbye to the concrete box he'd called home for the past ninety days. He felt strangely connected to this place.

On most days, he would fall into his well-worn morning routine, an emotional sparring match with the ghosts of his past. His demons were ever-present, lingering at the edges of his consciousness, stubborn and relentless. Today, however, the mental battlefields were temporarily abandoned, and he set his sights on the future.

He rubbed a tender spot along his cheekbone. The previous day's violence was tattooed onto Kelly's body, each bruise and cut a memento of the physical hell he'd pushed through.

He sat on the edge of the worn mattress and thought of Embry, his little girl. Images of her flooded his mind, bringing with them a deluge of emotions. The upcoming custody battle loomed like a daunting mountain peak, shrouded in uncertainty. Re-establishing his bond with her was priority one.

The prison had given him a small box to compile his sparse belongings. Among them, a photograph of the two of them at Fenway Park, their smiles frozen in a happier time, lay atop a pile of her drawings. They were powerful totems, warding off the darkest days of his incarceration, talismans against the soul-crushing loneliness. He vowed to tell her one day of the magical strength her drawings had bestowed on him, the invisible cord that had tethered him to hope during the relentless days and nights apart.

Three resounding knocks against his cell door snapped him from his thoughts. Metal springs squeaked loudly as Kelly rose from the cot and moved to the back wall of the cell. He widened his stance and pressed his body against the cold concrete.

A voice, comfortably familiar, cut through the lingering silence. "No need for that today. You're no longer a prisoner. In my opinion, you never were."

Kelly turned to find Hopper looming in the threshold of his cell.

"Got your stuff?" Hopper's eyes traced to the cardboard container resting on Kelly's cot.

"Not much, but it's all there."

Hopper then lobbed a plastic bag onto the bed, where it landed with a soft thump. "It's the clothes you came in with. Take a moment to change out."

Kelly shed his prison uniform with the frantic urgency of a firefighter responding to a crisis. He discarded the jumpsuit among the heap of worn sheets and scooped up the cardboard box cradling the remnants of his former life.

Then he stepped out of the cell, an act as momentous as it was simple. He allowed himself one last look, an intimate farewell to the iron and concrete confines that had been his world, before he and Hopper began the final, solemn procession along the hallway.

The path led through imposing secure doors and into the very corridor where chaos had first unfurled. The signs of the carnage had been scrubbed clean, yet an invisible imprint lingered. Faint traces of a bloody past were stained into the worn linoleum, a morbid testament to the madness.

Kelly's gaze drifted down the hall toward D-Block's access door, a place where anarchy had once held court. Silence replaced the cacophony of earlier. "Riot's secured?"

Hopper nodded. "National Guard arrived in the dead of night. Backed up by the State Police, they regained control. Watt's absence threw his troops into disarray. Domino and his crew have been ousted. Hard to believe we owe Nickel and his Irish gang for that." Hopper just shook his head. "As for the rest, the instigators have been singled out and isolated."

"What about Bentley?"

"It's a hell of a thing," Hopper mused. "An inmate risking everything, for a guard, no less. Warden wanted to give him an award for bravery, but can you believe he turned it down. Said it'd tarnish his rep."

"Sometimes all we have is our reputation," Kelly said, thinking of his own and the tarnish it now carried.

"Gladstone's hanging up his uniform." Hopper rubbed his hands together as though shedding the taint of the man's incompetence. "Good riddance."

"No one really knows how they'll stand up when the storm hits. Not until it does."

Hopper spat into his cup in agreement. "Guess he knows now."

"How's Doyle faring?" Kelly asked as they approached the imposing metal door leading to the heart of the control center, the final gateway to the inmate release area.

"He's a fighter. His back's broken, but the doctor believes he'll walk again." He paused, his gaze falling to the polished floor. "It looks like his career is over."

"Pass on my gratitude," Kelly said. "He treated me with decency in here. I just wish I got to him sooner."

"He left something for you." Hopper reached into his cargo pocket and pulled out a sliver of silver. He extended his hand, dropping a silver chain into Kelly's palm.

A pendant hung from the chain. On it was an embossed image of the archangel Michael, standing with sword in hand and his foot pressing down upon the devil.

"Worn by his father before him," Hopper explained. "He said there's no one more deserving of it than you."

A knot of discomfort tightened in Kelly's chest. "I can't... it should stay with Doyle. With his family."

The lines around Hopper's eyes deepened. "He figured you'd say that. He told me to tell you, let this shield you on your next journey."

With a deep, solemn nod, Kelly slipped the chain around his neck, the pendant resting against his heart, a symbol of protection and the silent promise of justice.

"Now let's usher you toward freedom." Hopper made the call over his radio, alerting the control station of their incoming passage. A metallic groan echoed as the heavy door yielded.

Kelly turned back to face Hopper, a lingering question still on his mind. "And what about Watt and Goliath?"

"Watt is set to become the latest addition to our ISO wing." Hopper grinned. "As for Goliath, his transfer to supermax is already in the works. In light of recent events, they've expedited. He'll be out of here by dawn tomorrow."

"That's good news." Kelly paused for a moment. "Thanks for everything."

"Just remember, a day can make all the difference. Don't waste a single one." Hopper shook Kelly's hand and returned inside.

Kelly pivoted toward the designated pathway for departing inmates.

The icy coating atop the snow crunched under his weight as he walked the exterior corridor hemmed in by chain-link fencing crowned with razor wire. At the far end stood a solitary guard, a gatekeeper between Kelly and the world that lay just beyond.

Kelly had entered the gray and come out the other side. He didn't look back. His sights were now set on the future.

44

The sun had broken through the gray clouds as Kelly took the final few steps of his long walk to freedom. Light bounced off the glistening snow, temporarily blinding him, the months of his dim quarters making the adjustment more difficult. He reached the cage's end, the gate the only thing now separating him from freedom. A guard stood at the ready. He was heavily bundled, but his body trembled nonetheless. He gave Kelly a once-over before speaking into his radio.

A moment later, the gate buzzed. The guard gave the handle a yank. The iced-over latch resisted as if beckoning Kelly to remain. With a little extra effort, it was open. The guard offered no parting words, just a simple nod of his head for the prison's final sendoff.

Kelly stepped through. The air beyond the gate felt fresher, as if he'd passed through an invisible boundary. He inhaled deeply, accepting it as his reward for his time spent inside.

He looked across the lot to a sign designated as the prisoner pickup location. Underneath it he saw an older-model sedan, heavy tints obscuring the driver. Kelly didn't need to see who was behind the wheel to recognize his oldest and most trusted friend. He had begun making his way toward the car when he heard a familiar voice call from behind.

Kelly turned to see Bentley crossing over. He looked different, lighter.

He smiled as he shuffled across the snowpack littered with rock salt that added an extra crunch to his steps.

"Glad I got to catch you before you split," Bentley said, his breath captured by the cold air.

"Me too." Kelly smiled. "So what's next for you?"

"Just takin' it one step at a time." Bentley shrugged. "Less likely to trip up that way." He looked around and then over at the car Kelly was headed to. "I see you got yourself a ride."

Kelly nodded. "Need a lift? Heading back to your neck of the woods."

"Thanks, but I'm straight. My people'll be rollin' up soon enough. Plus, can't be seen rolling 'round town with a cop, ex or not. It's bad for my rep."

"I get it." An awkward pause followed. "Listen, you ever need anything, I mean anything, you come find me."

"And how do you suppose I do that?" Bentley asked, stuffing his hands deep in his pockets and pulling his coat tighter.

"Pops's Gym. I'll be there. And if I'm not, he'll know how to find me."

"Sounds good."

"So you haven't given any thought to what you're going to do now?"

"Not really. Well, maybe a little." Bentley shrugged. "Inside those walls, you get these big dreams. Soon as you're back on the street, they get squashed."

"Doesn't have to be that way."

"Says you. But I come from different stock."

"You and I aren't as far removed as you might think."

"Maybe."

"For what it's worth, you're one of the bravest men I've met. Badge or no badge, you could do a lot of good in the world." Kelly slapped his shoulder. "You're just a hero in hiding. Maybe it's time you take off the mask."

"We'll have to see 'bout that." Bentley looked up at an approaching SUV. The driver flashed the lights and tapped the horn. "I've gotta jet. Looks like my ride is here."

"You be safe out there."

"You too. Don't worry, you ain't seen the last of me." Bentley hustled off. "I'll catch you on the flip, Michael Kelly."

Kelly watched as Bentley made quick work hustling his way across the lot to his ride. And like that, his sherpa was gone. He then began making his way over to the sedan. The passenger side door swung open and Bobby McDonough leaned across the seat, looking up at him with the same mischievous grin he'd had since they were kids. "Well, don't you look like a steamin' bag of shit."

"Good to see you too, Bobby." Kelly slid inside and closed the door. The warm leather of the seat melted away the cold.

"Your face looks like it's been through a meat grinder since I last saw you."

"Long story." Kelly rubbed his hands in front of the vent, feeling the sting of his damaged knuckles as they thawed.

"Yeah, I heard." McDonough cocked an eyebrow. "Nickel said you're a tough Irish prick. Best compliment I heard him give a guy."

Kelly gave him a questioning look.

McDonough laughed. "Surprised I knew about it? Hell, word spreads as fast in there as it does on the street, maybe faster."

Kelly held back a smile, pleased his time with Nickel had furthered his advantage with Walsh's crew, knowing it might serve to speed up his time-line before he could return to his old life and shed the cloak he now wore.

"Where to?"

"Right now, all I want to do is see Embry." Kelly's heart kicked. The thought of seeing his daughter was a defibrillator bringing him back to life.

McDonough put the car in drive and pulled away. He looked over at Kelly as they passed by the prison's main entrance. "Given any thought to my offer?"

Kelly was quiet for a moment, once again weighing the risk versus reward. "Tell Walsh I'm in."

McDonough broke into a full smile and punched Kelly in the shoulder. "Never thought I'd see the day. Finally going to have a saint among us sinners."

Kelly felt the pendant over his heart, gifted to him by Doyle. And just like the archangel, he set out on his quest to vanquish the devil from Boston.

THE MEMORY BANK

When a series of high-profile deaths is linked to a lethal conspiracy, Detective Morgan Reed must risk everything to uncover the truth.

Technology pioneer Dr. Gerald Price is at the height of his scientific career. After years of research in the field of memory augmentation, he's just made a world-changing breakthrough.

But his life's work is mysteriously cut short by a fatal overdose in a seedy motel.

All evidence points to a suicide, and the case is closed...until Detective Morgan Reed begins working a series of similarly strange deaths.

As Reed joins forces with Detective Natalie De La Cruz to expose the lies and corporate treachery at the heart of the suicides, they discover a shocking plot that will put thousands of lives at risk.

In a world where cutting-edge technology meets dirty money, Reed and De La Cruz must navigate the labyrinths of an impenetrable network to save countless innocents from certain death...as their own lives hang in the balance.

SHEA & BYRNES deliver an explosive techno-thriller that will keep you up all night—perfect for fans of Michael Crichton and David Baldacci.

Get your copy today at
severnriverbooks.com

ABOUT THE AUTHOR

Brian Shea has spent most of his adult life in service to his country and local community. He honorably served as an officer in the U.S. Navy. In his civilian life, he reached the rank of Detective and accrued over eleven years of law enforcement experience between Texas and Connecticut. Somewhere in the mix he spent five years as a fifth-grade school teacher. Brian's myriad of life experience is woven into the tapestry of each character's design. He resides in New England and is blessed with an amazing wife and three beautiful daughters.

Sign up for the reader list at
severnriverbooks.com

Printed in the United States
by Baker & Taylor Publisher Services